# ARCANE KNIGHT

## AN EPIC LITRPG FANTASY

### ORDER & CHAOS
### BOOK 5

## TIMOTHY MCGOWEN

ILLUSTRATED BY
## RICHARD SASHIGANE

EDITED BY
## CANDACE MORRIS

RISING TOWER BOOKS

Fantasy / LitRPG / Gamelit

# BIBLIOGRAPHY OF TIMOTHY MCGOWEN

**Haven Chronicles**
Haven Chronicles: Eldritch Knight

**Short Stories/Novellas**
Dead Man's Bounty
Exiled Jahk (https://dl.bookfunnel.com/c10uz8peaf)

**Last Born of Ki'darth**
Reincarnation: A Litrpg/Gamelit Trilogy
Rebellion: A Litrpg/Gamelit Trilogy
Retribution: A Litrpg/Gamelit Trilogy

**Order & Chaos**
Arcane Knight Book 1: An Epic LITRPG Fantasy
Arcane Knight Book 2: An Epic LITRPG Fantasy
Arcane Knight Book 3: An Epic LITRPG Fantasy
Arcane Knight Book 4: An Epic LITRPG Fantasy

**The Elemental Realms**
Nexus Guardian Book 1: A Fantasy LitRPG Adventure
Nexus Guardian Book 2: A Fantasy LitRPG Adventure

Arcane Knight Book 5: An Epic LITRPG Fantasy

Order & Chaos

ISBN: 978-1-956179-29-3

First Edition: October 2023

Published By: Rising Tower Books

Publisher Website: www.RisingTowerBooks.com

Author Site: AuthorTimothyMcGowen.com

# REVIEWS ARE IMPORTANT

**Every review matters, get your voice heard.**

Follow me on Amazon to get informed when my next book is released!

https://www.amazon.com/stores/Timothy-McGowen/author/B087QTTRJK

Join my Patreon for early Chapters!

https://www.patreon.com/TimothyMcGowen

Join my Facebook group and discuss the books

https://www.facebook.com/groups/234653175151521/

# SPECIAL THANKS

I wanted to give a special thanks to those that helped bring this book to its current state.

Candace Morris - Editor

Dantas Neto - Proofer

Sean Hall - Proofer

I would also like to mention my patreons and thank them for their extra support!
Jesse Butcher, John Percival, Brad Gibson, Destin McMurray, Alvaro Miyazawa, George Clark

Thank you.

*I dedicate this book to all the many friends I've made in the Indie Book Publishing space. Your encouragement and zeal have helped me tremendously in the past few years.*

# CONTENTS

# LEAVE A REVIEW & CHECK OUT MY WEBSITE

Don't forget to leave a review! You can follow this link to do so after you finish reading! My Book

Get an exclusive short story to read if you subscribe to my newsletter at https://authortimothymcgowen.com/

# PROLOGUE

"Lucian Vargas," Vikari said, her voice filled with as much venom as it had when she'd last addressed the Council of Chaos.

"I come at the command of the Lord of Chaos, whose command cannot be ignored," I said, each word as painful to utter as the next. Only months before I had held a position of great honor and power, now I find myself reduced to the most menial of tasks.

"Has the stranger of our kind finally accepted his role? A bit too late, as I hold the means to set myself above even his power," Vikari said, twirling a blackened blade, energy thrumming off of it.

I watched her for a moment, and in that instant, I realized why I'd been sent here. This offshoot and her small band of followers had grown much more powerful than even I'd expected. Sending anyone else short of our best would surely have been a sacrifice before her mighty power. But I wasn't just anyone, I'd fought more battles and survived longer than any other of my kind. This child with her new toy was nothing to me.

Or at least that should have been the case. Instead, I felt an unfamiliar sensation run down my spine. Was that fear? Did she truly wield enough power to make even I, the great Lucian Vargas, tremble in fear? Surely my senses were being affected by something, that sword couldn't emanate the kind of power that I was feeling.

I squashed the old companion running down my spine, fear had no place in my task and what lay ahead. If I were truly facing death and I'd been sent here by the direct request of the Chaos Lord, then that meant he either wanted me gone or had faith in my abilities. We'd spat in the face of tradition when we last turned against the Chaos Lord, but he'd come back with an iron fist and reunited all of us, except Vikari and her crew. This was the final act to unify our people for the upcoming conflicts against those vile beastkin.

"He stands at the head of us all, as it was always meant to be," I said, my message was clear, despite not saying it. She needed to step in line and end her wild experiments or suffer the consequences.

A gust of wind blew in from the south, with it the

scent of ocean air. I'd tracked Vikari and her influences into the Elven Lands, but it was unclear to me what she hoped to accomplish here.

"He ought to have come himself, the mantle of Chaos Lord would have only hastened my plans. You can feel it, can't you? The very source of power beneath us throbbing and pulsing in rhythm with our Chaos. The time of the Chaos Lords will end, and all shall be covered in the blanket of Chaos. In the end, only I will stand at the head of the new world."

I felt something shift in the air and I summoned forth my power, throwing aside a strike of pure chaotic energy. The trees all around shattered as if made of glass and I was thrown off my feet, despite turning the attack aside.

"To me!" I called as I twirled through the air, and I felt the veil over my companions fall. Two of my most trusted Chaos Knights, each nearly my equal in power, appeared on either side of the lone Vikari.

Feldren, known for his incredible speed, knocked aside the sword she held and grabbed hold of her arm, just as Talon, a more talented weaver of Chaos you'd be hard pressed to find, firmly grasped her left. I was neither a fresh-faced recruit nor one as foolish to waste words when I had my opponent in a compromised situation, so I made it to my feet and shot forth like an arrow from an impossibly strong bow.

I moved so fast that the air cracked, and my sword

whistled as I brought it down. But as fast as I moved, she moved faster and with much more power than should have been possible. Energy crackled off her, flaring all around a black and red aura. Both Feldren and Talon went flying, their bodies aflame in Chaos fire. The Chaos Flame wouldn't be enough to kill them. Every being of Chaos could control it, and it didn't harm us as severely as one might expect.

My blade was turned aside by hers just as I reached striking distance. The force of the blow nearly made me lose control of my sword, but I held on tight, kicking back and out of the way of her counterattack. However, I hadn't moved far enough. As she sliced down, a line of energy travelled off her sword and struck me in the chest.

That single attack sent pain through my body unlike anything I'd ever felt before. Covered in Chaos Flames my body smashed through a tree some distance away. My mind struggled to right itself and my breath came in ragged pants. I hadn't expected to face death today, but that is what I'd encountered.

Whatever she had done to get this power, it was unlike anything I'd seen before, including that of a Chaos Lord. I saw his gaze in my mind's eye as I tried to determine my next step. I could betray him and join forces with her, but it didn't feel right. He'd spoken of a future filled with prosperity and rest, something my soul very much desired.

I was an old dog of war, beaten and left out to die so many times, but I wouldn't fail in my mission. Not one given to me by our Chaos Lord. Tradition be damned, I didn't keep the faith for such ideals. It was the power in his words, the truth I felt that turned me to his cause.

"You better have meant it, Chaos Lord, ruler of the Eastern Clans. For the sake of Chaos and Order, you better see this task through," I spoke the words and saw a black bird flutter down on a branch of a tree that hadn't been demolished from our fight. It seemed to incline its head at me, and I felt the strands of magic, chaotic as they were, that weaved the bird to life. "So, you will know the outcome of this battle regardless of if I return. So be it. I won't sacrifice life without meaning." Closing my eyes, I reached out to Talon and Feldren, only to find that the latter had perished already.

Speaking aloud but also into the mind of Talon, I said, "Flee and report our failure. I will delay our enemy."

I felt him receive the message, but I couldn't tell if he'd follow the orders. While we Knights of Chaos had a reputation of unpredictability, there was still a certain hierarchy that we tried to obey.

Rushing forward, weapon ready and knowing that my life was forfeit, I prepared to give it my all. My speed, so incredible, the air cracked around me twice. I smashed into an unsuspecting Vikari, taking my blade across her armor, and throwing her back. Talon lay on the ground, right where she had been on the verge of ending his life.

I extended a hand and helped him up.

"I will not flee," he said, gripping his warhammer and cracking his neck to the side. His voice, low and rumbling, was pleasant to hear. Perhaps together we might get lucky, perhaps not.

"Then together we will end this bitch, and the Chaos Knights will be all the better for it," I said, my words portraying more confidence than I felt.

Just then, several of her followers along with a few Chaos Knights among their ranks, began to appear around us. It looked like we'd get a chance to leave a dent in her forces after all. Talon and I did not hesitate to attack. With my first move, I took the head off one of the weaker followers, just a cultist in black robes. My next attack threw a lesser Chaos Knight into a tree, where I sensed his back break.

The battle continued for less than a minute before she returned with her terrible power. Talon fell first, and I took a mortal wound to the chest only seconds later. The raw power that spilled off her was impossible, completely unreal.

"As much as it hurts me to say it," I said, spitting blood out before me. My sword was far enough away and my life force so weak that I couldn't do much more than kneel in pain. "Order is coming for you!" I shouted vehemently. "And you aren't ready!"

I heard her hideous laugh and three words before darkness took me.

"Let them come."

# CHAPTER 1
## HOME FOR NOW

**M**ab had been right; we did need a drink after being teleported from such a distance. Only minutes after arriving, it felt like my insides and outsides were being stretched in all directions at once. If not for holding several pieces of my broken armor and my newly acquired sword, I'd likely just have laid out on the ground. As it were, I sat in front of the formidable weapon while Alayna, Emory, and Ismene talked animatedly about what had just happened.

I wasn't paying any attention to their words, instead, my eyes were fixed on the sword of truth, the Shard of the Ordu, and it was mine. I had fed it all my spare essence, keeping only a few thousand for myself, yet still, the blade didn't so much as pulse a drop of power. My memories were clear from the dungeon, I knew what this weapon could do and how it felt to wield it at full strength, and this wasn't it.

What had Merlin said? I needed to feed it several million essence? I stood suddenly, remembering the gems Merlin had stored in the back room. Certainly, one of those massive gems, brimming with endless amounts of essence, wouldn't be missed if they were just sitting around.

My mind came spinning in on itself as I stood, and I took in the room around me. The thick black oak table was sturdy enough for me to catch myself before I swooned over the bench. Sitting back down, I decided I still needed time before I tried anything.

The room bustled with a low hum of conversation from locals and a few lower-level adventurers. Bright cloaks, mismatched armor, and weak level gear, all the trademarks of lower-level adventurers. My eyes rolled across the locals, and I recognized several people, though by the looks they gave me, the recognition didn't go both ways. The fireplaces were burning again, the cool night air filling the room each time someone opened a door.

I hadn't remembered it being night when we arrived, but so scrambled were my thoughts from the teleportation that I could hardly be bothered to remember.

Emory had a large smile on his face, but I didn't know why since I wasn't paying attention to the conversation. Nevertheless, I returned a smile when he looked my way.

He truly was a titan of a man, and though he was larger than me, we both knew that with my superior attributes, I was easily his match in strength. Given our close friendship, this was a fact that neither of us would even think of testing. I found myself reminiscing of that friendship and simpler times. He looked at me with a curious expression, but I quickly looked away.

My eyes then came to rest on the beautiful Ismene with her striking purple eyes and straight black hair that fell over her face. She met my gaze and smiled. Ismene and I had given so much and would have given even more to get to where we were now, powerful adventurers. It felt like almost no time had passed since we last sat at this table, talking about how we would make her an Awakened. We had gone and hunted giant rats, nearly getting her killed in the process, and if not for the kindness of Merlin and his unusual powers, she very well may have perished. She gave me her signature, 'are you okay?' look and I nodded, before turning my attention to Alayna.

Oh Alayna, I thought as I put an arm around her and pulled her close. The warmth of her touch was enough to push away some of the grogginess that held so firmly in my mind. She turned her vibrant purple eyes on me and leaned forward. I kissed her softly, closing my eyes and letting the darkness wash over me. Emory and Ismene were lifelong friends, but Alayna was so much more to me. It felt as if in her arms I was safe from all else, no matter how dark and horrible. Flashes of the war couldn't threaten me when I had her close, nor the pain of those who I'd lost. That list—the number of which had grown over the last few months during our expedition—haunted most of my waking hours.

"I hope it was worth it," I said, my voice cracking as I trailed off into a cough. I ran my hand across the blade thinking of all the impossible tasks I'd accomplished to get to the point where I was now. Then it hit me how much more still needed to get done and I sighed.

Alayna put her hand atop mine, drawing it closer to herself. "We did it. We actually did the impossible. You are one step closer to putting the world right again. But I just can't help but wonder."

"Wonder what?" I asked, her warmth merging with mine as I held her close.

"The elves and my cousin, our companions," she said, raising her brows at me when I didn't immediately get where she was going. "Did they get transported back as well, and if so, where are they?"

"I'm sure he sent them back to wherever he thought they were meant to be," a voice said. I turned to see Mab hanging over us, a free hand polishing a glass. "Mind if I sit?"

She sat without waiting for an answer. She was a dark-haired woman with a wild look in her eyes. "Tell me about your travels and try not to miss any details."

I looked at Alayna who just shrugged. We had nothing to hide at this point and it might do me good to go over the facts.

Starting at the beginning, I went over how we'd ended the conflict in the Southlands and made plans to bring peace to the Easternlands. Then how I'd maneuvered us into being able to join the elves with Alayna's help. I even told her of the essence grounds that were overflowing with power, though I didn't really know why I divulged that information. It was like she was pulling all the facts and secrets she wanted out of me, and I was unable to stop her.

Finally, we got to our airborne adventure. I told her about our losses, the monsters we came up against, and the endless hordes that met us before Merlin appeared.

"Oh, how like him. Fixing a problem he caused in the first place! But you made it here, so you must have faced dear old Arthur and lived to tell the tale. How wonderous your tale is. Do you mind if I record it for you? I believe the history books will one day want an account of the great Caldor Miles and his adventures. But we can talk in more detail later. I believe you've got an item or two you wanted to plunder from the back room of our dear Merlin's pub?"

"How did you?" I began to ask but she just put her finger against her lips and winked at me.

"Follow me and I will show you to what you need," She said, her eyes as wild as ever.

I did as she requested, picking up the sword and taking it with me. My mind reeled at the sudden motion, but I managed to stay on my feet and follow her to the back. The eyes of my friends followed me the entire way.

The savory smell of stew reached my nose and my mouth watered. I needed to get me a bowl of that stuff, but I had to stay focused for now. I had wet my lips with some sweet ale and felt all the refreshed for it, but it wasn't anything against the hunger that was beginning to grow deep in my stomach. The floorboards creaked underfoot, and I was brought back to reality. Mab had led me to the back room and the table was filled with items once more.

"You may take two items of your choosing, but no more," she said, and my eyes hungrily passed over the table.

There were weapons, armor, gems, trinkets, books, and more sprawled over the table. First, I went for a gem similar to the one Merlin had given me before and found that it contained an impressive six-hundred thousand essence. I checked the others and they all had less. Taking the largest of the gems in my hands I transferred the essence into me, while immediately transferring it into the blade from my own core. There was an odd sense to it, like I was drinking myself full while a part of me leaked it free.

By the time I finished, a shiver ran up my spine. It seemed now that the runes on the surface glowed ever so slightly brighter. Had I not been staring at them for so long, I might not have noticed the change. I reached out to pick up the next biggest gem when Mab cleared her throat.

"Perhaps you ought to look over all the items. You seem to have broken your armor, for instance."

She had a good point, but I had every intention of getting my armor fixed. I ran my hand over some of the armor and, sure enough, none of it compared to the free slots and reinforcement enchantment that my 'Lord Black's Enchanted Armor' gave. Though, there was another item that drew my eyes: a book as thick as my clenched fist and looked to be even more ancient than Merlin. A gem was set into the center of the cover, yet despite my profession bonuses, I got no sense of what it did.

I opened the first page and read the title.

"Guide to the Path of the Titans."

"Ah yes, one of the oldest texts that our dear Merlin had, but he's walking much further down that path that he no longer requires the text. Perhaps it would be best that a younger mind got a look at it? Take the book and read."

Her words were like a command, and I found myself taking the book into my arms. However, I purposely refrained from reading it. Though her strength and iron will be formidable, mine was equally so. The temptation to flip through the pages was difficult, but I continued to resist. Mab let out a crackling laugh upon realizing I had successfully defied her.

"You might have what it takes after all. Good luck, son of Elkor, mighty slayer of cities."

With a casual wave of her hands, the table was cleared instantly, yet the book and gem remained in my possession. I put both in my inventory and made my way back to my friends. Stew had been delivered to each of them, and a hot steaming bowl was waiting for me as well. I dug in without a word, enjoying the flavors and zest of the amazing food with each bite.

"That Mab lady is a bit old for you," Emory said, chuckling as he polished off his stew. "I mean I know you said you liked older ladies, but something tells me she is much older than she looks."

"Excuse me," Alayna said in mock offense. "The only lady Caldor is having is me, so if Mab wants some, she'll have to get in line and wait her turn."

Despite having a mouthful of stew, I felt my face flush, which made them all laugh the more for it.

"So, when are you going to make an honest man out of my Caldor?" Ismene asked, not at all wary of calling me her Caldor in front of Alayna. Neither were the jealous type, but the wording of it made me cringe a bit. Nevertheless, I kept on eating my stew, enjoying each bite until I reached the last one.

This time Alayna blushed, and we exchanged a look as

I finished off my last bite. It wasn't like we hadn't thought about it, but we had long lives ahead of us. Or at least we hoped as much, both of us having taken the life extending perks and reaching levels that most Awakened didn't.

Alayna surprised me by responding first. "I could say the same about you and my cousin."

"Oh, she's gotcha there," Emory said, loving every moment of the tense back and forth.

"Quit it," I said, shaking my head. "We all have lots of life to live yet. We don't need to make decisions now, we are young still, lets act like it." And with that, I took a pull of my ale, draining the cup and calling for another.

The rest of the night passed by in a blur as we talked, joked, and reminisced. So much had changed for all of us over the past year. Each one of us had the potential to be some of the strongest Awakened in the land, and not a small amount of that was owed to us by the devastation done to that city where we power-leveled so hard.

I glanced at my character sheet with a thought and couldn't believe the progress I'd made.

Name: Caldor Miles | Classification: Arcane Knight | Species: Human

Level: 52, 834,750 Essence to Lvl. 53 | Essence: 4,003 | Reputation: Rank 5, 13%

Health: 2,790/2,790 | Mana: 3,150/3,150 | Stamina: 2,300/2,300

Health Regen: 259 Per Minute | Mana Regen: 158 Per Minute | Stamina Regen: 210 Per Minute

Constitution: 259 (74 Base) | Intellect: 315 (80 Base) | Endurance: 210 (77 Base)

Core: 97 (74 Base) | Concentration: 144 (74 Base) | Strength: 386 (76 Base)

# CHAPTER 2
## SWORD PRACTICE

Now that the sword had a bit of essence in it, I wanted to test out its possibilities. To that end, I'd taken Emory, Ismene, and Alayna out to the middle of nowhere to spar. I had no intention of going full force, as my power still stood a head above the rest, especially with the sword in my possession. However, I'd learned time and time again that in the heat of battle, insights could be gained.

We were a few miles east of Creeshaw in an opening in the trees, and I couldn't sense anything more than a few stray signs of wildlife for miles, so we were alone. The wind came in sharp and cool as the seasons were in the throes of change, but I barely noticed. My loose white tunic fluttered against my chest, as if the wind wanted to rip it off to show my muscles beneath.

I took a moment before we began our sparring and closed my eyes, feeling my essence. It pulsed and flowed through my body like a cool summer's breeze. I could focus down to the smallest part of it and feel it as it worked to strengthen my body and soul. My core was like a bright star, shining with incredible power, ready to blind me if I looked too long. I averted my spiritual gaze and slowly opened my eyes to my surroundings.

Black oaks with yellow leaves swaying against the sudden gust of wind that was so common in the area, the ground covered in dead leaves. Across from me were my three opponents. Emory was equipped with his best armor and weapons: shining steel armor pulsing with runic formations beneath the surface and a powerful sword that nearly glowed with power, barely perceivable by the untrained eye.

Meanwhile, Ismene had her set of leather chainmail armor and a bow at the ready. She was the one I'd need to watch out for, as her unique abilities could trick and trip me up. Then there was Alayna, in her glorious white and gold armor. With the faceplate down it was hard to tell if she was taking this seriously, but with how she held her mace I doubted it—she'd decided against bringing her spear, saying she preferred the new mace she'd gotten commissioned recently. It hung at her side, as if it were too much weight to be bothered with, and every now and again she swung it up as if to get ready to attack but then just let it swing back to her side.

"Remember," I said, shouting into the space between us. "Do not hold back or hesitate. I'll do the same."

Of course, I only half meant that, as I didn't plan on using any skills or spells. But my skill with the sword was nothing to sneeze at anymore. Through countless hours and battles, I'd honed my skill to a razor's edge. Michael would be proud, I was sure, almost as sure as I was that he would still find something in my form to correct. I smiled, thinking about the sword master and how he'd promised to look after my siblings. With him at their side, they couldn't fail.

"Let's get this foolhardy exercise started," Ismene said, sarcasm in her tone masking the worry I knew she felt for Zander. All of them had wanted me to teleport to the Elven capital and make sure that everyone had arrived, but I wasn't ready to teleport again, and I needed to figure out how to use this sword at its full capacity. It took priority over every other concern, though, I too was worried for our friends and companions. Kora would be very useful at a time like this, her strength and potential much greater than even my own.

Many times, she'd proved that the wisdom of a dungeon could be turned into a deadly strength and that was the kind of challenge I needed to push myself further. Of course, I also needed thousands and thousands of essence, but not for my own advancement, but that of the sword. It was a curious thing, this sword. When I'd wielded the fake version of it in the dungeon, the power had been intoxicating and over-whelming, yet I was so eager to power the blade back up to its full strength. Did I have the willpower to even wield this sword? It was a question that haunted my inner thoughts.

"Begin," I shouted, raising my sword, and readying myself.

Ismene shot first, releasing a seemingly normal arrow right for my unarmored chest. I deftly sidestepped, expecting the arrow to fly harmlessly by. However, just as it was only inches away from my chest, it exploded with a sudden surge of essence. The force of the blow sent me back a few steps. Though I was unharmed, smoke drifted up from a hole in my shirt.

"I said, no holding back," I remarked, laughing as I stepped forward to meet Emory, blade against blade.

Ismene cursed as Emory's beefy form blocked her next shot, and Alayna just watched, swinging her mace as if she were bored.

With a mighty clang of our weapons, Emory and I locked blades. We both knew plenty of ways to break such a hold, but we didn't. Instead, Emory grinned in my face, looking like he was on the verge of laughing.

"I'm as strong as you now," he said, chuckling as he increased his push, forcing me to take a step back.

I smiled but said nothing.

With a heft of my own, I pushed back, and he flew back several feet, our sword lock broken. He should know that he isn't a match for me, not yet at least. He'd been putting his attributes straight into Strength for some time now, and eventually he might outpace me, but not yet. We clashed again, but this time I avoided giving him a sword lock, striking against his armor several times before kicking him in the chest. He fell to his knee, panting.

"That all you got," he said between huffing breaths of air. "I'll handle you all by myself, you just watch."

Alayna appeared by his side, her full-faced mask still down and she rested a hand on his shoulder. "Rest a moment, while I teach my lover a lesson in humility."

I smiled. She could certainly try, but I had a ten-level advantage over her, along with an increased number of attributes. Moreover, I'd been trained by Michael and Fran, there was no way she could match me with that unwieldy mace she used.

"Bring it on," I said, realizing this was the first time I'd ever sparred with her before, though I'd seen her fight plenty of times.

She advanced toward me at a steady pace, and I raised my sword to meet her blows. The first one nearly knocked my sword from my hand; the force behind her mace swing was twice as hard as I'd anticipated. But I quickly got the hang of it, ensuring not to catch the full force of the attack on the blade's edge—something Michael would have lectured me for if he'd seen it. I was overconfident and it showed.

I teased her, striking her in the chest lightly and even scoring a head shot that left a scratch in her pretty armor. That was when she decided to stop playing with me. Her form burst into golden light, and it almost appeared like she had golden wings spreading out of her back. Suddenly, she was my match in speed and strength. She struck out and knocked my sword out of my hand. As I'd spent the night before bonding the weapon, I rolled out of the way of the next strike and the sword returned to my hand immediately.

My instincts told me to activate a skill or spell, but I resisted, wanting to keep a fair match. An arrow slammed into my exposed, unarmored thigh just as I pivoted around to avoid another slamming blow. Just as I faltered, a lance of light smashed into my chest and this time, I felt the blow. Blood dripped down my chest and suddenly, the idea of fighting without armor didn't seem like a smart choice.

Ripping the arrow free through gritted teeth, I caught her next blow just as the aura of golden light faded around her. To my surprise, she kicked me in my wounded chest and disengaged, slapping Emory on the shoulder as she backed off.

"You're up big man," she said, lifting her visor and

showing a row of gleaming white teeth. "I'll buff you, but I've just used up my most potent offensive abilities."

Emory got to his feet just as Ismene stepped forward, an aura of green around her and a massive polearm in her hands that I'd never seen her use before. But she swung it about with practiced ease and I found out soon what the aura was doing for her. Her speed was off the charts. It wasn't just me that had picked up a few new tricks, and I was learning that my friends had much more to offer than I'd been giving them credit for.

"My turn!" Emory screamed as he emanated an aura of his own. His was a reddish color that I'd often attributed to bosses enraging in dungeons, so I instantly guessed at what it must do.

Forgoing the use of his shield for the duel, he cut a swath in the ground as his long sword dug in and sprayed dirt in my direction. I didn't let it distract me, especially since I had to keep my eyes on Ismene as she suddenly moved as fast as me. Weaving back and forth, I avoided both attackers—Emory, slower but now seemingly a match for my strength, and Ismene, much weaker but mirroring my swiftness.

Back and forth we moved. I landed one or two strikes, but fighting two opponents at once, while occasionally dodging a lance of light from a third, was no easy task. I found myself pumping a small amount of essence into the sword, as I had with my previous weapon, but no boost of power came. Instead, the sword soaked it up greedily.

I felt the barest of surges from within and power crackled up my arm. Although, whether it did anything, I couldn't tell. I moved the same speed, my strength remained the same, and yet, as I fought, it did seem easier to track the movements of all three of my opponents. But I was ready to attribute that to the weapon itself, as it was so different than the overwhelming sense of power it had given me before. But the longer I held them off the more I was able to predict their movements perfectly.

It got to the point that I'd fought them both to a standstill and if I were willing to use a skill or spell, I'd have taken care of Alayna as well. Several times I had to restrain myself, as my instincts told me when to strike with a well-placed Lightning Strike that would take her out of the fight. There was a stillness that came with using the sword, like my entire being was focused beyond anything I'd experienced before.

The fight was over, they just didn't realize it yet. I swooped in, kicking Ismene right off her feet and sending her smashing into Alayna. Then, in the same motion, I swung my sword right into Emory's armored chest, and followed up with a strike to his exposed neck. I held off from actually cutting him, but he froze, eyes wide as I held the blade there.

"The fight is over, I win," I said, finally letting myself

take a full breath. I felt the stillness withdraw and suddenly my mind felt foggy when compared to the crispness that I'd been experiencing.

"Mind moving that sword?" Emory asked, his eyes still locked on the blade at his throat.

"Oh, sorry," I said, removing the sword and letting it hang loose in my hand. "You two alright?" I asked, calling over to the jumble of legs and arms struggling to stand.

"I bit my lip," Ismene complained, but finally she made it to her feet and glared daggers in my direction. "That kick broke two of my ribs. You owe me a drink. Overpowered brute." She said the last bit under her breath, but I heard it just as easily as if she'd spoken it aloud.

"Did it work?" Alayna asked, pulling her helmet free and her blonde curls spilling over her face.

"I think so," I said, looking at the sword and trying to decide if I could attribute the effects to it or my own abilities. Deciding that it must have been the sword, I shook my head vigorously. "Yes. It worked. I'm unlocking the powers of the sword, but now it just needs an immense amount of essence and I think I might know where it can get it."

"Where's that?" Emory asked, cracking his neck to the side, and rolling his shoulders. I could tell he still wanted to fight, but I'd learned what I needed and there was little point for us to duel otherwise.

"Well, I need to cleanse the ley lines, right? And the ley lines are filled with essence, so if I go to where the corruption started, then maybe I'll be able to charge up the sword and fix the Prime Mana Shrine as well. It isn't the perfect plan, but it's the best I got."

Alayna and Ismene both tried to speak at once, but Ismene spoke louder, and Alayna allowed her to take over.

"We need to check on the others first," she said, her expression strained. Alayna nodded; likely she was going to say something similar. They were right of course, but I still didn't like the idea of opening a portal or teleporting yet.

"Give me a day to recover and I will go check on them," I promised, looking each of my friends in the eye as I did so. They nodded, knowing that I was a man of my word. I could tell just by looking at Ismene that she'd prefer we not wait at all, but short of flying over there with Ares, I wasn't ready to summon forth the magic just yet.

We headed back into town after the sparring session, each of us ready for lunch. Our bodies operated at peak efficiency, but that also meant that we hungered for more and more food. Unless, of course, it was a higher quality of food that would sustain us with a smaller amount, but there was a reason why larger portions of food were so common for adventurers. We fought hard and we needed to eat hard.

# CHAPTER 3
## RECOVERY

Sitting in the warm bath, I found myself alone for the first time in longer than I could remember. With that sudden realization, came the darkness. It wrapped around me like a noose and with it, the names, and images of so many dying. I clenched hard on my wash rags, trying to will away the darkness, to no avail. It was like I was back on the field of battle and no matter how fast I moved or how hard I fought, my friends died all around me.

My body shuddered and I could feel myself on the verge of breaking. It was like the weight of all my grief decided to appear all at once and without friendly faces around, I couldn't see the way out. Suddenly, my sword appeared in my grip and a stillness surrounded me. The pain was still there, but a distance had been erected between it. I could now see it logically and dismiss it if I wished.

I didn't. Instead, I let the names flow through my mind in perfect clarity. I accepted that this was my reality, but that it didn't make me any less of a man. No less of a warrior, a friend, a partner.

I was enough, the weight of this darkness be damned!

I refused to surrender.

I refused to be beaten.

The words of my father and his ideals filled my head. He'd tell me that one can only do as much as they're capable of and that if the goodness I brought into the world outweighed my failures, then I should mark myself as a successful man. It was hard to believe those words at times, not to mention the fact that I still didn't know if he was truly alive or what had happened to him, but in the end it was enough.

My father, as I knew him then, spoke truth into my soul and strengthened me. I let the sword fade away, knowing that I could pull it back for strength at any moment, but I was good for now. I finished bathing and wiped tears from my face that I hadn't realized I'd released.

I thought I'd hidden away any sign of my episode, but the moment I saw Alayna, she rose from her seat and pulled me into a tight hug. "I love you," she whispered in my ear, and I felt myself strengthen all the more for it.

"I love you too," I said, and I meant it. Our life and

our relationship weren't perfect, but my feelings for her had blossomed into something stronger than anything I'd ever felt for anyone else. I couldn't imagine a life without her by my side. Despite every bit of my life being filled with danger and potential harm to those around me, I'd keep her as close as I could and together, we would triumph over the world and anyone willing to challenge us.

She led me back to the table with our friends and we enjoyed a second lunch, each of us needing to gather our strength. A few times, my hands began to shake slightly, but a stray touch by Alayna or with a bit of hard focus, I had it under control again.

Looking up, I was surprised to see Cam enter the bar. He was supposed to have moved to Blackridge and yet, here he was getting a drink and sitting at a table with his wife and child. I didn't get up yet, but I decided I'd go see him and maybe understand why he hadn't left already. It had been a while since I was able to check up on him and I was curious how he was getting along. So, finishing up our meal I turned to Alayna.

"I'm going to go visit an old friend, did you want to come? His name is Cam, I've told you about him, I'm sure," I said, and Emory perked up hearing the name.

"He the one you and Kora gave the metal arms?" Emory asked, then before I could answer he continued.

TIMOTHY MCGOWEN

"I'd love to arm wrestle him and see just how strong those arms make him. Can I come?"

"Why don't you boys go, and the girls will see about doing some shopping and relaxing while you're gone," Alayna said, leaning in to give me a soft kiss.

"Or we could go visit Emilia and see if she could use a hand around the farm, with all her kids out being adventurers," Ismene suggested. This caught my attention, as I'd never known Ismene to be great friends with my mother. They got along fine, but she never went to randomly spend time with her.

"Oh, that sounds lovely!" Alayna said, and I knew my opinion didn't matter at that point.

Emory and I decided to wait for Cam and his family to finish eating and leave, so as not to interrupt their meal. We headed out to their small farm a little while after they'd left.

***

We found Cam working on some trees on his property, having finally purchased some of the acreage around his cottage. The sun was out in full force, but he worked with a speed that didn't seem quite normal, his hands zipping from here to there, cutting free parts of the trees as he went. The new arms he'd been given were working well, I could see.

"Slow down," I said, keeping my tone jovial. "You're making me tired just watching you."

Cam had worked up a good bit of sweat, his long coat covering his tunic all but, in the front, where it stuck to his chest. He also had one of the signature wide-brimmed hats that orchard hands used to keep themselves cool from the sun. Short of his metallic arms, he looked like any other orchard worker.

"Here to work for me?" Cam asked, a sly smile spreading over his face. "I'll take the big guy, but you don't look like the working type."

I laughed, Cam laughed, but Emory just grunted before saying, "I'm not a farmhand."

"He's just teasing," I said, shaking my head at Emory. "Our friend Cam has a persistent humor, despite how shorthanded the war left him."

Cam nearly bust a gut as he started to laugh uproariously. It had been a poor joke, to be sure, but it was the kind that he liked, so I went for it.

"Left shorthanded," Cam said between laughs. "That is just perfect."

"Speaking of the hands, how is your control?" I asked. I had plans to improve the model he was using, with Kora's help, but I hadn't found the time to do anything just yet.

In answer, Cam reached out a hand and grabbed hold

of a wrist-sized branch, snapping it off with ease. Then he took the thin bark and gently peeled it back.

"I can both crush anything I've come across and be as gentle as a feather. For the first week or so, it was difficult figuring out how to do one or the other, but I managed to figure it out," Cam said, a far-off look crossing his eyes. "If I'd had these back during the war." He shook his head, not finishing his thought.

"It still would have been hell," I said, seeing where his train of thought was headed and not wanting him to set any blame on himself for faults that were my own.

"But I could have done so much more and now, here I am living out a life as a farmer. With these," he looked down at his arms and paused, then after a moment he sighed and continued, "I could do so much more now."

"Are you not content in your new life?" I asked, surprised that Cam was being so forthcoming with his feelings like this.

"It isn't that," Cam said, his eyes darting to his cottage where his wife and child would be. "I just feel a responsibility to do more. Surely you still have use for someone with my skills. I'm not saying I want to jump right back into another war, but I could do more than this."

My mind went through response after response for several long moments, but I couldn't come up with the words that would work. So instead, I stepped forward and held out a hand. He took it and we shook. His grip was powerful, but not so much so that I wouldn't be able to wrench my hand free if I wanted.

"What happened to you moving out to Blackridge?" I asked. "You told me you sold everything when I saw you there."

"We thought we had, but my wife convinced me that we should finish the harvest first, so we spent some time in Blackridge and then came back here," Cam said.

"I've got plenty of positions that would be a good fit for you if you took the plunge," I assured him.

"We are still planning on it, just wanted to finish off the season before we sold the property back," Cam said, his face a mask of eager enthusiasm.

"Don't sell your cottage just yet. Hire someone to tend to it so that you've got a way back if life doesn't suit you in Blackridge. That is, if you choose to walk that path. There are other major cities and I do not doubt that there is plenty of work, including being a scribe, which I think would suit you just as well."

"Blackridge," Cam said the word as if tasting it and he nodded. "Perhaps a job as a guard would suit me."

"Or a general," Emory offered, as if he knew the least bit about military operations.

Cam laughed and shook his head. "No, I don't think they want me standing on the sidelines." To show his point he squeezed the branch he was holding and basically disintegrated it between his fingers.

"If battle comes again, I'd be honored to have you fight by my side," I said, then a thought occurred to me. Ever since Ismene had such trouble with Awakening, I'd not really followed through with my plan to shout out the nobles' secrets from the rooftops. However, Cam would be a wonderful addition to the ranks of Awakened if he could survive.

I decided to take a look at him and see if I could see what Merlin had seen when inspecting Ismene. Opening my magical sense, I scanned Cam, focusing with all my mind to the task.

It was like looking at the sun at first, with so much life around Cam and the trees, but my inner eye adjusted to the point where I was feeling as much as seeing. Without an idea of what a core should look like, I wasn't going to make much headway. Cam's center was bright, but nowhere near the impossibly deep shine like Emory's core. Did that mean that he didn't have what it took or perhaps the level and time Emory had advancing had changed his core?

I decided not to offer Awakening to Cam just yet but make a mental note to go view other people to get a baseline on understanding what I was seeing. It was rough knowing something that could possibly help Cam and keeping it to myself. I found myself wanting to at least ask his opinion on Awakening, to see if it had changed from any earlier viewpoint he might have had. It wasn't like his level as a soldier and the skills that came with it weren't already benefiting him, perhaps he liked his circumstances as they were?

"Cam, if you could suddenly become Awakened and walk the path Emory and I have been on, would you take it?"

Cam looked a bit taken aback, rubbing the back of his head with his mechanical arm before sighing. "No point in dreaming of the impossible. Sure, when I was younger, I yearned for the chance to be special, but I'm a married man with a wife and child now. I want to do something special with my life, but I'm not sure I'd want to be a full blown Awakened. There is much more responsibility and a certain weight to that calling that I'm not sure I'm up for."

I nodded, understanding now more than I ever did before Awakening myself. "You've got wisdom beyond your years," I said, patting him on the back. I still wanted to go through with sensing others' cores to get an idea for who might be ready and safe to push over the edge to advancing to a Sparked.

"Come on in for some tea," Cam suggested suddenly, wiping sweat from his brow. "It's cold, we've got a new contraption that creates ice for us and it's been a life changer. Had to figure out something to do with all the extra gold we had." Cam added at the end, elbowing me lightly in the ribs as we walked. I pushed him in mock retaliation, and he pretended to stumble into a tree, which had Emory laughing out loud.

It was nice seeing Cam and knowing that he was doing alright. He had an infectious personality that left me wanting to laugh and be lighthearted. Any trace of the darkness that threatened to overtake me, might as well have been nonexistent around Cam. He had come out of the war better than most and I wished I could ask him how he does it, but for whatever reason, I couldn't bring myself to do it. It felt as though admitting that I wasn't doing perfectly would, somehow, spoil his own triumph over the many horrors he experienced.

# CHAPTER 4
## MAH'KUS

The visit with Cam and his family was a pleasant reminder of how not everyone had been lost in that horrible war. His wife and child were so loving, clinging to Cam as he recounted the days of work that led up to him purchasing the orchard. He didn't mention anything about moving to Blackridge, but I guessed that was likely a conversation to be had with his wife in private. As evening came, they invited us to stay for dinner, but I declined, wanting to go down the road to visit my mother.

So, as it were, we said our goodbyes and left. Emory left me then, saying he wanted to go surprise his family for dinner, so I said my goodbyes to him as well. He was a loyal friend, and a part of me was relieved he hadn't suffered through the worst of the war by my side, opting instead to clear out monsters or pursue quests of his own.

As I walked down the road in the evening light, I took a look over my quests. I had several still active, from Restoring the Balance Part 2 to a vague quest given to me by Lord Variyn to root out the Chaos. It was so general that the rewards weren't much to look at, but it was part of my calling, regardless of his meager quest offerings, so I didn't worry about it.

I examined a quest I'd received from the mysterious Mah'kus, 'Seek the Blade of Order' and wondered if he'd return to give me a part two or if he was finally done meddling in my life. As if my thoughts summoned him to me, a figure that I recognized appeared from behind a tree.

He had dark hair and deep brown eyes filled with humor, as well as a small smirk on his lips. He wore simple clothing that, for once, actually seemed to be of a local style. However, he still stuck out, as his fashion was more appropriate for a noble and not something you'd typically see in Creeshaw. He had a black silk shirt with a tight-fitting purple vest, and dark tan pants that laced up the side with purple string. His boots rose high, reaching his knees, and I noticed the sparkle of a dagger's pommel peeking out from his right boot. I found it slightly amusing to see him armed; from my understanding of the being known as Mah'kus, he could obliterate my existence with a stray thought, no weapon required. When he spoke, his voice was warm and deep as it always was.

"Not done with you just yet," he said, placing a

comforting hand on my shoulder. His touch spread a warmth through my body, and I really did feel a deep measure of comfort just from his mere touch. "And I don't think you need a part two for that quest, do you? Now that you've retrieved the artifact, all that remains is for you to restore the balance. But I would urge you to be swift in your execution of your duties."

"Once I've checked that my friends have made it back safely, I was planning on checking out the Prime Mana Shrine for any signs that I can help it," I said. Running my plan by a god seemed wise enough, but Mah'kus grimaced. It was an expression he only held for a moment, but he was silent for several more before speaking.

"Do what you must but remember that time is of the essence, and your adversary hasn't been idle. Several more Prime Mana Shrines have fallen, I've marked them on your map for you. A little extra help shouldn't hurt." With a wave of his hand, I felt a rush of information hit me and I pulled up my map to see four areas marked.

Surprisingly, there seemed to be a pattern of sorts. The Prime Mana Shrine in Variyn City formed the top position, while the shrines in the Elven lands and the Easternlands sat on either side, and the one in the Southlands occupied the bottom, creating a diamond shape. Was there a method to her madness or was she just trying to spread the rot out as much as possible?

"There is a method, and with the fall of the Elven

Prime Mana Shrine, magic for all in this continent will be weakened. You should begin to feel the effects within weeks, and within a month you will struggle to cast even the most basic spells or skills. The System in place here is very reliant on a continuous stream of magic, like a complex webbed network, to stay functional. If this Chaos Knight is successful, you will find that in your most dire time of need, the powers of both the Order and Chaos will fail. I believe the enemy has somehow communicated with this girl and directed her on this path, but I can't be certain."

"Enemy of who? You and your kind? Can't you use your power to fix the ley lines and just end her?" I rapidly shot my questions at him, as he was being surprisingly open about the situation.

"Enemy of all living kind. I've told you this before, but it needs reminding. I am dead and as such, my powers are limited. Do I have the force of will to purge the ley lines? I might, but in doing so I reveal myself to the enemy and seal the fate of this planet. Could I cut the string of life that holds this Chaos Knight up? Easily, but the more action I take, the more action the enemy will be able to take. It is a tentative balance that must be maintained. So, as they've chosen their champion in her, I have chosen my own in you. Do not fail me, and I promise that when the time comes you will know what to do," Mah'kus said, his gaze steady and full of confidence.

A sudden thought occurred to me. "Do you know if my father is still alive and where I can find him if he is?" I asked, biting my lip when I saw his expression fall.

"I know a great many things but know that I've told you all that is required for you to succeed at this time."

"He is alive isn't he," I said, reading between the lines of his response.

Mah'kus just put a grin on his face and raised a hand in a half salute. "Farewell, Caldor Miles. Remember, that however hopeless the path forward may look, you are on the right path. Continue forward."

A sudden gust of wind forced my eyes closed and when they opened again, he was gone. Left alone with my thoughts, I couldn't help but be frustrated with the being known as Mah'kus and his insistence on messing with my life. Though, I had to admit, I always felt a bit better after talking with him, like my very soul was being refreshed.

\*\*\*

"These girls are a hoot," my mother said, drinking deeply from her glass of wine.

I looked at the trio, all of them drinking and giggling over one thing or another. I'd found them sitting in the newly extended portion of the house where several couches had been placed for lounging, opposite a massive fireplace.

"The changes look good," I said, gesturing to the roaring fireplace.

"Your father and I always wanted to expand the house but with how tightly he held onto the purse strings, we could never justify it," my mother said, then her expression darkened a little and she added, "I wish he was still around to see it. I was just telling the girls how much you look like your father and, based on the stories they've been telling me, you act just like him as well."

"I don't know about that," I said, not seeing myself in the same honorable light that I saw my father. "Surely, if I was more like father, I'd have never gotten myself mixed up in a war."

"He went to war, but unlike him, you came back from it," my mother said, and I felt a pit in my stomach from turning the conversation in this direction.

"Sorry, I shouldn't have brought it up," I said, looking to the side, unable to meet my mother's eyes.

"My sweet Caldor, thicken your skin. I will be alright." Her voice was suddenly a bit mocking, and I looked up to see her grinning at me.

"Perhaps we've had enough wine for the night," I said, grabbing the spare glass Alayna had gotten for me when I arrived and pouring myself some. "Or at least let me catch up first."

What followed was an enjoyable night of drinks and snacking with three women that I loved very dearly. It warmed my heart to see Ismene, Alayna, and my mother getting along so well. One of the additions to the house had been more rooms, giving Michael his own and freeing up my old bedroom. Ismene took Michael's room and Alayna and I retired to mine. A look from my mother as I escorted her to her room, she was very tipsy, had me laughing.

"Where else would she sleep?" I asked, responding to her unasked question.

"She's a lovely girl and I wish you both the best," my mother said, chuckling. "But none of that in my house before you're married. You will be marrying her, won't you?"

"It's very late, let's get you into bed," I said, pushing her covers aside and helping her into bed. "If and when we get married, you will be the first to know, I promise."

"Good, good," she said, already half asleep as her head hit the pillow.

"Good night, mother. I love you."

# CHAPTER 5
## PORTAL TO THE ELVEN LANDS

"Gather up, I'm opening the portal now, but I don't know how long I'll be able to keep it open," I said, focusing my mind on the task at hand. There were a dozen ways this could go wrong. I wasn't the best at portal formations, despite Warrick's help on the subject, but I knew haste was important now and I would not fail.

Mah'kus had made it clear that I should be working on fixing the ley line issue as soon as possible, but I couldn't focus on that until I'd made sure that my friends and comrades had made it back safely from the dreadful Isle of Avalon. With that thought in mind, I began the process of opening the portal. It strained me but after several long seconds, I felt the process take hold and the air before me began to shimmer.

I'd focused on a place I knew well enough, the shipyards. It was where Warrick was meant to wait for us, along with additional military forces, however, a small space had been seared into my mind that was meant to receive portals and teleporting folks. So, when the shimmer turned into a window to that very spot, I let go of a breath I'd been holding. The strain continued but I felt more confident now that I had it open that I'd be able to keep it open for at least another minute, maybe even two.

Emory went first, followed closely by Ismene then Alayna. Finally, after I saw them each move through the portal safely, I stepped through myself and let the window fade away as my concentration faltered. With a shimmer of air, the window closed, and we were left standing in a busy shipyard. I looked around and was surprised with the amount of activity going on around us.

An elf approached from not far off asking us where we transported from and whom we needed to speak with. I informed him that we were part of the expedition that went out to the Isle of Avalon. After telling him our names, he quickly excused himself.

Looking around the large shipyard, I saw several damaged ships that I recognized. It appeared as if Merlin had returned not only the people, but the vessels that made it to the end as well.

"I apologize for the delay, but it was believed that you

had perished, and I needed to halt the plans for your funeral and inform those who required it."

We'd waited for no more than ten minutes, remaining respectful to the elves and their ways. While we waited, I didn't see anyone I recognized, but that made sense in a way. All those that went would be needing medical attention or be on some sort of leave of duty, given all the crazy adventures we'd experienced. Then, to my surprise, a tall willowy figure in flowing grey robes suddenly arrived in a flash before us.

"Warrick, what are you doing here?" I asked Warrick as he strode down the stairs to meet me.

"I came here when you didn't open a portal to Blackridge, and I told those fools you weren't dead. Though, my own detection spells caught no sign of you from half a continent away. Where did that fool, Merlin, send you?" Warrick asked, not waiting to hear an answer from me as he reached forward and pulled me into a tight hug.

"He sent me home to Creeshaw," I said, smiling up at the confident blue eyes of my father's closest friend and my truest mentor. "What have I missed?"

Warrick shrugged at my question, an odd sight from a man so old and powerful as he. "Forget that nonsense for now, everyone is fine and dandy. Let's go get a drink and discuss that weapon you've recovered."

He looked down at the sword I kept sheathed at my side. Although I'd bonded with it, I'd felt wrong about not having it on my person at all times, like if I let it out of my sight, it might get lost. It was an odd sensation to have, considering how I was tied to the weapon from my special class perk, but it was how I felt, nonetheless.

"Alright then, you all coming?" I asked, turning to my companions, but more familiar faces were approaching, and I saw that I'd at least lost Ismene to one such newcomer.

Zander wore black armor with white edges and carried himself like someone that had a broomstick firmly up his backside. As stiff and arrogant as the man could be, I'd grown accustomed to him and it hardly bothered me any longer. However, Ismene was a different story altogether. She was infatuated with him and the moment she saw him, she rushed forward, falling into his arms.

For his part, Zander blushed and wrapped her in a hug just as firm. They shared some words, I was too far to hear them, but I could imagine what they were. Alayna settled her soft gaze on me, and I nodded with a smile, knowing that she wanted to reunite with her cousin as well. Emory turned to me, rolling his eyes and shrugging as he followed behind them.

"I think it might just be us," I said, looking back to Warrick and winking at him.

"As I intended," he said, putting a comforting hand on my shoulder and leading me away.

As we walked, Warrick filled me in on what I'd

missed. About a day ago the entire expedition had appeared just off the coast and rescue airships had to be sent out before any monsters could claim the floating ships, since they'd appeared not in the air but in the actual water. By the time rescuers arrived, some of the crew were beginning to come to, but the vast majority of them were still unconscious. Warrick explained that to do what Merlin did would have taken a hundred or more Awakened with Warrick's power, and even so, he wouldn't have attempted it because the effects it might have on people physically.

Which explained the next part of what he told me. Over half of those sent back were being treated for internal wounds. Something about needing advanced healers that could resettle the very essence of their bodies and place organs back where they were meant to be. It was all a bit much for me to process, but I was suddenly glad that everyone who'd returned with me had come back in a single piece. Or at least I hoped there was nothing wrong with us, perhaps we ought to get checked after all.

I told Warrick as much and he said he'd done a quick scan of us already, seeing no displacements or lasting effects. A part of me wanted to remind him that he was not in fact a healer, so perhaps I should consult with one instead, but I didn't. I was too eager to discuss with him the sword and what lay ahead for me. By the time we reached the place Warrick was leading me, it became clear it was a personal room of his, but drinks had already been set out.

It was tea.

"This tea won't do anything to me will it?" I asked, only half joking. Warrick had been instrumental in repressing my Spark using our weekly tea meetings as cover. I had forgiven him already, but I couldn't help myself when it came to messing with him.

"I deserved that," Warrick said, shaking his head. "It's a black tea that will awaken your mind only and tastes quite lovely."

"That's good," I said, pulling free the sword and placing it down on the rectangular wooden table with a soft clink. "Have a look."

Warrick shifted in his seat, the red velvet making a sound beneath him as he did so, before finally reaching out and taking up the sword. His eyes closed and I could easily guess what he was doing, examining it with his magical senses. After a solid minute of holding it, one hand on the hilt and the other on the flat of the blade, he opened his eyes.

"I sense nothing special about it," he said. "How strange. I would expect something from such a legendary artifact."

"I'm still feeding it," I said, holding out my hand for the sword. He passed it to me, careful to keep the edge from nicking my skin. "According to Merlin, it requires several million essence, just as a start, to begin to unlock its original powers. Which are substantial and addictive."

Warrick looked at me with an expression I'd grown accustomed to, an almost fatherly gaze. "You will be careful, won't you? Such artifacts are sometimes best to have remained lost. Yes, yes, I know you need it and why, but tell me what you've learned of its powers and this addictive quality you claim it has."

So, I did, going through the entire events of my journey and sparing no detail that might be too small. All the while, Warrick listened intently, hmming and ahhing in all the right places. By the time I finished my tale, ending it with the appearance of Mab, he was on the edge of his seat.

"You say the sword made you feel unstoppable, as if you could reshape the very matter around you?" Warrick asked. I could tell this part of the story had gotten him excited by the way his mustache twitched. It usually meant he wanted to ask a question right away but was too impatient to wait for me to finish.

"It was a power so incredible," I said, "that I can't imagine how devastating it is to be wielded in the wrong hands."

"I know firsthand what the artifact can do in the wrong hands," Warrick said. "I think we ought to be grateful that the weapon wielded by that Chaos Knight wasn't as deadly as the one you described. She had many more tools and machines at her call, but they were all controlled by the sword. I think perhaps she doesn't know how to use the sword at its full capacity either. You will have that advantage over her when you face her in battle."

"If I can find her," I said, shaking my head. "All I can do right now is try and fix the damage that she's done. I meant to start my attempt at healing the ley lines where the first Prime Mana Shrine fell, but I don't know what I will be able to do if I can't get a hold of at least another million or so essence. You wouldn't happen to have any gems filled with essence laying around?"

"I do not," he answered, but he paused suddenly, eyes going wide and then his face fell. He tapped on his lips a few times before raising a finger in exclamation. "I do not, but I bet the Elven Queen does! Surely, she'd be willing to part with a million or two for the betterment of all those living."

I'd only met the Queen briefly before, but she had seemed like the sort to understand. She had, after all, allowed me to go forward with the expedition that allowed me to get the sword in the first place. How much more of a burden could asking for a million essence be? If it were a matter of coin, I had so much that I'd gladly give it to her if it meant accomplishing my quest.

Of course, if it were just a matter of buying monster cores or collected essence in the millions, I'd just do that. But I knew that that amount wouldn't be available for sale in any capacity. If it were, I'd be more worried about Lord Variyn setting off another powerful detonation and ruining more lives. I was actually worried about that, but I tried to not let it show.

"It would be worth a try," I said, and Warrick nodded along.

We spoke further about the sword, and I went over again how I felt when using it. I also told him that I was fairly confident that I'd be able to resist the effects this time, now that I knew what to expect. He said that he wasn't sure he could resist it but patted me on the back, saying that I was likely to be just fine with it. I almost told him about my meeting with Mah'kus and the additional fallen Prime Mana Shrines, but I hesitated.

It wasn't like Mah'kus had specifically told me not to share his meetings with anyone, and I'd told of his meetings before, but I didn't want to worry Warrick.

"Any news from the East or when are you expected?" I asked, remembering part of the bargain we struck with the Eastlanders that required Warrick to be present after his show of power against the Chaos Knights.

"I've given them the means to get a message to me, but I don't plan on answering that call until Newaliyn's armies have gathered in full force. You see, I'm not as invincible as I might seem some days. After the events with that wretched lady, I'm much weaker than I ought to be. My power comes in spurts and blasts," he said, and I took a moment to truly look at him.

As I studied him more closely, he indeed seemed more haggard. The bags under his eyes were the worst I'd ever seen on him, but he was standing under his own power and had a quick step at that. How bad could it possibly be for someone who showed off as much power as he did? While he might have acquired a few more wrinkles than I remembered, it was hard to really say.

Determined not to focus on his shortcomings, I looked him in the eyes and saw the power reverberating within. "You'll be fine," I said by way of comfort.

Sipping at the tea, I savored the pleasant flavors. It was such a notable difference ever since hitting my latest threshold and breaking through it. Each little herb and flavor played over my tongue at once, but I could also experience them individually and really appreciate each note. It was because of this that I noticed that lack of a flavor that I'd grown used to, a sort of minty flavor that had accompanied all the different teas he'd given me. I realized without having to ask him that it had been the elixir used to suppress my Spark, or perhaps a strong flavor to help mask it.

We finished our tea and sat in silence for several long minutes. Neither of us needed to say a word, both content to be in pleasant company. After a time, Warrick pulled out a book and I did the same. Alayna found us some time later while I was in the middle of a very exciting bit of information about theoretical uses for monster cores, including such ideas as using them as substitutions for those that could Awaken. Whoever had written this section—it was a gathering of works from various authors —hadn't known the secret that noble families held close to their chests.

It was an interesting read though, suggesting that by placing more powerful Cores in the chest and infusing them with essence, one might attach them to an individual, enabling them to access essence-driven abilities and spells. It theorized that it might have to operate outside the system that normal Awakened operated, but the author wasn't entirely sure, as infusing essence wasn't a secret that anyone knew at the time. So, his theories had been just that: theories. And it was a good thing too, because the processes this person suggested looked like borderline torture.

\*\*\*

"I need an audience with the Queen," I said, directing my words to Adathin.

Alayna and I sat beside his bed as he was still resting from having to have several organs replaced in the correct positions. He looked like hell; his sheets were as white as a cloud, and his face not far from the same color. It was like he was trying and succeeding to do a Zander impression, which was unfortunate, considering his complexion had been notably darker before his return by Merlin.

Adathin coughed, crimson blood staining a cloth he held over his mouth. "I can try to arrange a meeting, but I'll need to know why if I am going to have any chance of doing so."

I nodded and Alayna put a comforting hand on my back as I dove into it. I explained about the sword and what I needed to do. Then went on to explain that according to Merlin, I needed several million essence to get the sword ready. His expression went from placid to confused to outright horrified when I told him how much essence I needed.

"I'm not sure anyone has that amount of essence just sitting unused inside cores," he said, ending his words with several painful sounding coughs. "But I can see that you are serious, and I will try my best. Can this Merlin be trusted after what he did to us?"

"His word isn't the only thing I have to go off of," I said. "I've fed the sword half a million essence of my own and I've felt it begin to do...well, let's just say, it's done something, just not much."

"I'll send out a petition to the Queen at once," Adathin said, and he signaled to a waiting healer. She gave him a pen and paper, all the while glaring in our direction. Satisfied that he'd get it done, I left to go have dinner with

Fred, Fran, Kora, Emory, Alayna, Zander, Ismene, and Beth.

It was a fun night of drinks and revelry that ended far too soon. The Queen had provided an entire eating hall to us, despite us taking up only a small amount of the available space. Fred was his usual self, and Kora stayed close by him. They often spoke in soft tones to each other. About what, I couldn't be sure, but it warmed my heart to see Fred being more animated in his speech.

Fran stayed close to Emory, and I thought maybe there was something happening there as I watched them flirt back and forth, but I didn't say anything. It was a fun show to watch; Emory wasn't exactly a ladies' man and Fran hit him with sarcasm and teasing more than anything else.

Zander and Ismene sat beside Alayna and me, but they were more affectionate, and after a while, I almost wanted to move down a few spots. For the sake of Alayna, I didn't, and after a few drinks, I didn't care anymore. Beth was her normal social self, going from group to group and injecting herself into conversations with ease. All was well that night, and I knew I would remember it for months to come. All was in harmony and at peace. If only it could stay that way.

# CHAPTER 6
## A QUEEN'S REQUEST

My meeting with the Queen came two days later and I found myself standing outside her royal throne room awaiting my turn for an audience. To say I was feeling a bit nervous would be an understatement. My heart rate accelerated and sweat ran down the side of my face. The Queen would already know what I wanted, and I just had to convince her that the great cost would be worth it.

Before I had much more chance to think about what lay ahead, the doors opened, and my name was announced. The throne room was much the same as I remembered it before, tasteful banners and works of art covering the walls. However, it was the centermost throne that, once again, caught my attention.

It was clearly a throne of some kind, but it looked as if

it were grown straight out of the ground and carved into a suitable seat for a queen. The colors were green, brown, and gold, all mixed together in such a way that it played tricks on my eyes the longer I looked at it.

Upon the throne, was a single figure with bone straight brown hair atop her head, with the occasional braid running here or there. Her eyes, cunning and expectant as I approached, were the deepest of blue. It was like staring into a swirling ocean of colors with specs of white that gleamed with power. She had a proud bearing, same as before, and emanated power that if I'd been any weaker, might have already forced me to a knee.

I knew by experience that she could and would eventually pull her aura back, so I followed protocol and bowed to her as I reached a dozen paces from her. The powerful aura that made even breathing difficult, suddenly vanished and she spoke.

"Please shield your aura as I taught you," she said, her tone revealing a hint of annoyance that I hadn't remembered to do so.

I closed my eyes and focused on sensing my aura. When I'd first attempted to do this, I'd had very little success, but I'd been practicing and with a good amount of effort, I suppressed it as best I could.

"Better than before, but you still burn like a raging flame in my senses. Keep practicing," the Queen said, her gentle smile putting me at ease as I raised my attention to her. She gestured to a seat beside the throne, which had appeared as if out of nowhere, but I was used to it. I took a seat beside her so that we could get into the tough matters.

The silence stretched and after a time, I realized I'd have to be the first one to speak if I wanted to broach the subject. Taking a deep breath, I prepared myself for the inevitable refusal that would be coming, before diving right in.

"You know why I'm here and you know I wouldn't ask if it weren't important," I said, but the Queen just smiled and nodded ever so slightly, obviously wanting me to continue.

"I need as much essence as can be spared to help accomplish my quest to restore the balance." Taking another steadying breath, I prepared to continue but she held up a hand and my lips closed.

She let out a sigh that reminded me of a parent who was frustrated at a child. "Is that the sword, the one created by the Ordu?" She asked, gesturing to the sword on my hip. No one had said anything about me carrying a weapon around, but the last time I'd been here, there had been a distinct lack of arms, so I still found it odd.

"It is," I said, standing and drawing the sword. I placed a hand on the hilt and the flat of the blade, offering it to the Queen to examine. I wasn't worried that I'd lose the sword, it was bonded to me in a way that couldn't be easily broken thanks to my Arcane Knight class.

The Queen didn't take the sword from my grip, but instead leaned forward and ran a finger up the blade. The runes shimmered as she did so, and my eyes went wide. I'd never seen it react so visually from just the barest touch and wondered what it meant.

"I've infused it with a few hundred thousand, but I'm afraid if you want more, I will require a task to be completed, and it won't be an easy one," the Queen said, and I reeled from her words.

I had no issue doing practically anything to earn the right to activate the blade, but her effortless display of essence infusion threw me off. I thought that it had been a secret that I held and of course those who'd learned it since, but that hadn't included the Queen.

"You can infuse essence?" I asked, ignoring all else she had said.

"It is an ability I learned many years ago, but I would appreciate your discretion in keeping the secret. You see, you aren't as unique as you might think, but you must learn to keep your secrets, for sometimes the world isn't ready for the change that they imply. Be wise, young Caldor Miles. Now, back to my request, I can provide just a hair over a million essence to be used to empower the tool of the Ordu, but are you willing to risk your life to earn it?"

"I'll do whatever is necessary," I said without hesitation.

"Good. I need you to remove Lord Variyn from his position of power. I do not care how you accomplish this or by what means, but he has placed himself in direct opposition to not only the Elven nation but to all who follow Order. Pledge to me that you will remove him, and I will grant you all the essence you require," she said, her eyes remaining firmly pressed into my own as she spoke.

Why would she want Lord Variyn to be unseated? Did she somehow know of my plans to deal with him myself and she was just giving me a reason? No, that couldn't be it, I'd told only one other person of my plans and Alayna wasn't one to share that kind of information lightly. There was more going on than I was aware, and I wasn't sure I wanted to be in the middle of it.

"You are asking something that amounts to treason to my entire nation," I said, and just hearing the words made me think that perhaps this was a test. Should I agree to it or refuse? I needed the essence, but showing myself to be a disloyal traitor would certainly have implications beyond just my actions.

"I have thought long and hard on this," the Queen said, her gaze unyielding. "The blame for his actions, despite the knowledge you provided, lies at his feet. That King Newaliyn allowed this to happen under his watch, disturbs me, but I believe you are in a unique position to deal with Lord Variyn and avoid a potential civil war."

"Civil war?" I asked, not following her logic. The

nation of Newaliyn was almost always at war but never had it been called a civil war. Unless she thought... "You think he intends to attack the King?"

"The destructive power of his weapon has gone to his head, and I have it from trustworthy souls that he intends as much. He has begun to collect essence in earnest again and yet, King Newaliyn does nothing. It is hard for those who, like I, have reached the heights of our level to fear someone so far beneath us, but this is the way to keep the human nation together. As a baron under House Variyn, if you struck a blow by removing Lord Variyn and then marrying his heir, Lady Alayna Variyn, you'd be put into place over House Variyn and the weapon could be put to rest."

I was too shocked to speak. I tried several times but didn't get more than a word or two out before I fell back into silence. She was deadly serious, and I didn't know what to say. On the one hand, the idea of marrying Alayna didn't sour in my mouth, but I hadn't seen our paths going quite that way so soon. On the other hand, the Queen meant to put me at the head of House Variyn.

Was I ready for something like that?

The sheer volume of what I didn't know about politics and maneuvering could fill an entire library. In the end, it came down to what I'd already planned on doing. I was going to kill Lord Variyn and now I could do so with the support and resources of an entire nation.

My words came out shakier than I wanted but I said them regardless. "I'll do it."

I'd already planned on dealing with Lord Variyn, so why did I feel a weight press onto my shoulders the moment I made the declaration? It was like the reality of it was finally coming to bear and I needed to deal with it now, instead of later. But how I would accomplish such a task was beyond my understanding, and I still had no idea of a plan yet.

The Queen inclined her head, a grim expression on her face. "I wish I didn't have to ask this of you, but it is the reality of our situation. I will give you the essence you require and help mend any gear that you have by our best smiths. I believe you are fully capable of challenging him one on one, but you will need to be wise in how you accomplish it. He has resources and men at his command that will overwhelm you. I would suggest an ancient human rite, Morsocare."

"Morsocare?" I asked, I wasn't familiar with the term and its pronunciation was odd, like it belonged to another language entirely.

"Yes, it is a challenge that one ranked as Baron or higher can issue to their Lord or a Lord to their King. Essentially, you issue a challenge for a duel to the death, staking their position and power on the outcome. The challenge cannot be declined. However, if you challenge him in private, he will likely just have you killed by overwhelming force. So, you must find a way to challenge him publicly to prevent him from outright killing you."

"I understand," I said, letting out a breath of anxiety-filled dread. What was I getting myself into?

"Good, now let's get that tool working," she said, snapping her fingers.

The doors opened and several large chests were brought forth. It turned out that each of them was filled to the brim with monster cores and one by one, I began to feed the sword. At the suggestion of the Queen, I vowed to speak to no one of my plans, Alayna included.

The task of filling the sword with a million essence took hours and hours. My armor was collected, and I was told my items would be fixed by the time I finished, so skilled were the artisans in the Elven Kingdom.

Each core had a large amount of essence, but even with ten thousand inside each one, it would take many monster cores, and most were smaller than that. The gold cost of such an amount was ridiculous, but I tried not to think about it while the hours drained away.

The sword began to glow and shimmer with power and as I infused the last cores into it, I felt a measure of the sword's power thrum through me. It was intoxicating as I held the sword and felt the extent of the power. Despite what Merlin had said, now that I'd fed the blade nearly two million essence total, I could sense that it was less than one tenth filled to its true potential.

There was just enough essence that I might be able to fix one of the Prime Mana Shrines and purge a measure of the corruption. However, to truly purge it completely, I would need an almost impossible amount of essence. But one impossible task at a time. I'd made plans now and I was going to keep to them. Without saying my goodbyes to my friends, and happy to have them somewhere safe, I teleported back home.

I instructed my mother to go to Blackridge Keep where my forces could protect her for the next few months, and I felt confident that Michael could keep the twins safe. It took much more effort and convincing than I anticipated, but eventually I got her to agree to go along with Cam. Since I'd already set Cam up with a place and farm out in Blackridge, it was easy to get them settled. I didn't interact with my generals at Blackridge, instead sending a message with Cam that they ought to be on guard in the coming months, along with a sealed letter to Cron to expect someone to try and take control of Blackridge, but that he should defend it with his life.

Next, I teleported outside of Variyn City, ready to enact the first part of the plan. I would clear the ley lines here and fix the Prime Mana Shrine.

# CHAPTER 7
## PRIME MANA SHRINE

My activities had taken me much longer than anticipated and I found myself standing outside the main gate of the city in the early hours of the morning. Despite this, commerce and trade started just as early, and several wagons weaved their way into the city from distant towns and villages. It wasn't particularly dangerous to travel at night or the early darker hours of the morning, but it wasn't the safest either. So, it wasn't surprising to see each wagon with one or more enforcers standing nearby with hands on swords or wielding spears.

These would be lower-level adventurers gaining a good measure of essence rewards from quests posted to the boards outside an Adventurer's Hall. Progression in the early levels went fast for me but I was reminded of Emory's progression and how he'd accomplished only half a dozen levels or so in a year. In comparison, I'd gone from Sparked to one of the strongest in the kingdom in a matter of years. It was a struggle for me to remember how many months had gone by since my Awakening, no matter how hard I bent my mind to the task.

An odd sense of loneliness washed over me as I approached the road and fell into line behind a wagon bursting at the seams with kelt fruit. Had it been the right move to disappear like a specter in the darkness? Should I have trusted my friends with news of where I was headed or perhaps even a notion of what lay ahead for me? I steeled myself and my resolve hardened as I decided that I had indeed done the right thing. My plans were still shaky on how I'd get Lord Variyn to accept my duel to the death, but I had one thing I needed to do if I were to save the kingdom and ley lines.

I would fix the Prime Mana Shrine and purify as many of the ley lines as I could with the little juice the sword had in it. That brought my hand to the hilt of my sword, I could hide it and call it to me at a moment's notice, but I found myself hesitant to do so. Something about having it there and feeling the mighty power that lay within stayed my hand. It felt like I could change the very shape of reality while I held the sword, and though the pull wasn't nearly as strong as it had been, there was temptation there as clear as day.

A part of me wondered how far I could push the

power. Would I be able to simply make Lord Variyn cease to exist? Not killing him per se, but rather, willing his very life force from existence through the pure force of the magic contained within this instrument of the Ordu. I thought back to what the Ordu wielder of the sword had done, making the hydra weaker. Perhaps I could at least do that. Lord Variyn was a powerful foe, that much I couldn't doubt, but had I stopped enough to consider if I was a match for him? In terms of raw power, I was skeptical that he could rival me, especially given how easily I have taken on so many stronger opponents without even infusing my body with essence.

Yet, there was a whisper in my mind that reminded me of the raw power he had used to fight back the Chaos Knight and the terrible rage that had followed when his brother had fallen.

What would Zander do when I killed his Uncle?

The thought came upon me so suddenly and without preamble that it staggered me a step. I'd helped Zander grow stronger than he would have ever likely reached without my help. Would I now be making an enemy of him by killing his uncle? And, more importantly—a reason that genuinely made me pause for a moment— what would Ismene's reaction be if Zander chose to avenge his uncle? Would she hate me for bringing pain to the one she'd grown close to or would our friendship weather such a blow? The uncertainty of my path forward caused me a pain in my stomach and, for once, I almost wished for the simplicity of war.

Despite all the horrors I'd faced, what I had to do had been clear. I was what I was, and I did what I did. Sure, I beat myself up over those I'd lost, and war was never truly so simple, but it had a certain straightforward charge to it that my path lacked right now. I knew what needed to be done, I had some idea how to accomplish it, but the consequences of my actions weighed heavily on me.

What if the King himself didn't agree or like the actions I took, surely, if he wanted another Lord to be raised up, he'd handle it himself? And then there was the request from the Queen, one that hadn't come as an official quest I realized, but instead a foreign kingdom had set me to task with a mind to kill one of the sitting House Lords. If I hadn't already planned to kill Lord Variyn for the awful crimes he'd committed against Order and all those innocents, I'd probably find myself more suspicious.

The time finally came that I was allowed into the city, waved by the guards through without so much as a second glance. It was common enough to see armored and armed individuals like me entering the city at all times, but I'd grown accustomed to being recognized, so it struck me as odd that the two guards hadn't realized who I was. Surely it was just my own pride getting in my head and not something worth being suspicious about, so I forgot about it after only a minute. The guards that ran the entry gates were a part of the Guardsmen's Guild anyway, which operated separately from the Variyn Keep guards. I was just finding monsters in shadows when there was nothing.

The city was as alive as ever, smells filling my nostrils and sounds of activity filling my ears. I watched as a small family—they had two small red-headed children—that I recognized from many months before, exited a bakery, the scent of the bread they carried reminding me that I hadn't eaten in several hours. I decided that perhaps it wouldn't hurt to stop and grab myself something to eat.

The building I focused on had a simplistic design, bricks whitewashed that went halfway up the front and reddish-brown stained wood artfully placed above. I read the sign aloud as I entered, "Bran's Breads." It had been written across a black oak sign swinging above the door. I passed by the family as I entered and I realized that the kids' hair had turned black, an occurrence that I barely remembered had happened the last time I'd seen them. Before I could turn and ask them about it, they were gone. I turned around completely and looked back and forth but saw no sign of them.

I continued inside and ordered four sweet rolls with a wonderful glaze on them and promptly paid. Going back out of the little establishment, I slowly made my way toward Variyn Keep, devouring the sweet rolls one at a time. Each bite was like a wonderful performance of flavor, layered with sweetness at every note. By the time I'd finished, I was reaching the outer walls of the keep and decided to do something a bit peculiar.

I approached the front gate and used Blink to put myself past the barely awake guard and deeper into the complex surrounding the keep. I glanced over my shoulder and sure enough, he hadn't noticed me. I hoped I didn't get the poor guy in trouble, but I wanted privacy for the first part of my plan.

In the early morning hours, it was fairly easy to get to the side of the keep undetected. The massive garden surrounding the Prime Mana Shrine had been rebuilt, but the sense of Chaos from the incident was still thick in the air. By the time my eyes reached the ruined Prime Mana Shrine, my stomach was in knots from the feeling of Chaos. However, as my hand rested upon the hilt of my sword, I got a feeling of peace and tranquility. I'd be able to undo the damage, I knew it as surely as I knew my own name.

I stepped up to the ruined mass of stone and scripts. It had been an infinitely complex structure that I couldn't hope to create by my own knowledge, but what I could do was restore what had once been. The sword was capable of so many feats, and turning back damage as if turning back time was one of them. But first I needed to dive deep into the ley lines beneath and try to cleanse what I could. For that, I opened my mind to the sword and pressed the flat of the blade against the ruined stone.

Immediately, I felt my sense of self dive deep into the planet and down to where the ley lines interconnected the world. It was like touching a vast network of lights flashing through pathways of immeasurable length. At first, I lost myself in the flow of it and it was almost like I was being swept away, but a sudden wrongness inside the flow of essence brought my attention into sharp focus.

This essence was meant to be pure, to be untainted by either Order or Chaos, instead it flowed in a natural state someplace between the two. But this perfect harmony had been set askew and now I saw what I had to do. Using the power of the sword, I injected Order into the ley lines. Slow at first but then faster as I got the hang of it. I needed only to do enough to set the balance right again, so as I worked, I kept my mind open to the feelings of the ley lines.

After a time, I felt a portion of the balance begin to be restored, but more than that, I felt that the changes I'd made would reverberate throughout the system making greater change. Pulling my mind back out, I put my mind to the task of repairing the Prime Mana Shrine. I'd drained a measure of the sword's power already, but I knew instinctually that there was more that I could do before I used up this charge. So, I went about feeling my way through the Prime Mana Shrine and the remnant pieces left around it from the destruction.

One piece at a time, I drew it back together until the

Prime Mana Shrine looked like it had once before, except for the many hundred cracks and several small missing pieces. Next, I pulled on the intoxicating power of the sword and flushed the raw energy into the Prime Mana Shrine. Suddenly and all at once, I felt it form together, and with it came a voice in my head.

"Didn't think I was going to make it back, you did well, wielding the power of the Ordu," Arb said, the world around me had reformed into a dark hallway with Arb sitting on a massive throne of white and black.

"Glad to be of service," I said, surprised that I'd been taken into the Prime Mana Shrine just then. "Was there something I could do for you?"

"No, but I believe I can do something for you," Arb said, chuckling to himself.

"Like what?" I asked, stepping forward and curious what Arb had in mind.

"How would you like a new Class ability that merges the effects of your bonding and Arcane Armor? I call it Armor Bond. It would allow you to permanently bond a suit of armor and when you cast Arcane Armor on it, the effects will last weeks, instead of days."

"I mean, I wouldn't say no to such an ability, but I don't have much essence left to spend. How much would it cost?" I asked, completely aware that I'd literally spent all but a thousand essence to empower the blade of the Ordu.

"This one is on the house," Arb said, grinning like a madman. "Stand still and let me grant you this gift. I'll even bond your current armor for you, never know when you'll need quick access to armor."

I did as he commanded and waited for the ability to be passed down. It hit me all at once and in an instant, I knew what Armor Bond could do and how to enact it.

Armor Bond: You can bond a set of Armor. Bonded Armor can be stored in the ethereal plane and summoned and dismissed with a thought. Furthermore, Bonded Armor cannot be destroyed, doing so will cause the Armor to shift back into the ethereal plane and be restored to the state it was in at the time of bonding. Any armor modifications require you to re-bond your chosen armor. Additionally, if you cast Arcane Armor on Bonded Armor, the effects will last for an extended period of time with additional effects. There is no cost or cast time for this ability. This ability cannot be upgraded and has no further tiers.

I reeled at the usefulness of my new ability. No longer would I have to worry about maintaining my armor and the effects of my Arcane Armor would be enhanced when cast on the bonded armor. It was almost too good to be true, but I looked up at Arb, ready to thank him anyway. But, to my surprise, I found him gone and myself back in the garden where the Prime Mana Shrine stood, and I wasn't alone.

Several guards had halberds leveled in at my direction and one of them was yelling orders at me, but I didn't hear him at first. It wasn't until my mind cleared a moment later that I heard him clearly.

"By order of Lord Variyn and for the crime of treason, you are commanded to stand down and come with us!"

I recognized many of the guards around me, some of their faces appeared sympathetic, but I guessed that was done on purpose. It would be much easier to cut my way through unknown faces and flee than it would be to kill those I'd trained with and had even played some cards with at least one of them.

Despite not wanting to be free of the blade, I let the Sword of the Ordu fade into the ethereal realm, along with my armor. It left me wearing nothing but my underclothes, but I didn't care. This might just work out in my favor if I could play things right.

"Take me to Lord Variyn," I commanded, but the head guard, a burly man who I didn't recognize, just sneered at me.

"You'll be heading straight for the dungeons."

And with that, I let them lead me away, their weapons ready the entire time.

# CHAPTER 8
## PRISONER

As they walked me through the Keep, I couldn't help but go over all the ways in which I could escape. With my weapon and armor able to be called on at a moment's notice and my spells being enough to deal with these guards with ease, my hand twitched as I restrained myself. It wasn't uncommon for Awakened individuals to be taken prisoner and I knew there would be some methods in the dungeon to keep my abilities from being activated, but I couldn't help but wonder if those safeguards could hold me.

Should I just escape and try to find Lord Variyn on my own, then hope that others were around to hear my challenge, or would it make more sense to just allow myself to be taken prisoner? I didn't have a perfect answer to either question, so I let them guide me through the familiar twists and turns, while servants and nobles rushed to be clear of our path. I thought I caught a glimpse of Non disappearing into a servant's corridor, but I couldn't be sure. However, I did see a very surprised Merlin the cook, his eyes all but hollow from the overworked conditions he'd suffered under Lord Variyn.

He tried to step up between us and the guards, but he was immediately thrown aside and a quick look from me held him in place. Now wasn't the time for heroics and they couldn't truly contain me, I reminded myself. I wondered if Non would try his mind controlling abilities on me to prevent me from escaping? I'd grown much stronger since his last attempt and I was confident that my defenses would be enough to at least attempt a proper resistance to his skills.

We reached stairs that led down into the dungeons, and I sighed as I felt the pressure from several runic scripts carved into the wall. They were indeed meant to suppress my abilities, but I could still feel my connection to my spells' mana that infused them, so I wasn't worried yet. But the deeper we went, the more oppressive the feeling became, until I wasn't sure if I'd be able to summon even a Firebolt to my hands if I wanted.

Surprisingly, my skills seemed unaffected as of yet, I even used Speed Burst to ensure that I could indeed still do it. The world slowed down for a while until finally shifting back to normal speed. If I could use my skills but not my spells, then I wasn't completely helpless. Still, the urgency of escape called to me, and I had to suppress it once more. The ability to use my skills, suddenly didn't seem so impressive when I made it to my cell. Bars of greenish metal that I didn't recognize, outlined the cell and heavy chains were placed on my wrists, neck, and ankles.

I was no longer in any position to escape. For what it was worth, though, the guards hadn't taken any of my belongings, leaving my rings and necklace in place, an oversight that left me still able to access my inventory. But when I tried to pull out an item into my ring hand, I found that even my inventory didn't seem to work down here in the cells. I felt weaker and more helpless than I had since uncovering my Spark.

The guards left me alone with my thoughts then, and I sat in the darkness of my cell thinking of ways to escape. A single torch lit up the dungeons, its blue mage light casting an eerie glow around the surroundings. I tested the strength of the metal chains and they creaked against my efforts. If I had just a measure more strength, I could likely break the chains, but I didn't have any essence to waste. I summoned forth the Sword of the Ordu without any effort at all, but it was hard to hold with my hands behind my back as they were.

The sword had been drained to next to nothing, taking with it the intoxicating sense of power. There was more essence inside of it than when I'd first received it, but still nowhere enough to do any more than shimmer in the dim light. I let the sword disappear and instead summoned my armor, it came just as easily, and I focused on casting Arcane Armor on it.

The task of doing so felt like wading through a thick muck, so cut off from my own Mana as I was. But after some intense concentration and several long minutes, I got the cast off and the translucent blue settled around my armor, then faded to a barely perceivable sheen atop it. I unsummoned my armor then, sure of my ability to call it back at a moment's notice now.

"You've shown yourself to be more powerful than any we've held in this dungeon before. To so easily summon and cast a spell here is no easy feat, you should be proud," a voice said, it was familiar, and it only took me a moment after he finished speaking to place it. Non had come to interrogate me.

"Here to pry secrets from me?" I asked, not hiding my intense dislike of the situation I'd found myself in. I wasn't sure how I felt about Non, but he was just as complicit with the destruction and death of so many lives that I barely saw him as any better than Lord Variyn. That heat rose in me and I wanted to suddenly yell at the man, but I held my tongue for the moment.

"My abilities are just as suppressed as yours down here," Non said, pulling out a bench from the darkness and sitting where I could just make out his bald head and deep-set eyes. "Tell me why you've decided to betray Lord Variyn. Help me understand and perhaps I can help you avoid a death sentence."

When I didn't answer immediately, he went on.

"It would be a shame to put down one of the rising stars of your generation, but he will do it if he feels it is necessary. So, help me help you, by explaining yourself."

How could they even know that I meant to betray them? What had I done to give away such information when I'd told only one person and in secret. Surely, Non's reach, and ears didn't venture so far as to have heard my most inner thoughts? There was critical information that I didn't have, and I needed to figure out what that was before I said another word. So, I waited to see what information Non would give, normally he was the quiet type, but I felt like he was probing for something specific, so eventually he'd say something to give me a clue.

"I'm not used to such interrogations or the techniques that I might need to rely on here, my abilities are such that a simple command gives me all the information I need. However, you are far too strong and unpredictable to be allowed free of restraints, both physical and magical. So, tell me, why did you ally yourself with the elves?"

And there it was, he thought I'd defected to help the elves for some reason. I had no problem being truthful and telling him exactly what I thought about that. "I have no more allied myself to the elves than you have."

That caught his attention, and he furrowed his brow. "If that is true, then explain to me your presence there and how they obtained secrets only known to House Variyn? You think we wouldn't notice a fleet of flying ships being prepared or what that means to the peace of the borders between our land and the elven territories?"

Again, I found I was able to answer honestly, as I hadn't been the one to give away such secrets, Alayna did. "I did not give the elves any secret information or any information that would aid them in the creation of flying ships."

"And yet, you don't deny having been in the elven nation, how do you justify your actions? Even if you weren't the one that passed the specific information, you surely know who did and can testify to that fact. You are a good and honest man, Caldor. Tell me who gave the elven nation our secrets and why do they ready a fleet of such ships against us?"

I chose to ignore the request to give up Alayna, which I wouldn't do if my life were on the line, which it probably was, but that didn't change anything. "They readied a fleet not for war but for exploration. We were a part of an expedition to uncover truths and recover artifacts that might help all of the Wyrd, not just the Kingdom of Newaliyn."

I knew it was a stretch to get Non to care about the state of Order and Chaos, but I had to at least try. If not for the actions I'd done and that of the elves there would be no world left to worry about territories or borders.

"First you commit our forces to a pointless war in the Easternlands, convincing even the King, but now you try to spin a tale so tall as to justify your own traitorous actions. I'll ask you again, who gave the plans to the elves? Was it Farstoon, Emet, Alstar, or perhaps even Alayna? I know of the relationship budding between you two, did you lure the heir to House Variyn into being a traitor to her people?" His voice rose from barely a whisper to just below a shout as he spoke, but I ignored him. Instead, I'd decided that I'd just count the bars in my cell.

One, two, three, four...

After a time Non's patience waned and he let out a loud sigh.

"Special containment shackles are being prepared, when they are finished, you will bend to my will and be stripped of your titles by Lord Variyn himself. Unless, of course, you give me something I can work with? Are you truly so eager to lose Blackridge Keep and all that you've cultivated and worked so hard for?"

"I am not a traitor, Lord Variyn is," I said, venom in my words. I turned my gaze on Non but I didn't see surprise or shock on his face, instead, he just smiled and nodded.

"Very well," Non said, nodding some more. "I will return in a few days with your shackles. Food will be brought to your shortly, we aren't barbarians after all."

And with that, he stood, and without so much as the sound of his steps, he was gone, melting into the darkness.

\*\*\*

The first day wasn't so bad. They provided food, stale bread, and a small amount of water, but my body had passed enough thresholds that I could go weeks without eating or drinking before it became an issue. So, the fact that they only gave me a toddler's share of food and drink was still better than nothing. The guards that delivered the food were always ones I knew very little about, even their names eluded me.

It was difficult to tell time down in the dungeon where the blue flames of mage light were the only indication of light. But I still had access to the system and checked through my skills and menus regularly as a means of passing the time. Turns out, I'd nearly maxed my Swordsmanship skill, bringing it to an impressive 952 out of 1000. Though, what that meant was still a bit rough in my mind. According to the skill's description, it would raise my base damage. But how did one truly quantify sword skill? Was reaching a thousand the end of my journey or just the beginning?

Michael had spoken of the Swordsmanship skill as one of many that I ought to learn, but he thought like a weapon master, not a swordsman only. I had, of course, picked up several other weapon skills from his training, but none were over five hundred. Then there were skills like my Perception and Mana Sense. Both of which were something I just did and didn't have to think about anymore, but neither had reached over seven hundred and fifty. Only Inspect had been maxed at 1000 out of 1000, but what that meant, I didn't really know, as I didn't feel like I got much more information on items or people than I had at the start.

Hell, half the time I got less information, though, that might be my own mental filtration system going into effect, as it provided many lines of useless information that I would normally just ignore. By what felt like the fifth day, I began to practice accessing my mana, despite the restraints and runic scripts in place to prevent me from doing so.

It was impossible at first, and I thought perhaps my casting of Arcane Knight—a class ability—might have been a fluke, but eventually I began to sense my mana swirling around my aura both within me and without. I started by pushing mana through the channels that naturally formed within my body, using the tiniest amount of essence to ease the process and make it possible. With the combined might of my mana and essence, I used only a few points at a time, as I had almost none to work with, and I began to make progress.

I wanted to start off with something that would help my senses relax and show that perhaps the darkness wasn't as thick and foreboding as it appeared. I cast Light, using only a single hand to do the motions made it harder, but not impossible. With a spoken word and a flush of mana, a globe of light appeared before my face, blinding me from the rest of the cell.

The first thing I noticed was a bucket that I'd left alone this entire time and whose purpose I could guess but had no intention of using. Next was the scope of the cell that I was in, it was easily ten paces by ten paces, twice as big as I had thought it was when only the dim blue light had shone.

Focusing my mind, I moved the light globe out through the bars, revealing a stony walkway that led off to the left but ended in a dead end to the right. This entire cell was the only one, from what I could tell, down this hallway, as if keeping me alone were a top priority or something. I heard a faint noise, footsteps, in the distance and I released my spell, plunging the room back into darkness.

# CHAPTER 9
## BARON'S END

It turned out to be several footsteps, and in the middle of them all was someone I hadn't expected to see here at all: Galt. Standing tall and proud, he led several guards I recognized and a few I didn't. At first, I thought perhaps he was here to rescue me, but in his hands were chains that seemed to glow in silvery light from the many hundreds of runic lines of script. These were the binding chains that Non had promised, and they were being delivered by Galt.

A mix of emotions ran across my face and through my heart, but I knew Galt was loyal to Alayna more than anything else. So why had he returned now? He'd taken time off to go on the expedition with us to the Isle of Avalon, but surely Non would be aware of his attendance? Wouldn't that put him under suspicion as well? The cell door swung open, and Galt signaled for the guards to take up position outside, each of them lowering their weapons as if cornering a wild beast.

From this distance, I saw into his dark eyes and what I found there wasn't encouraging. Galt, the ever proud and powerful guard, seemed ashamed and wouldn't look me in the eyes.

"It's good to see you," I said, but the words came out raspy until I cleared my throat. It had been some time since I'd talked at length and the lack of water had left me dried and my throat parched.

"And you," Galt said, as he removed my manacles only to replace them with the silvery glowing ones. I felt a great force press around me as he clicked the final pieces together. The chains wrapped around my waist and connected down to my hands and feet, ending around my neck. Whatever they'd done, it was enough, that much I could tell just from wearing them for seconds.

It was like the feeling I'd had when my powers had been suppressed by Tim, the old wizard and traitor to House Variyn. But, unlike when he'd done it, I could find no way to press against the force holding me in check or bring myself to even feel the powerful aura around me. It was like they'd found a way to cut me off entirely from magic. The feeling wasn't one I enjoyed, and I groaned as I stood, even my body feeling weaker than it ought to.

"I'm sorry," Galt whispered. "Orders are orders, but don't worry." He looked back at his guards and lowered his voice that only my enhanced body, crippled as it might feel right now, was able to pick up his next words. "I won't let them kill you, Alayna would never forgive me."

I smiled at Galt, picturing him standing between me and the powerful Lord Variyn, but as heroic as it might seem, he wasn't a match for him, and it would only end in his death. "I've got a plan," I assured him, winking.

"Good, because all my plans were thwarted before I had a chance to do a single one of them," he said, his voice rising to be heard by his guards, but he didn't seem to mind. "These boys are all loyal to me, and to you. We ain't much, but we will treat you with the respect you deserve. Lead the way, Caldor Miles, leader of the free people of Blackridge Keep."

I looked at him and he nodded. So, Blackridge Keep had split from House Variyn already. Surely, Lord Variyn had sent troops thinking to obtain Blackridge Keep without a fight, but he'd been thwarted and Cron had done his duty. I felt pride swell in my chest and I just hoped all those involved were safe. Surely, they'd have backed down if the forces against them were too great. But no, Cron would fight tooth and nail, despite the odds.

"Thank you, Galt," I said, standing tall. "Where are we headed?"

"To the throne room where Lord Variyn awaits you," Galt said, and he put a gentle hand on my back to lead me toward the exit. I took the guiding hand and walked the familiar route to the throne room. This time was much different than the last time I'd walked through the halls. Servants bowed to Galt and our procession, several nodding their heads to me, but I didn't understand until Galt spoke next.

"Word of you healing the Prime Mana Shrine has spread through the city and you are being hailed a Champion of the Ordu. They speak of you as if you are the very Ordu come back to bring Order to the world. Lord Variyn will be in a tough corner now, but I've never seen him so hellbent on taking someone down. To outright arrest you like this, just shows how far gone he has become since losing his brother." Galt spoke in a whisper, but I heard each word as clear as day.

Merlin the cook, ragged and as tired looking as ever, stood in the hallway holding a platter filled with food. I was forced to stop in front of him, or risk bowling him over.

"I tried to sneak you food but, damn them to hell, they kept a tight lock on you. Here, eat this and know that we stand with you," Merlin said, his voice as ragged as his looks. He handed me a meat pie, and I took it in my chained hands, stuffing it into my mouth as carefully as I could, as hungry as I was. He then raised a drink to my lips, and I took in a sweet wine, draining the cup and feeling refreshed. It must have been a kelt fruit-based wine because my powers surged in response and I thought for a moment I might be able to push back from the bonds holding my powers back, but it faded soon after.

"Thank you. But stand aside before they decide to punish you. I'll be fine," I added when he didn't immediately step aside. Merlin the cook, an old friend, nodded his head and stepped aside, pulling himself into a slight bow with the rest of the servants around him.

We reached the throne room with no more interruptions. I was filled with mixed emotions, worried for those showing such respect toward me and proud at the same time that I'd made such an impression on so many people. I'd seen so many familiar faces and several whose names I knew, like Miss Meldry and John Shettal. Each of them had bowed their head in respect to me, but suddenly, with the throne room looming before us, I couldn't help but think of it as a very pleasant goodbye.

"We have to stay out here, but I have keen ears and I'll be ready should we need to act," Galt whispered, and nodded his head with cold confidence in his gaze.

"Just let it play out, he won't strike me down the moment I arrive, and if he does, perhaps he will knock these chains off and I'll show him how much I've improved," I whispered back, but Galt didn't look convinced.

"Do not underestimate his abilities, he may be a healer, but he is a damn strong one."

"I understand," I assured him and stepped forward,

pushing open the throne room doors with my shackled hands.

I didn't know what I expected when I entered, but this wasn't it.

The entire throne room was packed with familiar faces, Lords, and Ladies of House Variyn. Men and women, I'd fought in war with, and other older members who had avoided the war, but held positions of power in House Variyn. For some reason, I'd expected that he'd confront me alone, but this was anything but.

Several Commanders, now Barons or Lords of several territories, met my gaze and inclined their heads. It was clear to me that I wasn't among just enemies here and it swelled my heart. This wasn't going to be a cut and dry situation for Lord Variyn, so why had he risked it based on such flimsy evidence.

After speaking so highly of how he needed someone of my power in his House and making me a Baron, now he has chosen to cast me aside? I was missing a vital piece of information still, and I needed to figure out what it was. As I walked slow and steady toward the throne and Lord Variyn, who sat atop it, what I had missed suddenly became clear.

In his eyes I saw madness. The way he looked at me as if he were a wild animal and how he barely kept his composure. It was so different from the cool and composed Lord Variyn I'd come to know. Then, as I neared, I recognized something coming from him that I was uniquely qualified to sense: Chaos.

Through the dark circles around his eyes and the aura of Chaos he gave off, I knew something terrible had befallen the Lord of House Variyn. Somehow, he'd been turned to the side of Chaos or in some way was being influenced by Chaos. This was no longer just a task that I hoped I'd be able to complete, no, this was now my responsibility to deal with, this threat. If Chaos had infected the very heart of House Variyn, then how far could its reach be now?

That Chaos Knight was proving to be more of a threat than I'd realized. Not only had she taken out several Prime Mana Shrines, but now, if she'd been able to bring someone as strong as Lord Variyn to the side of Chaos, infecting him with her essence, then who was safe from her influences?

When I finally got within twenty paces of Lord Variyn, he met my gaze, and a shiver ran down my spine. This truly wasn't the same person I remembered, and I would do well to remember that.

"Caldor Miles, you come before me, accused of treason," Lord Variyn said, his voice the same as ever, if perhaps a bit more gruff than normal—but that could have been my imagination. I knew I wasn't expected to speak yet, so I just stared him down, awaiting his next words.

"You have conspired with enemy nations and sold precious military secrets to them. Moreover, we have it on good authority that you've sworn an oath of service to the Queen of the Elven nation. Do you deny these charges?"

I blinked, holding my eyes closed for several moments longer than I ought to, as I readied my response. It was clear no matter what I said, he was here to see me in chains for the rest of my life, or worse. No reason to beat around the bush; I would go straight to challenging him in front of all these witnesses.

Taking a deep breath, I spoke, "As a Baron of House Variyn I challenge you to Morsocare."

The quiet whispers that had been going through the hall burst into a hiss of words and shocked gasps. From what I understood, Morsocare wasn't something declared lightly. Although, I was in no position to declare such an event, if I was to be stripped of the very title that allowed me to do so, but I had to try. He would be forced to accept, as he'd not stripped me of my titles just yet. All of this I knew because of the Queen of the Elves, and from the expression on Lord Variyn's face, he was thinking the same.

But he pulled himself together, his face going flat as he spoke again. "I hereby charge you with treason. You are stripped of rank, lands, and privileges. As such, I will not honor your Morsocare, as you have no authority to declare such a challenge any longer."

A sudden roar of conversation filled the hall, the Lords and Ladies, Barons and Baronesses not happy about a Morsocare being set aside so quickly. It was part of the very law that ruled the entire Kingdom of Newaliyn and a right that allowed them peace of mind against a House Lord who acted contrary to the betterment of the kingdom. I took all this in as voices competed for Lord Variyn's attention. So loud and uproarious were their words, that I couldn't tell how many were in favor of it being upheld and how many were arguing in favor of Lord Variyn.

Lord Variyn, for his part, had a smug smirk on his lips and snapped his fingers. The doors opened and the guards approached. "Take him back to his cell to await his execution. Tomorrow his head will be mine." His voice turned to a snarl as he spoke, and the room quieted. Suddenly, the other Lords and Ladies weren't so eager to meet my eyes or speak out in my regard. If Lord Variyn could announce so casually the execution of a war hero and champion of the Ordu, then what safety did they have?

I saw their expressions and guessed at their thoughts easily enough. I found I couldn't blame them. There was a certainty in the chaotic glean of Lord Variyn's eyes, but I wouldn't be taken down so easily. As Galt led me from the room I began to work my way past the chains that bound me. It was hard, but without the combined runic formations of the cell and the chains, it might be possible.

Galt said nothing as we walked, but he looked at me several times, sweat beading down my forehead, before finally he leaned in and whispered. "Here's the key, wait a few hours and I will clear the way for your escape. Wait for my signal and be prepared to teleport away."

I looked him square in the face and shook my head. "He can't just ignore my Morsocare. See that word is sent to the King and he will have to honor it. I'm not ready to flee yet, but when I am, I will let you know. Keep the key, I don't want you being pulled down with me if I can help it."

We spoke in hushed whispers, though with other guards and a few loyal servants the only that could over-hear, we probably could have spoken louder.

Then we turned a corner and Non stood blocking our passage, several guards flanking him as well as what looked like cloaked wizards. "I need to speak with you." He turned to Galt and added, "Alone."

***

For a tense moment, I thought that Galt was going to attack Non, but after sharing a glance at me, to which I nodded, he stepped aside. The guards standing beside Non, came forward and took me roughly by the arms while the two wizards began to chant softly, and I felt additional layers of suppression wash over me. There was no way I'd be able to lash out against the combined force of the chains and these powerful wizards. Still, I had no doubt I'd be able to activate my skills, as they were more concerned about keeping me from accessing my mana.

"Follow me," Non said, leading us off toward a servant's corridor and out of sight of Galt and the guards he'd assembled.

The path forward took many twists and turns, but eventually I thought I recognized where we were. We approached the room I'd first stayed in when I was brought to the keep. No guards were posted outside leaving only the ones Non brought at our side. Non pushed the door open the moment we reached it.

"Stand guard and keep the suppression active," Non commanded, then led me through the door, leaving the guards outside.

Before I could say a word, Non pushed on a section of the wall and it opened up to another hallway. He moved me through it until we reached his familiar entry to his office with the doors that opened and shut automatically.

"What do you want with me?" I asked, getting frustrated by the run around and seemingly endless twists and turns of the day.

"We are in a secure area where we may speak freely. Tell me, did you notice the difference in Lord Variyn? Is that why you challenged him to a Morsocare, or were you perhaps just looking for a way out of your predicament? Tell me the truth."

His final sentence warped the air as he infused his power into it.

"I want him dead," I said, before I could help myself. It was like the words wanted to be said and I couldn't do anything to stop them.

"So, its personal, why wait till now to challenge him? When did you decide you wanted him dead?"

I tried to resist but words poured out of my mouth unbidden. "I was only recently informed of the Morsocare and I decided he needed to die for the crimes he committed against humanity when he let loose the weapon."

"Do you know what affliction has befallen Lord Variyn?" Non asked, leaning forward and exerting his full force on me.

"I sensed the stain of Chaos on him. I believe he has been infected by the Chaos Knight." I hated that I had no control over what I said, so I decided to add to it, at the very least giving myself a sense of control. "That is why my quest is so important. The Chaos Knight will continue to erode our leaders and the very fabric of magic. If I don't get a chance to cleanse the rest of the damage that has been done to the ley lines, we will all die."

"Only speak when answering my direct questions. Do you understand?"

"Yes." It pained me when I tried to speak more, and I hated every moment of the experience.

"If you were to take Lord Variyn's position at the head of the House, would you kill all those that had a hand in the devastation in City Blalor?"

"I hold Lord Variyn and myself as the responsible parties, no one else."

"Interesting. And do you think you can beat him if I were to ensure that the Morsocare went forward?"

"I know I can." I surprised myself with the answer I gave, as I surely still had doubts, but apparently, I was more confident than I felt.

"Good. I will return you to your cell. If I am successful, then you will get your chance to cross swords with Lord Variyn. If not, then you will likely be executed for your crimes, fabricated as they might be."

With that, Non led me back to the guards and I was sent to my cell to await an outcome that I had no control over. It was hard to feel any of my mana down here and in the chains, but I did my best. I pushed and pushed until finally, I was able to ignite a single light spell, small as it was.

# CHAPTER 10
## VISITORS

The next day came, but no execution followed, as I'd feared. So, I settled into a peaceful meditative state where I pushed the boundaries of my magical ability to resist my restraints. The longer I kept at it, the less effective the chains and even the scripts in the prison became. It was like I was working out a muscle that was already strong, just not strong enough. With each repetition, I pushed my strength further and further. Days went by with no food or water delivered to me, until after what felt like a week, footsteps sounded down the corridor.

I heard shouting, but it was so indistinct that it might as well have been nonsense. The footsteps increased in pace and suddenly the blue mage light gave way to the most beautiful sight. Alayna, carrying a platter of food and a large mug of some kind.

"Am I dreaming," I said, my voice cracking from unuse.

Alayna looked behind her suddenly, but whatever she was waiting for never came and she set the platter down on a nearby bench. Then, coming over to the cell she opened it with a silver key. Only then did she speak.

"We only have a few minutes. If he finds out that I've visited you, I might end up down here with you. Eat and drink swiftly." She turned and moved the platter over to me, filled with meats, pies, vegetables, and more. I feasted, not taking any time to savor a single bite, instead, stuffing in as much as I could before the dream ended.

She spoke as I ate and I listened, eager for any news of the outside world.

"Blackridge Keep has maintained their independence, none of the forces sent to do battle with us have been willing to draw swords. Your generals say it's because of your reputation in war that keeps them back, there have even been large numbers of soldiers sneaking away from their commander to join forces with our side. We've been careful with them, wary of spies and assassins, but Cron has been wonderful."

"The elves have promised a battalion of troops and several sky ships to come to our aid if we need them, but the Queen seems to think you have a plan and that we should wait and see. Did you really challenge him to a

Morsocare? The King has now gotten involved, and rumor is that Lord Variyn will be forced to accept."

I nodded in the right places but kept stuffing my face with as much food as I could get into my stomach. My strength had been starting to falter, but with new sustenance I would be fit and ready when the time came. The mug she brought turned out to be nothing but water, but water never tasted so sweet as it did in that moment. With my mouth finally clear, I spoke to Alayna.

"I love you," I said, reaching out and hugging her the best I could in my chains.

"I know," she said, pressing her cheek against mine. "I love you too, but I'm mad at you."

"I know," I said, pressing my face harder against hers. It had been stupid not to at least tell Alayna my plans, but I was worried she'd try to talk me out of it, and I needed to do what I did. "How is everyone?"

"Emory wants to cut his way through Keep Variyn and get you out, and he isn't alone," Alayna said, chuckling. "Even Zander was ready to take up arms against his uncle for throwing you in prison. He's been rather quiet ever since he heard that you issued the Morsocare challenge. He knows what it means, and I don't know if he knows what to think now. He and Ismene have stayed mostly isolated now, but Ismene is almost as bad as Emory with her calls to fight our way to you."

It warmed my heart to hear such news, but I had to assure them somehow that I didn't need saving. "Tell them I have a plan and it doesn't involve dying. So, unless I'm being taken in front of an executioner's blade, do not try to save me." Not my most inspiring words, but they'd appreciate the bluntness.

"Galt told us as much, but he insisted that I give you this key. It will unlock your restraints and allow you to train properly. He also told me to tell you that you should not underestimate Lord Variyn and I have to agree. His combat abilities are far less known than his brother's, but both were considered geniuses of their generation. If nothing else, he might be able to just heal through all the damage you send his way."

"I know," I assured her. "But I have a plan, flimsy as it might seem right now, I have an answer to dealing with his healing." My plan was simple, hit him so hard and so fast that he couldn't heal through my damage. Thinking upon it now, it seemed silly, but I was a fighter that relied on instinct more than plans. So, when the time came, I would either win or I'd lose.

"Of course, you do," Alayna said, pushing herself closer to me. "I wish you didn't have to take this burden, but I know you are able to handle it. Stay strong and do what you must."

With that, our meeting ended. She stood, handing over the key to my restraints, then leaned in and gave me a quick kiss. I accepted it, kissing back with passion, before she stepped away and back into the darkness.

She didn't lock the gate, but it wasn't shackles or a cell door that was keeping me here any longer, so I ignored it. Using the key, I rid myself of the chains and felt a weight lift off me. Then something strange happened, my power seemed to flare all around me as if my aura had grown wings and wished to fly me away. I focused on my aura and dampened as best I could. Then I checked over my menus to see if I had changed something or earned some special ability, but I saw nothing.

I had access to the same amount of mana and when I cast a Light spell, the same amount was used, yet the light seemed just slightly brighter than normal. Which was saying something, considering the suppression bindings would still be holding my magic down in the cell. Whatever I did, there was definitely a change, but it was very odd that it wasn't something being shown in my menus. As best as I could figure, that meant it might be outside the bounds of the Ordu's system, but what did that mean?

I summoned my armor and sword then, wanting to work up a sweat and get some training done. At first, I focused on strike patterns Michael had taught me, just moving my body for the sake of moving it, but after a while I decided to work in some of my skills.

A Phantom Thrust broke apart the cell door, my aim

had been off by just an inch. I cringed suddenly, hoping that wouldn't attract any attention and force me back into those chains, but after several minutes of waiting and no alarm going up, I continued to train. I went from using Speed Burst to combining Power Strike with both Swift Strike and Force Wave, cutting through more of the cell's metal bars. I didn't know what metal was being used here but it hardly seemed secure enough.

All the while, I tried to sense the connection I held with the sword, this ancient artifact of the Ordu. I felt like I should be able to do something, despite the small amount of essence left inside the sword. And the harder I trained, the more I felt a whisper of unyielding power from the sword. It was almost as if the sword itself was a tool that could unlock access to something greater.

At times, my mind and aura would sync with the blade. My movement would become even greater than if I were using Speed Burst, but it would hamper after a moment of use. I tried something when I realized I'd lost a bit of mana during one of those moments of clarity. To my surprise, it was extremely easy to harness my aura and guide my mana through my arms, feeding it into the blade.

The effects were instantaneous. The feeling of over-whelming power flooded me, and I could feel myself being overtaken by the sheer force of it. I cut off the mana and dropped the blade, it was warm in my hand. It clattered onto the floor where I left it as I stared in shock. That had been the power I'd felt when the sword was at full strength, the ability to tear the world apart or reform it as I wished. But the longer I examined the feelings and the power that came with it, the more I realized how wrong I was about it.

It had empowered me, no doubt, but the ability to change and reshape reality required essence, so despite feeling like I could, I knew it shouldn't work that way. I picked up the sword after some time and repeated my experiment.

This time, I put only a dozen mana into it and felt the power blaze to life. I tried to reshape the cell door, but nothing happened, as I suspected. Instead, I got the distinct impression that I was missing something, but as I focused on the cell door, another impression came to me. I could sense the very essence of the door and the metal. I pulled and suddenly a wave of essence was released and consumed by the sword.

My mana depleted a moment afterward, but I stared blankly at the place the cell door had hung.

Nothing was left, not even a glimmer of dust or a speck of anything that would speak to the cell door being there a moment before. I smiled and fed the sword more mana, activating it.

After long experimentation, I came to my conclusion.

The mana I fed the blade was activating it to full power in brief spurts, but to do anything, the sword required essence. However, it can also take essence in from the world around it. By using my mana, I could slowly harvest and store essence within the sword. This made me wonder if I'd be able to use it on a living being and see if it is as easy to reclaim as natural matter. I suspected not, and I didn't have a target just yet to test it. It seemed that activating the sword came with a few benefits. For one, it appeared to strengthen me physically. However, it also toyed with my mind, filling it with whispers that made me believe I was stronger and more powerful than perhaps would be wise to trust.

Ultimately, I decided to practice my sword forms and skills all while pushing mana into the sword. The experience was electrifying, and after a long day of practice, I was able to better control the addictive impulses the blade fed me. After a week, because no one was checking on me or even bringing me food any longer, I had it down to perfect science.

I was able to push mana into the sword, sucking out pockets of essence from the wall—evident by the pockmarks left by my attempts—and even managed to find some of the runic bindings within the wall, extracting the essence from them as well. I had mastered turning it on and off to reduce the mental effects, but it was still a struggle not to feel invincible while wielding the Sword of the Ordu. Though, doing so enabled me to have access to combat potential that I hadn't had before, making me even stronger than I had been when taken prisoner.

When I slept, I put the chains back on me, focusing on sensing my mana through them until I got to the point where I hardly felt the suppression attempts on my aura and magic.

After what felt like an eternity, during which I lost all track of time, I heard footsteps echoing down the corridor. I let my armor melt away along with the sword and took a bite from a kelt fruit I'd taken from my inventory. I hadn't been hungry for days now, since none of the suppression effects were working on me any longer, but denying the kelt fruit's regenerative proprieties in my current predicament would be foolish.

Galt appeared, shielding his eyes with his hand. Only then did I remember I had half a dozen Light spells active simultaneously. I mentally reached out and extinguished them all but one, the blue mage light just not being enough for proper illumination.

"It is time," he said, his eyes darting from one corner to another. The cell had been reduced to no more than a hole in the stone now, as the metal, rich in essence, had been almost entirely consumed. Most of the distant runic formations had been sucked dry as well. "The hells did you do to this place?"

"I got bored," I said simply, and picked up the chains

meant to bind me. I had no intention of putting them back on again, so I summoned my sword and touched it with my mana. The moment I could sense the essence in the richly enchanted chains, I drained them away before Galt's eyes.

He chuckled and said, "Those cost a fortune and a half. Serves them right to think they could hold you for long."

"It's time for what? My execution or the Morsocare?"

"The King has arrived, and an arena has been set up outside of the city walls. Stone mages have been working on it endlessly for weeks."

"King Newaliyn is here?" I asked, my mind going over our last meeting and the offer he'd given me.

"Yes, he means to oversee the proceedings and Lord Variyn is furious about it," Galt said, his weathered face cracking into a sly smile. "Word is, Non and all of his advisors have stopped taking orders from him, stating that they would like to wait and see the outcome. Good thing too, because I heard he called for one of those devices to be used on Blackridge Keep. I did a bit of digging and he doesn't have enough essence collected by even half to do it, but the fact that he wanted to try boils my blood. I thought I knew this fool and he shows himself to be nothing more than a coward."

"Lead the way," I said, hearing his words but not really

knowing what to say. Then, catching a whiff of myself, I added, "Any chance we can visit the bath first, it's been a while."

# CHAPTER 11
## MORSOCARE

I was careful to unsummon my armor and weapons, not wanting to tempt fate. New chains were brought, to make it appear as if they could possibly pacify me so easily. It was an odd feeling, to be walked out into the sunlight after so long in the dark. The sun felt like it kissed my skin with the gentlest touch, but the brightness felt like needles stabbing my eyes. Galt said nothing, as he walked me out of the keep and into the streets, but the crowds cheered at my appearance, and I wondered what they could possibly be thinking.

Was Lord Variyn such a poor figure that they'd cheer the man who wanted him dead? Or perhaps it was like I'd been told earlier. Word of what I'd done to the Prime Mana Shrine had gotten out. They saw me as someone who had done the impossible, like the legends of the

Ordu. I tried to keep my composure normal, but I couldn't help but smile to see so many cheerful faces. Perhaps this entire ordeal wouldn't be so bad after all.

The arena that had been set up for this occasion loomed in the distance.

"They made that entire place just for the Morsocare?" I asked Galt as we walked. I couldn't help but think of Ares when I realized we'd be walking several miles to reach it, but it was a nice day out and she was safely tucked away in my inventory as a figurine. I know she didn't like to stay as such for extended periods of time, but I couldn't bring myself to let her free while I was imprisoned, she'd likely find herself chained up in the same way.

"Yes," Galt said, clearing his gruff throat and adding, "A Morsocare supported by the King is something we haven't seen in hundreds of years, it is quite the event. There has been a festival going on for an entire week, the general populace will take any reason to celebrate, it would seem."

I nodded along but said nothing more. I've always enjoyed a good festival, but obviously, I hadn't been invited. Instead, I'd been imprisoned until the very day when I was meant to fight to the death against a powerful opponent. Was it just? Hardly. Yet, having found a way to train, I was wholly confident in my ability to overcome Lord Variyn's powerful healing abilities.

What was more important to me was that I finally had

a chance to seek justice for all those who had fallen. Revenge wasn't a path easily walked, nor one that was without great pain, but today, that did not matter.

Today was a day of retribution. The spilled blood of those who had fallen cried out for justice, and in seeking it, I hoped my own pain would be lessened as well. Whether that hope would be realized remained to be seen.

With each step, we drew closer to our goal and further from the crowds that lined the road. The arena would undoubtedly have spectators, but in this moment, it was just Galt and me, walking alone.

"How has life been since I was imprisoned? Does Blackridge still stand?" I asked, there were countless questions on my mind now, but I asked only the most important ones.

"Lord Variyn has imprisoned several more of his court, Lords and Ladies, but as of yet, he hasn't tried to lift a hand against myself or Alayna. He must know where our allegiances lie, but I worry he has terrible plans in motion and only his death will set them to rest. So, strike true and don't be overwhelmed by his sheer force of spirit."

"And Blackridge?"

"It stands, but for how long I can't say. Reports have become harder to get as Lord Variyn pushes more troops into place in the region. It has cost us several miles of borders elsewhere, but he has a single mindedness these days, that remind me of a madman I once knew."

"I sensed the taint of Chaos on him," I said, not lowering my voice, as we were alone with not a soul around for at least a mile. "Could he have switched sides?"

"Chaos, you say?" Galt said, shaking his head. "If Lord Variyn has accepted Chaos after his brother fell to that awful fiend, then he is further gone than even I had guessed. Say what you will about him, but he loved his brother."

"Can I beat him?" I asked, biting my lower lip for just a moment before I pushed any sign of anxiety from my face.

"I've seen you do the impossible before, what is once more? You must win, for Alayna's sake and for the betterment of all House Variyn. If you allow him to strike you down this day, we lose a great agent of Order. The world will be a worst place if we were to lose you."

Hearing that from Galt surprised me. He'd always been a bit gruff and critical of me, but I took his words to heart and steeled myself against the upcoming fight. "I'm ready."

We walked in silence while my mind ran over battle scenarios one by one. I used what I knew of Lord Variyn and what abilities I'd seen him use, to come up with a plan different from my original, which was to go all out. The more I focused on his abilities, the more I realized that an aggressive approach right from the start would be unwise. He could use his most powerful abilities as well and block or heal through the damage.

What I needed to do was whittle him down until he had no Stamina or Mana to work with. It was the limiting factor of every Awakened, but I had an advantage in that department, as my attributes were much greater than my level suggested. I couldn't know Lord Variyn's level or his exact resource pools, but if he had more than my 3,150 Mana and 2,300 Stamina, I'd be surprised.

Of course, that meant I'd need to survive his magical and physical assaults as well, which would be no easy feat. I felt confident as I went over my new plan, that it held a higher chance of success and couldn't help but think that Alayna would be proud. She hadn't been the biggest fan of my first plan, so this surely must be better.

My thoughts came to a halt as we entered under an immense stone archway that led through to the massive arena. It was a wide-open hallway that had many doors leading to other places, however, my path was clear. Straight onward and into the sunlit arena. Ahead lay a similar hundred pace high archway to the one that I entered from the outside. Galt gestured ahead and stopped in place. Apparently, I'd be making the last bit of the trip on my own.

Guards lined the walls the further I went in, lit up by powerful globes of white light above their heads. But these weren't the guards of House Variyn, no, they bore the colors and crest of the King. None of them would meet my gaze, so I kept my eyes forward and marched through to the other side.

Light, powerful and blinding, hit my eyes as I entered the arena, which seemed to span about a quarter mile across. It was hard to tell because it wasn't flat, nor could I see to the other side, save for the high rise of the arena walls. The entire middle was covered with giant dunes of blood red sand. Several platforms rose out of the sand and were made of a dark black stone that reflected the light like a mirror.

"Welcome to the Crimson Arena," A voice said, echoing loudly in my ears. I turned toward the source of the voice and saw a giant projection of the King's face, who looked oddly excited. "Today is a historic day. We have not had a Morsocare for centuries, as most have forgotten such a tradition existed." His gaze turned and I wondered if he was looking toward Lord Variyn.

"However," he continued, "tradition can't be thrown aside when it doesn't suit our desires. The rules of this engagement are simple. As a Baron has challenged his direct superior, a House Lord, they will fight to determine who has the strength to achieve victory over the other. For only the strong shall rule."

His visage went quiet for a moment as his eyes flicked between me and what I assumed must be Lord Variyn on the other side of the arena. I still had chains around my ankles, arms, and chest, and I hadn't summoned my armor or weapon. Surely, he didn't mean to start it now with me at such a disadvantage.

"You have five minutes to prepare yourselves," his titanic gaze shifted toward me. "I suggest you use that time wisely."

A countdown took over the space where the King had been just moments before. No one came to unlock my chains, but I still had the key I'd been given. With nothing currently suppressing me, I used it and released myself from the shackles. The chains fell to the floor, and with several minutes to spare, I summoned my armor and sword. Searching through my inventory, I took out a kelt fruit and calmly ate it while the rest of the time ticked away.

After the five-minute preparation time ended, the King's visage returned, and he spoke a single word.

"Begin."

***

Red sand kicked up as I ran for the nearest black reflective stone pillar. It would be high enough to give me a viewpoint and determine where my opponent was, but I had to be on my guard, as he was likely making his way to higher ground as well. I found it difficult to run at any decent speed, the sand shifting and moving underfoot, but I made it to the base of one of the tower platforms and realized my mistake.

The closest platform was much taller than I realized, and I had no way to make it up the smooth glass-like structure. Turning, I examined the others and sighed as I saw the pattern. If I went all the way to the west, I would be able to get on the lowest one and jump to the next, but the taller ones were just too high for me. Resigned that I'd made a mistake, but eager to get onto one of the platforms, I made a beeline for the shorter ones.

I didn't need to reach the very shortest, as my Blink and ability to jump would be enough to make it to the third shortest, if only barely. So, twisting and nearly falling because of the damned sand, I moved myself toward the raised platforms. It was during this run that I saw the viewscreen shift and showed that there were indeed people in the stands. They seemed to be separated by a thick layer of stone, likely for their own protection. As I moved, I saw a familiar group of faces appear and my guts twisted.

Galt sat beside Alayna, Zander, Ismene, and Emory. I would have thought that Emory would have stayed at Blackridge to help defend it, but of course, he chose to watch the fight. They'd probably had to restrain him several times from trying to rescue me or join me in the fight. Sure enough, as the view began to shift, I saw Emory stand up and clench his fists in frustration. I had loyal friends, and it warmed my heart to see them here.

I reached the lower platform and readied myself for a jump, which was harder than anticipated, considering the state of the sand. Managing to get some decent footing, I flew up in the air, activating Blink at the last second to cover the final twenty or so paces. I appeared right at the edge and reached out, grabbing hold of the smooth surface. After nearly slipping because it was slicker than I would have guessed, I pulled myself over the edge and, for the first time, could see above some of the red sand dunes.

A figure in the distance burned with golden light. There were over twenty platforms in the large arena, and he was still a ways away, but he was lit up like a beacon. I kept my own spells and skills in check, gripping the sword and going over my plan again. I'd focus on using lower Rank spells and skills, the ones that cost less, but every third or so spell I'd hit him with something hard so that he'd need to keep his shields or guards at full power.

If I did it right, I'd be able to wear him down little by little. Jumping to the next platform, I saw him do the same, matching my speed easily. It would only be a matter of minutes before we reached each other, and I couldn't help but feel like I was walking right into the jaws of a terrible monster.

Platform after platform we drew nearer, but so far, no attacks had been thrown. Our destination became clear, a platform higher than the rest and four times the size. Lord Variyn got there first, and I followed his example, stopping on the other side, some hundred paces away.

He wore expellant armor of gold and white, but no helmet. He wielded a mace and shield, both radiating with the glow of several powerful enchantments. I could feel the full force of his aura blazing outward and slamming against me. Just by his aura alone, I could tell he was much stronger than I had imagined, that much was clear. But I was no push over either. I unveiled my aura and let the full force of it push against him as well.

To my surprise, he took a step backward, obvious shock on his face.

"You have grown in power, I see," Lord Variyn said, his words as clear as day despite the distance between us.

I reached out and felt his aura more closely, finding what I was looking for. "And you have betrayed your people and the memory of your brother," I said the words as loud and clear as I could, my eyes sharp enough to read the anger that flared on his face as I spoke.

"Do not speak of my brother you traitor!" Lord Variyn bellowed the words and lifted his mace up, then brought it down as if striking a blow. A shell of golden light launched for me, but it was slow, and I easily stepped aside, letting it pass within inches of me.

"The only traitor I see here, is you, Ceon Variyn," I said, dropping the honorific for the first time since I'd met him. "By the authority of the Ordu and the balance of Order and Chaos, I declare you an enemy and pass judgment upon you. I sentence you to death!"

I let my Fireball charge up with mana and Blinked forward to get close enough to let loose the attack, then hurled it toward his face. It was much more powerful than I'd planned and without meaning to do so, I'd added a tiny trickle of essence into the attack, making it spark with blue-green energy. The attack split the air as it burned through the space between us in mere moments.

A flash of golden light told me he'd gotten a barrier up in time and I backpedaled to give myself as much space to react to his counterattack as I could. My Fireball hit and it created an obscuring cloud of dust the moment it exploded. No counterattack came in the first minute and finally the dust began to clear.

Had I taken him out in a single attack? Perhaps my power was greater than I realized, and this wouldn't be a drawn-out fight after all.

The thoughts lingered in my mind as the familiar shimmering light shone through the dust, until a gust of wind cleared him completely. He hadn't raised a barrier after all, instead, it seemed he'd casually raised his physical shield and taken the entire full force of my attack on it. There wasn't as much as a smudge on the shield or Ceon Variyn.

"I gave you everything," Ceon said, fixing a glare in my

direction. "And you reward me by siding with our enemies."

"You're insane," I spat the words. No matter how hard I tried, I couldn't see why he'd be so upset at the elves learning of his flying ships or us visiting them. What was really going on in his mind for him to react this way?

"What other secrets did you give them? They are preparing a weapon to wipe us out, aren't they!" He was practically screaming at this point but suddenly his voice became soft and barely audible. "I had to find new power, new strength or my House would fall. You forced me into this, there is no other way."

"New power?" I asked, but I knew what he meant already. "Your choices are your own, but this day was coming from the moment you unleashed that weapon of yours."

"Weapon of mine?" Variyn said, shaking his head and letting out a forced laugh. "That weapon is as much your design as it was mine. I'd never been able to finish it without your insights and those of my daughter."

Bile threatened to come up in my throat as my rage boiled over. Hearing him say the words I'd told myself sickened me beyond reckoning and suddenly, I wanted to be cruel.

"What daughter is that, Ceon Variyn? Last I'd heard, you have no children that you can call your own," the moment I said the words, I regretted them and hoped that the audience couldn't hear our back and forth. I ignored the massive projection that showed the audience's reactions, realizing that, of course, they must be able to hear us.

Ceon Variyn's face went from confused to angry, back to confused, as his head tilted to the side. "What would you know. My daughter only befriended you on my request! Did you think she truly cared for you?"

That caught me off guard and I looked at the viewscreen, but it wasn't showing Alayna, instead, it panned over hundreds of audience members I didn't recognize.

I shook my head at his words, even if she had been nice to me at first by request of her father, we'd shared so much more since then. I knew she didn't care for her supposed father any more than I did at this point, but I couldn't help but keep my eyes shifting toward the projection to see if I could catch her reaction. That is when Lord Variyn decided to send another attack my way. This time, it was a spear of light, not unlike Alayna's own attack, but it moved with unreal speed.

I happened to feel the surge of power building up and looked back just in time to dive to the side. However, the attack wasn't as straightforward as Alayna's. Instead of just slamming past me and going away, it struck into the ground and golden crackling lightning sparked out, hitting me and taking several dozen Health points with it.

I rolled far enough away that the attack wouldn't keep hitting me, it wasn't a life ending threat, doing low damage overtime instead of high damage all at once. But any lost health was something I needed to avoid.

Variyn was there a moment later, having closed the gap and swinging down his mace at me while I made it to my feet. Gripping my sword in two hands, I swung and knocked his blow aside with ease. Then I followed up with a slash down his chest, but his armor was strong plate, and I wouldn't be getting through it without much more power. He took the blow to the chest and slammed me with his shield, staggering me back.

I followed up by activating Speed Burst and letting loose a stream of sword strikes. One such attack hit him right in the face before he could block, and I learned why he wasn't worried about wearing a helmet.

He had one on, however it was somehow completely transparent, not limiting his view in the slightest, while mine hampered my view toward the ground and the sky. When my attack smashed across his face, whatever made the helmet invisible flickered slightly and showed the form of a snarling bear's head. But a moment later it was invisible once more.

My attacks continued, him blocking one in three, but not a single attack getting through his heavy plate armor, and he hadn't used a single barrier or magical ability up close yet. That changed suddenly, as he began to move faster, and his form gave off a slightly golden glow. Soon he was moving faster than I could follow. Blow after blow rained down on me as my Stamina plummeted below half already.

This wasn't my plan at all, how had I let him get into an advantageous position like this? I had to put distance between us so my superior magical skills could come into play. I touched the sword with a stream of mana and suddenly my body moved faster for a moment. I parried his next strike and got a strike across his neck, hitting only armor once more. But the strike had been hard enough that he staggered backward, his head shaking as if to ward off a dazed feeling.

He'd gotten several hits on me, but my armor was special. It took the armor value and spread it across my entire body, so gaps in the armor that looked vulnerable were only visually so. Each strike he tried to score on lighter armored areas did nothing but smash against my own plate armor. However, I wasn't invincible, and each strike he delivered did blunt damage, whittling down my health by two hundred points already. Of course, my health regeneration was already working on closing that gap, but it was much closer during active combat.

I turned and ran, Blinking to give myself some distance. A spark of light from behind me was the only warning I got as a hammer smashed in front of me and chains of gold reached up out of the ground to hold me into place. I slashed down with my one free arm, activating Power Strike, and shattered the chains. However, the hammer in front of me had turned the ground into a shattered mess of golden light and black rocks. Stepping on the area burned, and I took another two hundred damage just getting out of the field he'd put down.

Turning, I decided it was time to show him what my spells could do. That also happened to be the exact time the platform began to spin and lower into the sand.

***

I had to slam my sword into the glass-like stone to keep myself from being thrown off, however, Variyn wasn't so lucky. He went flying off the edge and I thought for sure he'd take some damage from that, but he appeared a moment later with wings of golden power lifting him above the spinning and dipping platform.

That was just not fair, I thought, as it spun me beneath him, and he raised his mace to throw another slow but powerful globe of light. I wasn't going to wait around for him to mash me to bits, so I ripped my sword free and let myself go flying into the sand. Luckily, it had lowered relatively quickly and I hit the sand, throwing red dust up all around me. But the sand proved to be a difficult material to maneuver around in, and just as I made it back to my feet, a globe of light moved right toward me.

It was too close to dodge, so I raised my sword and let loose a Force Wave right into it, my Stamina dipped from the Rank 3 usage, but it was worth it. The spell was cut in two, but what I didn't expect was the wave of power that followed, throwing me right back off my feet. Rolling through the sand, I couldn't help but think that my plan was not going off as I'd wanted.

So, when I got to my feet and saw a golden hammer coming for me, I used Blink again and ran for a shorter platform. The largest was the only one to have disappeared so far, although I didn't know why or who was controlling them.

I made it to the platform without being hit by any stray attacks, and Ceon Variyn's wings of golden light had gone away. He now stood on a platform of his own, a golden blur in the distance. Jumping from platform to platform, I closed the distance. I needed to be within two platforms of him for most of my spells, so I just had to hope my bombardment of spells would keep him at bay.

When I got into place, he was channeling a spell to create a spear of light once more, but I ignored it for now. I poured several hundred into a Mana Shell that appeared around me, then moved on to my next clutch spell, Lightning Strike. He was just within range, and I saw it hit him the moment after he unleashed the spear. I rolled to the side and began casting my next spell.

The spear slammed down but the lightning damage

was absorbed by my barrier. Ceon, on the other hand, had taken a knee after my Lightning Strike had hit him. I guess being surrounded by metal armor didn't help when lightning fell from the sky. Deciding that I'd keep that type of attack up, I cast Channel Lightning. It wouldn't bounce around, but it could do consistent damage even to a single target if I held it long enough.

Lightning flew from my fingertips and for the first time, I saw Ceon Variyn raise a barrier. My Channel Lightning struck the barrier and lightning danced around it but didn't crack it. I let the channeling continue for a solid five seconds, and then threw down a Lightning Strike as it came off cooldown. I followed that up with a weaker Arcane Missile and a weaker Firebolt, each one cast at Rank 1. The idea was to not burn through my mana all at once but keep a steady barrage of attacks going his way.

I ignited the Light Blade on my sword, combining Power Strike, Swift Strike, and Force Wave. I released a cutting technique through the air, then shifted to channel a Rank 2 Fireball, using it without essence since I had so little left and needed to conserve it.

One after another, my techniques and spells slammed into his barrier. The Fireball was the last straw for it, and it shattered into pieces. Amid the dust and debris flying in the air, loud chanting echoed. Suddenly, a pillar of fire appeared over me and slammed down. It shattered my Mana Shell and burned me with terrible pain.

That single attack had done almost four hundred points of damage and more than that, it had somehow burnt away my remaining Stamina. I twitched in pain as I tried to stand, but it wasn't until I activated Stamina Surge that I was able to move. Over the course of five excruciating seconds, I stood, but Variyn was nearly upon me, mace glowing with a deadly golden light.

His blow caught me before I could get my sword up, smashing me backward and hitting me for another hundred points of damage. I was down and slow to get up, but he was there already, raining blow after blow on me until I coughed up blood from the ferocity of it all.

Despite all my spell casting, I had plenty of Mana left and I needed an edge. I cleared my foggy mind with a touch of essence and slowed time with Speed Burst. Then, dropping my sword and pressing my hand against his chest, I cast Firebolt Rank 3. The power of the attack blew him backward as I recalled the sword to my hand. Next, I infused Mana into it, my body reacting with the overwhelming sense of power and invincibility.

Casually I waved my sword and ate the platform beneath him, sending him plummeting down to the ground. Whether his spell was on cooldown or not, he didn't grow golden wings to save himself. Next, still feeding the sword mana and sighing at the new essence I'd collected, I began to eat away at one of the pillars. After only seconds, I'd eaten through the bottom, and it began

TIMOTHY MCGOWEN

to fall atop Ceon Variyn as he struggled to right himself in the sand.

It didn't help that I was eating away the sand at his feet to make it more difficult for him and laughing all the while. I felt invincible and so powerful! That was when my mana cut off. I wasn't out of mana yet, but pretty damn close, the sword had drunk it up like a thirsty wanderer in the desert.

The massive platform fell right atop him just as he finally made it back to his feet. Suddenly, a golden light flared, and I had to turn my gaze away, so bright was the light. I smelled a great burning stench that I couldn't quite place before the light dimmed enough that I could see what had happened. Standing atop the broken mess of the tower was Ceon Variyn, and his entire form glowed in a way I recognized. This was the same, or close to the same, ability that Alayna had used to multiply her speed, strength, and power for a short time.

With a sound like the crack of lightning, he jumped toward me, leaving burnt and broken pieces of glass-like pillar behind, some of it had even melted.

I managed to get a weak Mana Shell around me in the second I had as he closed the gap, but it wasn't going to be enough. His mace struck through my barrier, and I caught it on my sword. The blow sent me flying, but Ceon Variyn wasn't done with me yet. He moved with the speed of the gods, and I could only block one blow in five as he began

136

striking at me while running alongside my flying body. Each strike sent me further and faster away, but he kept pace.

Finally, we reached the end. We had been flying through the air for some time now, but I didn't know how. My back slammed against stone, and I heard cracks ripple up all around me, but still, the blows didn't stop. One after another, he slammed me senseless, unable to get a proper counterattack off or even a spell in my defense. My health plummeted to dangerous levels and suddenly, I felt the real probability of death coming.

The entire exchange had taken seconds, and to my relief, Variyn fell backward right between strikes as whatever ability or spell he was using cut off. I, however, was firmly stuck into the wall and remained some hundred feet above the sand, gathering my wits. Before unwedging my armored backside from the stone, I cast a few heals. First, a Restoring Light, followed by a Mending Touch and then a Lesser Heal, each one Rank 3.

Their combined healing took the edge off, but I was still in rough shape, and I needed to give my regeneration a chance to do its job. Although, I had no time to wait, as Ceon Variyn had already begun to gather golden light around himself in what I recognized as a golden hammer throw. I waited until he was about to send it into the section of wall I was currently sitting in, then pushed myself free.

As I fell, I aimed my sword to land a deadly strike upon him. He moved just enough out of the way, though, he was unaware that I had activated Phantom Thrust. I pierced out with my blade and its ethereal projection struck him right in the arm, this time it seemed to have hit a weak point, sinking in. Whether or not it was the nature of the skill or lucky aim, I'd finally wounded him.

My sword tip came back wet with red blood, and I slammed hard into the sand, kicking up dust. I leaned on my instincts as I rolled to get clear and back to my feet. I narrowly avoided a strike from Variyn, but I caught him on the leg with my sword, dropping him into the sand with me. Then I Blinked away, hoping to give my health regeneration some time to work.

I steadied my breathing and did everything short of closing my eyes, those I kept firmly on my opponent. "You are more of a worthy opponent than I'd have thought," I said, calling out over the distance between us.

He was taking his time to rise, but I didn't want to start fighting again. I needed to regenerate some health first, and I could already feel it working as it ticked steadily upward. This fight was not going to be an easy one, and I needed to work out a better strategy to deal with his over-powering melee abilities.

"You think I care if you stall for time," Ceon Variyn said, spitting red blood into the crimson sands. "You've only seen a measure of my power; I've got much more coming."

Then, as if to accent his point, the same golden nimbus of light that had given him such overwhelming power only minutes ago, flickered around him again. How he was able to use the skill so close together I didn't know, but I had to keep my distance or do something different, but he was just too fast.

The air cracked as he shot forward and I hit him with a Lightning Strike, smashing harmlessly on him as he came. I activated an essence infused Speed Burst and pushed essence into my body and mana into the sword. Suddenly, he didn't seem like he was moving so fast. Almost comically slow, he lurched through the air toward me. I could see his feet glowing with the intense light, each step shooting him forward faster than I could normally follow.

He raised his mace to deliver a deadly strike to my head, but I moved with such speed that it was hard for even me to follow. I struck with overwhelming force, aiming for his shoulder where I'd drawn blood before. The slash cut deep and threw him backward, though, only for a second. His feet hit the air and thrust him forward again.

Back and forth we fought with incredible speeds, but I cut mine off first, not wanting to cut my resources to zero before I'd made more progress. I had a handful of essence left, more if I could tap into the sword, and my mana was dangerously low again. Variyn struck me with his shield just as his own golden nimbus of light flickered out. I spat blood and felt several teeth loosen as I was thrown through the air. He was so freaking strong, this was ridiculous.

I landed in a spray of sand and got to my feet much faster than before. Whatever the rules were, no one had taken my inventory away from me, so I pulled out a Mana potion and downed it.

Sudden dread washed over me. Would I be able to win this fight after all? Ceon Variyn was proving to be more of an opponent than any other I'd faced so far in my life. I thought the application of essence and the sword's abilities would be enough, but he always seems to have another trick up his sleeves, ready to go. Thoughts of failure and the faces of those I'd lost ran through my head.

I whispered the names of those I remembered, letting each utterance give me strength. One by one, something inside me broke and I knew that this fight wasn't hopeless after all. No. I would end this, just as I'd planned originally.

I was done holding anything back; I needed to embrace the pain and my spells were as deadly as anything else, so it was time to make it rain fire! Spitting blood from my mouth and readying myself, I began to fill a Fireball with mana and essence.

***

Sizzling and crackling, I felt myself begin to take damage from the massive attack I'd prepared, but I pushed it even harder. Variyn was slow to get up and it would mean his death if I had anything to say about it. Finally satisfied with the amount of power in my Fireball, and sure I was about to blow away half the arena, I threw it with all my might.

Meanwhile, Variyn began to chant, and I saw a barrier flicker into place around him. But that didn't bother me at all, no matter the strength of that barrier it wouldn't outlast such a devastating attack. But there was something about the arrogant look on Variyn's face that made me wonder if maybe I'd overestimated my attack. In the brief moments before my Fireball hit, I sent a Lightning Strike followed by an Arcane Missile. The Lightning Strike hit first, cracking harmlessly against the barrier, while the Arcane Missiles kept pace just behind the Fireball.

Then, the Fireball hit and all worry about it being too little to get the job done went out the window. It struck with such overwhelming force that I was thrown off my feet and the viewing screen above flickered out of life for a moment or two. Once more, I was sitting in crimson sand and waiting to see if what I'd done had been enough.

The world stilled as I awaited the dust to clear. Thick and billowing, it refused to settle down, so I stood and began to step forward, too eager to find out what lay ahead. I'd closed half the distance between us when a sudden gust of wind blew away the remainder of the dust.

On one knee with steam rising off him in drifting waves, but still very much alive, was Ceon Variyn. My eyes went wide, and I stumbled back a step. How had he survived such an attack? Before I had a chance to do much more than doubt such an outcome, he rose to his feet and spoke.

"You've forced me to use my secret weapon, so now, see my full strength and tremble."

He raised a black gem in the air and instantly I felt an overwhelming sense of Chaos coming from it. It began to travel down his arm like slow drifting smoke. Somehow, he was using an artifact of Chaos to do something to himself, but I couldn't tell what.

His aura flared and suddenly the smoke tendrils covered his entire body, until a moment later they all disappeared. They left his armor black and his face a paler white than normal. It was a terrible transformation that left his aura flaring with more power than I'd ever sensed from him before.

"What have you done!" I yelled across the space, raising my sword in challenge.

"I have harnessed the power of the enemy into a weapon. And with that weapon, I will crush you once and for all!" Then, as fast as he'd been when using his golden wings, he flashed forward to meet me in combat, mace raised and ready to strike me down.

Waiting until the very last second, I infused my Speed Burst with a touch of essence and activated it, spending the last of my small reserve. The world slowed dramatically, and I saw the rage in Ceon Variyn's face. Next, I tapped into the blade by feeding it some mana. After I felt my connection with the sword wash over me, I struck down, knocking his weapon right from his hands. But his shield slammed into me, and I went flying backward.

I managed to keep my footing as I threw sand up all around me and came to a halt. However, my vision was obscured, and my ability ran out of time just as a thundering presence smashed into me again. I struggled to stay conscious as he battered me with attacks, and I couldn't imagine a way to defeat this foe.

Then, a terrible idea occurred to me through the waves of pain. With my health plummeting to under half again and my mind unable to understand what level Ceon Variyn must be to do this, I decided to do something I'd not tested, nor did I know if it would work.

Tapping into the sword that I barely held in my hand, I sent more mana into it. His prior blows had broken my concentration, but now my mind was as sharp as a razor. I'd walk the line and defeat this impossible foe. As soon as the connection to my sword activated, I began to pull in essence from all around me.

First the sand, the pillars, and then the very walls of the arena. I became a vortex of essence and when I felt like the sword had taken in all that it could, I turned my sights on the former Lord of House Variyn.

"Your turn," I said through bloody gritted teeth, his blows didn't stop, and I was near death.

I turned the suction powers against Ceon Variyn and began to pull. The sword resisted at first, his aura acting as a shield against such attempts, but it was his mind versus mine. My aura control pitted against his own and I'd gotten weeks of practice thanks to him. After only seconds delay, I broke through his aura and began to pull in his life force.

First, came the Chaotic energy that covered him, his blows becoming much weaker the moment I sucked it in. Next, came the power from his aura, which included thousands of essence. I could feel each blow growing weaker and weaker as I took everything from him. Level by Level I reduced him to no more than a normal human being without Awakened powers.

Something similar had happened to Warrick, but he'd been able to recover a great deal of his power. I wouldn't leave Variyn the same option. When I felt the power slacken, I pulled harder. His armor dissolved into essence, along with his weapon and shield. He stumbled back with pure horror on his face, but the intoxicating feeling of using the Sword of the Ordu held me fast.

I continued to pull on him until small chunks of his flesh began to be pulled away. He fell to his knees and began to beg me, but I hardly noticed as I took from him his flesh, his soul, his very essence of being.

A sudden pressure fell on me, and my head screamed. I'd run myself out of mana and the effects of the sword ended suddenly. It left me gasping for breath and looking at Ceon Variyn in horror.

What had I done? I'd wanted to kill him, but this wasn't death, this was torture. He looked like a shrunken human, barely enough meat and skin to indicate what he'd looked like before. His hair hung a mix of white and grey, so wispy that a nearby breeze might rip it free. His mouth opened and closed but no words came out.

I looked up to the viewscreen in horror, hoping that no one had seen what I'd done to him, but I saw the face of the King. He looked...satisfied? He nodded and gave me a thumbs down sign with his hand. I knew what that meant, but now that the deed had finally come due, I wasn't sure I could do it.

Stepping forward, dropping the sword in disgust, I kneeled before the naked form of Lord Variyn.

"No one deserves what I've done to you," I said, then seeing him trying to give a raspy reply, I leaned in to hear what he had to say.

A single word at first and it hit me harder than any blow.

"Mercy."

But he wasn't finished. He reached out and held on to me like a frail child.

"Mercy, please kill me."

I stood, gently letting him fall to the hard floor of the arena, all the red sand had been absorbed by me. Holding out my hand with my eyes closed, I summoned the Sword of the Ordu.

"For the crimes you've committed, I pass judgment for the betterment of all mankind. Goodbye, Lord Variyn."

My blade rose up as if on its own accord and slashed down. I forced myself to watch every moment and I added a new name to the list of victims that I should remember.

Ceon Variyn, victim of his own pride.

# CHAPTER 12
## LORD MILES, REGENT OF HOUSE VARIYN

The extent of the damage I'd taken and the sheer emotions I felt overwhelmed me as I fell to my knees and waited for death to come. Of course, I still had a solid three hundred health left and that number was rising as the moments ticked by, so I didn't die. Instead, several things happened around me, but I simply let them.

Guards appeared, but they didn't carry with them shackles, but blankets. The remains at my feet were taken away and I was covered as if I were some wet, sick child. Most, if not all, of my injuries were from blunt force trauma, so while my skin had broken here or there and my mouth was filled with blood, I didn't look as bad as I felt. They must have known this though, because as I dismissed both sword and armor, revealing a normal set of slightly bloody clothes drenched with sweat, they poured a potion down my throat.

Again, I let it happen, while they led me off the arena floor and to the doors to the east. There I met with someone I hadn't expected, Gavin Melantis, the captain of the King's guard.

"Before you go to meet the King, you must relinquish the weapon that you used to perform that final attack," His voice was firm and held none of the jovial tone it had at our first meeting.

I raised my hands to indicate that I was unarmed, but that didn't pacify him. He repeated himself, this time his voice much firmer.

"Relinquish the weapon," he said, his hand moving to the hilt of his own sword. "No harm will come to it." He added as if I were afraid that he could do any damage to it.

I shrugged and summoned the sword. Without another thought I passed it over. It wasn't like I couldn't just summon it back at any moment. To prove that point, I did just that and then offered it back up.

"A class ability?" Gavin asked, his tone telling me he was not impressed.

I nodded.

"Fine, but if you should try and activate that ability or any ability in his presence, we will strike you down before you finish your breath. If you found the former Lord

Variyn a challenge, let me assure you that we will be an impossible foe."

I looked him in the eyes, my frustration and exhaustion just too much for me. "I won't do anything, alright? I'm tired, I'm in pain, and I'm just done. Take me someplace to rest and I will see your King later, alright?"

Something I said stiffened his back and he drew out an inch of his sword. "You will go to him now and he is your King as much as he is mine. You dare show disrespect like this toward him in his presence and I'll..."

"Enough," came a familiar baritone voice that I recognized as King Newaliyn. "Walk with me Caldor, you may rest soon."

I looked up, barely able to keep my head up now that the adrenaline of the fight had gone. Potion or not, my body needed rest. But duty was duty, and I had a feeling that more responsibility than I cared for was on its way.

The King wore resplendent golden armor with a simple crown atop his golden curly locks. He had a short, trimmed beard of the same color and eyes the same striking purple. We were led, surrounded by his guards, to a small office with just enough room for the two of us to sit across from each other. After the door was closed, I looked up and waited.

"This room is warded enough that no one, not even my guards, will hear a word. So, Caldor, you survived."

"I did," I said, not sure what the King was looking for here.

"And you showed off an ability that will stifle any future Morsocare challenges, at least against you. What do you have planned next?"

"Sleep," I said, flatly. I knew he was looking to hear what my plans for the future were, but I hadn't had a chance to think beyond the fight, so I was just as curious about what came next as the King, in this instance.

He laughed and put a hand on my shoulder, his grip like iron. "Did you know that there is a soft cap to the levels you can reach as a human?"

I was thrown off by the sudden switch in the conversational direction, but my academic brain couldn't resist being pulled in by such a comment.

"Is it because the amount of essence becomes too great?" I asked, leaning forward, my exhaustion suddenly forgotten for the moment.

"Yes, at a certain point the requirement to just increase your level becomes impossibly high. In fact, by the mathematics of my scholars, it takes all of the prior essence up to level 100 to reach 101. And it only increases with each level after that. So, when I tell you that I am level 102, I want you to understand what I am saying."

This sudden revelation surprised me. He'd been so secretive and hadn't wanted to reveal his level before, but I would never have guessed that he was that high of a level. And despite that, he was a Paragon, so he'd be even stronger.

"I tell you this for two reasons," he said, before I had a chance to formulate a proper response. "First, to give you perspective, Lord Variyn was a powerful Healer and Champion in my kingdom, despite his failings, and he was level 79. You are...oh, you've learned to veil your aura, but regardless, I'd guess you've at least made it to your 50s. So, by the time you reach his level, you might think you can challenge me, but let me assure you that would be a mistake. I may only be level 102, but I've got the power of one twice that level and I wouldn't allow you to live long enough to use that artifact of yours."

There was sudden heat to his words, and I felt his aura flare, pushing down against me, but given all my recent training I resisted it without feeling overwhelmed. That surprised me, but I kept my face pacific as I regarded the King. If I understood the situation correctly, he was afraid of me or perhaps what I might become.

"I've decided to accept a position as a Baron under your direct authority," I said, thinking I might have found a way to avoid ruling over an entire House. If I could work directly under the King and perhaps join the King's guard as well, they could help strengthen me. I might not be a challenge to the King yet, but I would be some day, and I had to be sure that he didn't just kill me before that time came.

"No," King Edwin said, shaking his head but holding my gaze. "You will be installed as the head of House Variyn and marry young Alayna Variyn to help sooth matters. This is not a suggestion but a command from your King. I will give you special attention and advisors if you seek it, I know well enough that strength of arm isn't enough to successfully rule a House or Kingdom but trust me when I tell you it helps."

I didn't know what to say, so for several long moments I said nothing. Despite my desire not to be the Head of House Variyn, it appeared that I was now the Lord of the House. House Miles had a nice ring to it, but I didn't know how the name changes worked or why that would be important right now.

"I'm not sure I'm ready," I finally answered, being as honest as I could be. "There is just too much to handle and I've responsibilities to the Balance of Order and Chaos."

"And now as the head of House Variyn, and yes, we will be keeping the name, you've found yourself with overwhelming resources to accomplish your task. But don't worry, I'll have advisors sent and we can help you clean house of anyone still too loyal to the fallen head of House Variyn."

"Thank you," I said, rubbing at the back of my neck

and wondering at the responsibilities that awaited me. "I endeavor to be a loyal servant to the Kingdom and may your reign be long and prosperous." I was trying to be formal and polite, but King Edwin just chuckled.

"Relax, you've done it. You are the Head of a House and, given a few years, we will be near equals. Perhaps you might even succeed me when age finally takes me, or I decide to search beyond this world for the power that eludes me." His eyes went up to the ceiling and I couldn't help but think of Merlin. He'd spoken of ascending as if he could leave the world behind in some way.

I nodded to King Edwin and felt the mantle of responsibility fall on my shoulders. "I'm as ready as I'll ever be. What do we do next?"

"First, you bathe, sleep, and then and only then will the ceremonies begin. I'll have the necessary people informed and you can expect to be crowned by the end of the week."

"I understand," I said, and suddenly my exhaustion threatened to overtake me once more. Had King Edwin somehow been holding it back or had I just pushed myself too far too fast. Perhaps a mix of both, but whichever it was, I needed sleep soon.

With our meeting concluded, I left, escorted by Galt and several of the King's Guard to a bath. Instead of leaving, they stood guard around the tub as if they expected an assassination attempt that very moment. Thus, when it came, I wasn't as surprised as I ought to have been.

\*\*\*

The water was warm, and it easily seeped away my worries. It was so soothing in fact, that I fell into a deep sleep before I'd even scrubbed all the blood off my body. I was awoken by a sudden shout, and I sat up.

The guards were fighting against three figures, or at least, Galt and a few of the House Guards were, the two Royal Guards stood passively by, watching the exchange. One of the guards took a dagger to the gut and fell backward, but Galt was there a moment later, cutting down the black-clothed man. It was a very exciting few seconds, but the attempt ended without the Royal Guards having to so much as move an inch.

"I caught the last one trying to activate a device," Galt said, holding up a gem for me to see. It glowed with a fierce blue-green light and had several spiked prongs around it that would break the gem if pressed too hard. I barely had to scan it before I realized what lay inside and what this device must be.

"I think I know what this is," I said, careful not to squeeze it. I reached into it with my senses and drained away all the essence. "It's safe now." But I gave no explanation of what it was, instead, I tucked it away for further examination at a later date.

Galt seemed to understand without me saying, and he turned his back as I finished my bath. Lord Variyn must have had assassins in place, armed with miniature explosive devices meant to wipe me out. Had he sent them just in case he lost or were there those still loyal to him that I'd have to root out? These were questions I needed to ask Non, assuming he would be loyal to me. Time would tell, but for now, I enjoyed the warmth of the bath.

When I finished, I was taken to a place to sleep, still in the same arena where I'd killed Ceon Variyn, but I made no complaints. I needed sleep so badly that the moment my head hit the pillow, I was out.

\*\*\*

The next few weeks passed in a blur. There was a ceremony where I was named Lord of House Variyn, a few parties afterward and several advisors that were sent by the King to help me. I found them pompous, but helpful in dealing with the finer details. The message they brought was clear, the King had sent them to see to the House affairs and they'd take care of as much or as little as I wanted, so I let them do almost everything.

It probably wasn't the wisest approach to ruling, but I'd been rushed around so much in the past few weeks that

I couldn't be bothered with trade agreements and such when I had a wedding to plan. Alayna had been thrilled to see me, but I sensed that the death of her father, or at least the man that had a hand in raising her, was weighing on her. We spoke often but kept separate rooms, as was considered proper for an engaged couple.

Zander was a different story altogether. He'd been opposing me openly in meetings and refusing to talk to me directly outside of said council meetings. I thought I knew him well enough to say that he didn't care so much for the death of his uncle, but I'd been wrong. I knew that Zander had intentions of helping me during my imprisonment. Whether that was for Ismene's benefit or that he was acting as an ally, I was unsure. Given his attitude now, it seemed likely it was for Ismene.

Life settled into a rhythm, and though I wasn't particularly enthusiastic about an upcoming ball thrown in my honor, it was important to Alayna that we participate in such events. I wanted nothing more than to gather essence and fix the remaining damaged Prime Mana Shrines, but I was assured by my advisors that now wasn't the time for that. I only agreed when they assured me that, after marrying Alayna, I could leave the ruling to her and I'd be able to continue adventuring —provided I had a proper guard retinue, they emphasized.

What they didn't know was that Alayna and I had plans of running off after we got married, leaving her mother in charge for a time. She'd returned after hearing of her husband's death and Alayna and her had a new budding friendship that they'd lacked growing up. The days passed and the night of the ball came. Though I anticipated it wasn't going to be much fun, I found myself feeling a tinge of excitement. I reminded myself that this event just brought me days closer to marrying Alayna, and that was a thought that genuinely excited me.

# CHAPTER 13
## THE BALL

My mother fussed over my vest, but I assured her that I looked fine. She'd come from Blackridge only days after the Morsocare, along with Cam and several others that were serving as my personal guards. Galt had been training with Cam nonstop and risen him through the ranks to the position of Captain after only a few weeks by my own request.

This didn't sour Galt's mood at all, as he and Lady Variyn were openly in a relationship now and very little could remove a grin from his face. Cam and his new arm made him a powerful guard, plus his proxy levels he'd gained from war. I treated him as a close friend, often playing cards with him, Emory, Ismene, and Alayna when I could drag her away from her duties.

Duties she reminded me I ought to be paying more

attention to, but I just shrugged, telling her I wouldn't want to deprive my advisors from their work.

"You know," my mother said, adjusting my vest for the tenth time, "you don't have to accept all of this fanfare. I bet if you told them firmly enough, they'd even let you leave your position at the head of House Variyn."

I smiled, my mother had been throwing in gabs and attempts to get me to put the House title aside since arriving, but I told her the same thing I always did when she tried. "The King won't allow it and I am happy to serve my Kingdom."

She scoffed at that, knowing I felt just about the same, but understood that I truly didn't have much of a choice at this point. It wasn't the position I wanted, but it was what I was bestowed with, and I would do my best. Or, at least, I'd hire people able to do their best. No one needed a headstrong Arcane Knight to tell them how to do everything. So, I was content to let them act according to what they felt was best and relied on the advisors to tell me when they were wrong.

"That's enough, you should finish getting ready yourself," I shot her a look and she glared at me.

"And what if I want to go like this?" My mother asked, gesturing to her plain dress and her red hair falling around her face in natural curls.

"I mean, you look fine," I said, shrugging. "I'm in

charge, and I say you can go however you like, but be prepared for snooty women to raise their noses at you."

She laughed and bid me farewell with a gentle touch to my shoulder and a shaking head.

Alone with my thoughts, I couldn't help but frown. How had my life taken such a drastic change and why wasn't I out helping to stem the spread of the Chaos inside the ley lines. I could still feel the extent and reach of the damage, my quick repair had not been enough, but it had strengthened the power in this part of the Wyrd.

However, I knew that my time wasn't being wasted here, as much as it might feel that way. A time would come, soon, that I would be back out on the battlefield turning the tide of Order and Chaos. That time just wasn't now, so until then, I would do what I could here to strengthen my new House.

I poked my head out of the door and was greeted by a finely dressed Cam, in resplendent guardsman armor, his eyes as sharp as ever. By his side was Emory, wearing a guard's uniform and looking absolutely silly in it.

"Emory?" I asked, a bemused smile on my face.

"Hhmmhh?" Emory responded.

"Why in the hells are you wearing a guard uniform, I told you that you were invited to the ball as my guest."

Emory laughed then caught himself and mocked standing straight and at attention. "Sorry sir, I felt my presence would be better suited for guard duty, sir."

Emory had been absent for most of the war, and he hardly looked like a typical guardsman. His tall, thick frame made him the biggest guardsman I'd ever encountered. But if Emory wanted to play at being a guard, who was I to stop him from having a spot of fun. It wasn't like I was worried for my safety right now; assassins could try to take me out, but I had several tools at my disposal for such attempts. That list only grew, now that I had all of House Variyn's resources and some time to tinker around with my gems.

Not that I had much time to tinker, but I found a bit here and there between meetings. Either way, Emory was happy pretending to be a guard and Cam didn't seem to mind having an Awakened as backup. Powerful arm or not, he was still basically a normal man and could be killed as easily as one.

It marked me as odd, suddenly, to consider how easily mortals could be killed, for true Awakened were basically immortal if left to their own devices, and if they picked the right perks. I shook off the arrogant thought and reminded myself that these 'mortals' are the ones that bled and died for me when I led them into battle. And I would have to do that again.

Battle in the Southlands was a forgone conclusion at this point, but I needed to tend first to my Chaos issues. All this was secondary to the thing I didn't want to think about, going to a stupid ball in my honor.

"We should leave soon, Lord Miles," Cam reminded me, and I let out a sigh of resignation.

"So be it, Cam," I said, hanging my head in jest. "Take me to my doom."

"It can't be that bad," Emory remarked. "Just tell the stupid fucks to buzz off if they annoy you."

"Those 'stupid fucks' as you call them, are the pillars that hold House Variyn up. Guild masters, nobles, powerful merchants. I need to keep them all happy and working for the good of the city. Would you want to trade roles?" I asked Emory, knowing full and well he wouldn't.

"Oh sure," Emory said, moving to walk in front and doing a ridiculous impression of me walking. He shook his ass and held his chin so high that he looked like he'd hurt his neck.

"You are failing at being me or a proper guard," I said, laughing. We would encounter servants in the halls soon, so I needed to get myself under control. It was all about giving the proper outward appearance of strength and dignity, or so Alayna told me. A large part of me wanted to say, to hell with all of it, and do my sworn duty to the balance, but another part knew that this was part of that responsibility.

It wasn't just what I could accomplish with the swing of a sword that was important, but what I'd be able to do with it firmly in its sheath. Could I be the man that the King needed me to be, raising House Variyn to a new height of power and success? Could I even keep the House afloat after so many disasters? I honestly didn't know, but I'd be giving it my damnedest.

I thought I saw Non disappearing down a corridor and I almost went after him. He and I needed to have a long talk; our limited interaction thus far had been... limited. It wasn't that I truly thought he held any care for the deceased Lord Variyn, but he had been in his service for many years. How many plans of theirs were still ticking away in the background waiting to explode in my face?

We approached the side entrance to the ball, the one that would lead us right to the throne where Alayna would be waiting. Thoughts of Alayna distracted me even further. We'd had time together, but regardless of what she said, I knew it pressed on her that I'd killed her father. At least she wasn't openly opposing me as Zander did, another thorn in my side that needed to be dealt with sooner than later. I had to get him to understand why I did what I did, why it was necessary.

Then there was our upcoming marriage, all but forced on us by the King. He wanted realm stability and that came with having a Lord that was given the title by marriage as well as by challenge. I wanted to marry Alayna, I knew that I did, but I didn't like the idea of being forced into it. Yet, I knew my responsibility and would take the steps necessary to see it done.

Finally, I reached the door and took a deep breath,

readying myself for what I'd find on the other side. Pushing it aside with a nudge, I appeared from behind some tapestries. It turned out the private hallways that Non used were meant for transportation of the Lord and Lady of the House, but I didn't begrudge him for using such secretive passageways. They were safe and secure, thus perfect for someone who wanted to go about the keep without being detected.

"You took your time," Alayna said through a false smile. I strode up, donning a false smile of my own and nodded to several nobles who caught my eye before I sat down on the raised platform. The throne was stiff and not nearly as comfortable as I thought it should be. Emory and Cam stood on each side of the thrones, giving a clear message to the crowd.

"I've arrived much sooner than I'd care to," I said, giving Alayna my full attention, my false smile transforming to a genuine one under her gentle gaze.

"These balls are important, and we can't have you missing them all like you did before becoming the Lord of the House," Alayna said, keeping her voice low so that only the two of us could hear.

She wore a beautiful dress of red and white, with flowers that went from the edge of her dress all the way up to her hair. On the other hand, I wore a simple suit with no frills. Atop each of our heads were small silver crowns, the heaviest damned things I'd ever worn atop my head.

Though the physical weight was nothing, it was more the implied weight that threatened to crush my neck.

"Lord Caldor Miles and Lady Alayna Variyn, of House Variyn." I barely heard our names announced to the crowd, until I noticed everyone go silent and give us a slight bow of their heads. Alayna and I gave a returning nod, and the crowd returned to talking amongst themselves.

"As long as I can hide up here, I'll be happy," I shot a whisper at her, my voice rising a bit higher than it ought to, but still, I doubted anyone heard.

"Well, prepare to be disappointed then. Usually, the Lord of the House would give a speech of some kind, so if you want to avoid that then you should go down and mingle with the guests. Several Guild Masters require your assurances of their contracts, as well as a few prominent merchants that could use some reassurances as well," Alayna said, all the while maintaining her smile.

"Cam and Emory, stay up here while I assurance up some people," I said, standing and making my way into the crowd.

What followed was several hours of small talk, small promises, and much headache. It was like dealing with children at times, everyone wanting to know whether everything would be alright and that old contracts would be favored over any new ones I'd be making. I assured them that I had no intention of taking down the old

Guild system or replacing it, then had to ask where they'd even gotten such a wild idea. Turned out, an old friend was spreading false rumors about me, and it was just my luck that she happened to be attending this very ball.

"Regina," I said, approaching the diminutive woman wearing an over-the-top golden gown. "It is a pleasure to have you here." Then leaning down a bit, I added, "Any reason you're stirring up the Guild Masters against me?"

"Oh, why what ever could you mean?" Regina said, in a very Regina way of speaking. She had a glint in her eye and a grin on her face.

"It wouldn't do you well to start rousing the city against me right now. I've all the right to take action against you if I need to," I said, my voice firming.

"And I've ever the resource to counter you, but you mistake my intentions, young man," Regina said, taking a sip at her wine glass. "I meant only to stir up a little healthy competition among them. You know many of them have held their offices for far too long. It might do well for a few fresh-faced individuals to take their place."

"And I'm sure you have a list of such individuals that would be a good fit?" I asked, seeing through her thinly veiled plans.

I considered Regina for a moment and all she'd done for me, despite how we'd left things, I cared for her and her advice. "What if I were to offer you a position as one of my advisors? You'd have the power to change an official here or there. I could use you at my side," I said, meaning every word.

Regina made a show of consideration before shaking her head. "No, no, I'm far too busy with my growing enterprise. We've expanded into the capital, you see, which takes up much of my time now. With our latest discoveries, we believe soon that the world will seem much smaller. It isn't just the elves that can master traveling on those quick flying ships; you'll see."

I smiled. "You've figured out the flying runes?" I asked.

She shook her head again and stood on her tippy toes, I leaned in to hear her. "Nope."

I waited for her to say more but she just gave me a look. I returned the look and waited.

"Oh fine, all I will say is, traveling between certain locations is about to be much easier. We roll out several working locations in less than a year, so you'll know soon enough. Of course, I will be reaching out to you for certain permits to operate such a device within the city. You can do an old friend such a favor as to overlook certain missing information, can't you?"

I looked at her deadpan, before finally answering. "For you, Regina? Sure, as long as you can promise me that it will benefit the city in some way. I trust you."

Her grin widened. "That's what I like to hear! Now,

let's talk about your crafting training. I've got a few teachers that I think will suit you well and we can't have you being known as the student of Regina who didn't excel at his chosen profession. One, in particular, is Edward Nums and he is a master Gem Crafter and Enchanter."

We discussed the details, and it was agreed that I would find a room in the keep for this, Edward Nums, so that I could continue my profession leveling. It wasn't that I'd set it aside, I'd made great strides and bounds on it, just not recently. It was hard when aboard an airship to get much done, especially when physical training took precedence.

I caught sight of Zander and Ismene and made a beeline for them. Zander caught my eye and glared, but for once he didn't flee. It might have been due to Ismene holding him tight, but I liked to think he was ready to talk things over.

"Zander, Ismene," I said, inclining my head.

Ismene waved and I took her in. She wore a black and gold dress; it stood out among the crowd in a good way. Her violet eyes and makeup made her eyes pop, her beauty was striking. Meanwhile, Zander wore the latest fashion of a tight vest, black to match his date's, with gold trim on the pants and vest.

"Are these balls always so, dry?" Ismene asked, lowering her voice a touch as a noble lady walked by a bit too closely, likely looking to catch a bit court gossip to pass around the room.

"Have you not been offered a drink?" I asked, smiling and having a bit of fun teasing her.

"You know I didn't mean it that way," she said, her voice going a touch serious. Her voice went back to the overly cheery tone she used when trying to lift someone's spirits. "You know, I am thirsty, excuse me while a grab a drink. You two need to talk. Okay?" She looked to Zander then to me and I nodded.

"How are things in your territory, Baron?" I asked Zander, genuinely curious how his estates were doing, as very little reports had been given since I took power.

"I've done as requested and raised an army," Zander began, not meeting my eyes. "But I think perhaps they might be of use elsewhere, maybe even in the capital."

His words carried a hint of ambiguity, leaving me wondering where he was going with this. Did he mean their use in the capital as protection or as a means of taking over? I approached the matter with caution, given the underlying tension. "Zander, our main priority should be the Southlands for the well-being of the realm. I trust you see that as well."

He hesitated briefly, letting out an exasperated sigh. "So now you want our people to go and defend the South-landers? Shouldn't our priority be defending our own?"

"Going to the Southlands and meeting this threat

before it spreads to our lands is the only way," I responded.

He was silent for a moment, taking in what I had said, then spoke again. "After I heard about the Morsocare, that you challenged my uncle to the death, I was furious. And when you killed him you took my uncle from me after my own father died saving you. I've thought since then that perhaps it should have been you that lost their head, not my father, not my uncle."

I tried to interject a rebuttal, but he raised a hand to halt me.

"But I know you did what had to be done," he said, not offering anything more.

Meeting his gaze with empathy, I responded, "I'm sorry for what has transpired. Your uncle chose to side with the Chaos. It wasn't about choosing him or me; it was about the greater good. Can you truly say you'd want things to have gone differently?"

Zander's eyes softened a bit. "No, I suppose not. But it's hard." Even this small acknowledgement of weakness from Zander looked to be difficult for him.

"I can't begin to understand what you are truly going through. But remember, our roles come with responsibilities, not just to our families but to the entire realm. Let's ensure your efforts, your father's, and even your uncle's sacrifices lead to a brighter future for all."

With a sigh, Zander murmured, "I've pledged loyalty

to House Variyn, and that includes you. Even though I still think you are an asshole. Just... give me some time."

I nodded, hoping that time would indeed heal the rift between us.

Ismene returned, seeing us not attacking each other, and she smiled.

"I got drinks," she declared, handing Zander and me a drink.

We both gave her sheepish smiles and took a drink. It was a pleasantly sweet wine with a nice bitter undertone. I finished the glass far too quickly and excused myself.

The night wore on and I grew more and more done with the entire affair. After some time, I returned to the throne and with Alanya in tow, we left before the ball was finished. It was a common enough occurrence for the guests of honor to leave before the end, so we knew we wouldn't be missed. Our honor guard, Cam and Emory, walked behind us enough to allow us to talk.

"I spoke with Zander finally," I told Alayna. She walked arm in arm with me, but her mood seemed more reserved and somber than normal.

"That's good," she said, patting my arm.

"What's wrong?" I asked, knowing her well enough to sense that something wasn't quite right.

"Oh nothing," she said, though I knew that wasn't true.

"Please, Alayna, tell me and perhaps I can help?"

"It's nothing, it's silly really."

"Nothing is too silly a problem for you that I wouldn't give it my full attention," I declared.

"It's Galt and my mother," she said, lowering her voice a measure, though Cam and Emory were far back enough and having their own conversation.

"What about them?" I asked. As far as I could tell, their new open relationship was going swimmingly. It kept Lady Variyn occupied and out of most meetings, which was good because when she attended, everyone treated her like she was already running House Variyn now and not me.

"I just don't know how I feel about it all. I love my mother, but our relationship has always been strained. I know why now, and she's desperately trying to spend time with me, but I just don't know. It feels wrong."

I pulled Alayna in a bit closer, and side hugged her. "This can't be easy hearing from the man who took your father's life."

"Not my father," Alayna quickly interrupted me to say. She quickly turned to see if anyone was around to hear that, but we were alone.

"You know what I mean," I hedged, and she nodded. "You knew him as your father and the husband to your mother for your entire life. Of course, it feels strange to see your mother with someone else."

"And so happy, it kind of makes me mad that she is so

happy," Alayna admitted with a frown. "I feel like a horrible person even saying all this, but I don't know."

"It's natural," I assured her and seeing as she didn't respond, I decided the matter must be dropped.

So, we walked to our quarters, well, mine, hers were separate until we'd officially wed, but that was just semantics. Cam took position just inside our sitting room where he and Emory would wait until the night shift could relieve them. I had to give it to Emory, he was really taking this guard duty seriously. A part of me wanted to call more guards out and get a game of cards going, but Alayna needed my attention tonight, so I pushed that thought aside.

We ended the night in each other's arms, all the worries and cares in the world melting away in the embrace of a loved one.

# CHAPTER 14
## CHAOS BEASTS

Reports from several locations painted a picture of Chaos had spread throughout most of House Variyn. And not in the figurative sense, there were actual Chaos Monsters beginning to be sighted and found within the borders once more. It had been a while since they'd gotten so bad, thus, despite my advisors' disagreement on the subject, I'd put together a team to eradicate several of the more problematic threats.

Fred, Fran, and Kora hadn't joined our ranks until now; they had been held in the elven lands all this while. The Queen of the elves, with Warrick's assistance, had ensured they remained there, emphasizing that everything had to unfold as planned. Now, as part of our team, they were accompanied by my strongest members including Emory, with Kora leading a squad of her own. Also along for the ride was Cam and a half dozen other guards, including the ever-loyal Galt. They were adamant about ensuring my safety, leaving me with little room for refusal. While they might face greater risks than the rest of us, I had confidence that Galt would never let harm befall his fellow guardsmen.

Alayna had stayed behind, saying she had work to tend to with the wedding fast approaching. She'd even stung me with a few comments about me trying to get myself killed before the wedding. She knew me better than that, but still, the comments got me thinking. What would happen if I fell in battle now? The most likely outcome was that Alayna would take the throne and be the sole ruler until she married another. Or she could cede the throne and Zander could take her place. That was an interesting thought that I didn't care to entertain for very long.

Our destination was merely a few hours away by flight if I rode atop Ares. Still, since not everyone in our group had access to flying mounts, I stayed mostly on the ground. The first time I'd released Ares from her figurine after my imprisonment, she had been perturbed. Through our mental connection, she expressed her frustration for not summoning her assistance during my captivity and the subsequent Morsocare. We'd conversed mentally about it all, where I explained my intent to shield her from harm and that there were challenges that I felt compelled to confront alone. She was hesitant about leaving my side but eventually understood why I had done what I did. Nevertheless, she needed to stretch her wings and hunt, and I wouldn't confine her. Currently, she soared above, scouting and hunting. Reaching out to her through our bond, I sensed her tranquility. Despite everything, she was clear about one thing: she was unwilling to be confined to her figurine any longer, determined to stay by my side and defend me.

I knew that I could go further and connect my mind with Ares, sharing our sight, but it wasn't necessary right now, and doing so strained some unseen resource to do it for long periods of time. Upon thinking of resources, my mind wandered to the essence vaults I'd raided and the valuable information I'd gathered about Lord Variyn's schemes during a discussion with Non. He assured me that another explosive device had not yet been completed, but the stores of essence had already begun. As such, I plundered several hundred thousand essence from Lord Variyn's reserves and sunk it straight into the blade.

It wasn't enough to make that much of a difference, but it gave me an edge in combat now that I was getting the hang of using the sword. I also practiced in the evenings with Galt, activating the sword's abilities with only my mana. The sessions were more about familiarizing myself with the effects than getting any real practice, as Galt couldn't keep up with me any longer. I'd also had my armor serviced, several of the gems had been strained past their limit. I'd purchased replacements, instead of crafting them myself, but they were of the same quality as the ones I'd put together.

The countryside slipped into darkness as evening came and I made the call to make camp for the night. We were heading for a village by the name of Riverhelm, north of City Variyn. But it was still a day's travel at our current pace. Recent reports indicated that the town had been attacked at night and several villagers had gone missing. The final message we received detailed that a black wyvern was seen in the sky. Scouts had come back later with devastating news—the town had been destroyed, leaving dozens dead and nearly a thousand men, women, and children displaced by the destruction of their homes.

Already troops had been dispatched to lead the displaced citizens to a place where they could find refuge, but if the root of the problem wasn't taken care of, the entire northern part of my new kingdom would fall to the Chaos. That wasn't the turn of events I was looking for right now, or ever, truth be told. But this was more serious to me personally, as Chaos was my personal responsibility. Very few adventurers these days, especially inside of House Variyn, could handle a Chaos beast. Among those that could, I had most in my party right now.

After making camp, I settled down beside Cam and Galt. Fred and Fran had set up camp beside Kora and her team of Runeforged, and Emory seemed to tag along with Fran. Though I wanted to spend time with them, especially after everything, I wanted to make sure that Cam, Galt, and the other guardsmen knew that I had confidence in them and that I appreciated them joining us. So, I sat down by the fire and took a bowl of Galt's famous chili. Apparently it was more spice than anything else, but my tongue appreciated it all the same. Each bite was like an explosion of heat and flavor, but as an Awakened past so many thresholds, not only could I bear the heat easily, but I could also appreciate the subtle flavors he'd laced into it. Each bite stoked the fire in my mouth, but I didn't slow down until I'd consumed two entire bowls.

It wasn't so much as to make my belly bulge, but damn was it tasty. After that, I took time quenching the fire with ice cold ale that I pulled out of my storage ring. Because why wouldn't I save ice cold drinks and piping hot meals inside my storage right where I could pull them out at a moment's notice. It was good being an Awakened Adventurer most days, one of many perks I enjoyed. Looking around at our non-Awakened party members, I wanted to invite them to test their luck and become Awakened, but I knew Cam's answer already.

He was happy the way he was, and I didn't know if I truly felt comfortable offering the other guardsmen an uncertain opportunity that could result in death. Then there was Galt, an Awakened who'd chosen the life of a guardsman to raise up generations of powerful men to serve and protect. It was honorable, but at times I wondered how he happened upon the path, so I decided I should ask him.

"Hey Galt, can I ask you a question?" I asked.

Galt smirked, he was much quicker to smile or smirk these days, and said, "You just did."

"Hah," I said, shaking my head. "Then can I ask you a few questions?"

"Go right ahead," Galt said, his new cheery demeanor throwing me off for a moment.

"I was just wondering," I began trying to choose my words as carefully as I could. "How did you happen upon the life of a guardsman?"

"In my blood," he said, without hesitating. "My father was a guard, my father's father, and his father as well. Sort of a tradition in my family."

"But you're Sparked, aren't you? You never thought of taking the traditional route of being a dungeon diving adventurer?"

"Who said I never dived into a dungeon or two?" Galt asked, looking bemused.

"That's a story I wouldn't mind hearing," Cam said, taking a swig of his waterskin.

"Ain't much to it," Galt said, shrugging. "I ran with Bren, and that's how I met his brother and got my position. He was a great man, Bren. He kept his brother in check and without him, well you know. Besides, most of my progress came from those runs, giving me the strength I needed to lead my men and train them right."

That put a pit in my stomach for some reason and I couldn't put my finger on it. Bren had been harsh to Zander, but from all other accounts, he was a fair and honorable man. If he'd not died, I suddenly wondered if Lord Variyn would have gone down the same path of destruction. If Bren truly did rein in his brother from time to time, then it was Chaos that could be blamed for the fall of Lord Variyn. For if his brother had lived, perhaps his heart wouldn't have turned black.

Thinking of such matters put a bad taste in my mouth, so I turned to Cam, hoping for a new topic.

"How's the wife liking Blackridge Keep, or did she come to stay with you in the capital for now?" I asked. I felt a bit bad dragging Cam around and forcing him to be without his wife, but he'd jumped at the chance to become one of my personal guards, so travel was inevitable.

"She was at the capital," Cam said, taking another drink and clearing his throat. "But she's heading back to the farm to help tend to it. With another baby on the way, we felt it was only right."

"Another one?" I said, surprised. "Pretty soon you'll be swimming in babies."

"Yeah we are blessed so far," Cam said, his smile widening.

"Sounds like you should enjoy the time apart, otherwise you might make twins," Galt said, laughing at his own joke. This new Galt was going to take some getting used to, I decided, but I chuckled along with him.

"Not sure that's how that works," I said, despite having very little idea how the entire process worked outside the deed that planted the seed.

This got a laugh from the rest of the guards gathered around and the rest of the night was filled with cards, dice, and drinking. It was a fine time, filled with memories that I'd keep fresh in my mind to help stave off the darkness when it reared its ugly head. However, this trip, whether it was from the exertion or just being around these folks, had been pleasant and not once did I feel the darkness overtaking me. It was a rare occurrence to go more than a day or so without it, but I didn't think too deeply about it.

The next day came, and we reached the ruins of Riverhelm. It reminded me so much of Creeshaw that a pit grew in my stomach just looking at the burnt out remains of the buildings. The street into the town was scorched black here and there from the fire of the Chaos wyvern. Debris crunched underfoot as we traveled deeper into the ruins and the smells began to overtake all my other senses. It wasn't just the burnt buildings and flesh that assaulted my nostrils, but I swore I could smell the Chaotic energy infecting the land here.

And with that Chaotic infection seeping deep into the ley lines, I knew our powers, those of Order, would be weakened. But I didn't fear a single wyvern any longer. Weakened or not, my team would be a match for such a beast, and we would slay it.

"Ares," I called out and she finished a circle above, landing beside me and nuzzling at my hand. "We are going to take to the sky, Fred, stay with the troops, Fran and Kora, join us in the skies. We are going hunting. If we can, we will bring the wyvern back here, so be ready to fight."

"Ventus take the party and secure the area from below," Kora said, giving her commands to her gathered Runeforged.

"As you command," Ventus said, bowing.

Galt gave me a look that I could tell meant, don't split the party, but I knew my prey and I knew Ares was strong enough to outfly it. I gave him a reassuring nod before turning back to the two I'd asked to join me.

"When we find it, allow me to go in first and grab its attention. I will lead it back here, but Fran and Kora, keep a good distance away. You are there to help me fight on the ground if we can't lure it back to the village square," I said, and both nodded that they understood. Fran called forth her steed and Kora let wings of sparking energy form behind her. I got atop Ares and together we took to the skies, searching for the black stain against the reddening backdrop of the setting sun.

The weather was pleasant, if not a bit cold this high up, but flying always left me feeling a certain level of peace and tranquility. Fran didn't share that look, instead, her face was screwed up in concentration as her eyes traced the horizon, looking for the black wyvern that had caused so much pain and suffering.

Some would think I am foolish for taking a risk such as this, while all of House Variyn relied on me, but it was that very reason why I had to do this. I couldn't sit on the sidelines as Lord Variyn had done, destroying things at a great distance with uncaring malice.

No.

I was Caldor Miles, Arcane Knight, and defender of the weak, protector of the masses, bulwark against Chaos. If Chaos chose to stand in my way, Chaos chose death.

It was at that moment that I felt, not saw, the wyvern in the distance. Malicious and evil intent, hell bent on destruction. A moment later, its form, massive and black, rose above the tree line and into the air. It roared and even from a distance my ears tingled from the sheer ear-splitting sound of it.

"Go in fast and bring us in close," I said to Ares, though she'd read my intent seconds before I'd even spoken, and we were well on our way, outstripping Fran and Kora. I checked behind me to ensure they were following orders, both had stopped and hovered, awaiting to see what happened next, just as I wanted.

Sunlight warmed my face as I changed direction to flank around the massive wyvern. This one had to be at least a quarter bigger than the last one, easily twice if not three times Ares' length. However, that meant the massive wings had a bit more trouble keeping it aloft, and its movements were slow and sluggish. We came in like a dart, cutting in close. I pointed my hand out, sword forming in my grip, and let loose an essence empowered Lightning Strike, followed by a Chain Lightning.

The first strike cracked the air and smashed center mass into the wyvern's back. It roared, a simple roar and not an empowered attack, but it strained my ears regardless. If I weren't as powerful as I am now, it might have caused me to grow dizzy. However, I held my concentration and within seconds, my Chain Lightning ripped into it, traveling from wing to wing and dealing considerable damage.

With its attention wholly on me, I cut off the attack and slammed my sword into its sheath. I didn't like not having it firmly in my grasp, but if I lost it midflight, I could always call it back to me. There was a comfort to having it at my side that I couldn't explain, it just felt right.

With the wyvern locked on me, I saw its attack coming a mile away. Ares did as well, swooping low and turning around just in time to dodge a massive line of black flame. I could feel the heat of the attack as we increased speed, striving to stay ahead of the stream of fire. It wasn't until seconds later, when the fire cut off, that Ares finally took a breath and redirected our course back toward our two waiting friends.

"Move, move, move!" I shouted to them, waving my arms. I wasn't sure they could hear me, but they seemed to have gotten the message and began to travel back toward the town. The wyvern was gaining terrible speed and, despite its struggle to gain altitude, it appeared to be able to glide and dive just fine. The lightning attacks I'd thrown at it had damaged the left wing, but the cut was so small that the wyvern didn't seem bothered by it. Another stream of fire followed, but we'd outpaced it enough that we didn't even have to dodge this time.

"Turn around and let's go for another attack," I ordered Ares, not wanting to lose the wyvern's attention when we were so close.

We whirled and my stomach lurched as Ares went into a rolling turn. The edges of my vision blackened ever so slightly as the pressure of the turn hit me, but I remained conscious, and we dove down right atop the wyvern. I did as I had before, calling down lightning then channeling it to bring devastation to the beast. This time, I focused on the injured wing. My lightning flashed and blew straight through the leathery wing material, but we'd gotten too close too fast.

The wyvern flipped its entire body, lashing out with its claws. I summoned forth my sword and infused it with my mana, sending Ares a command to spread her wings and catch me in a few seconds. My words carried my entire intent, and I could feel her equivalent of a smile spreading over her face as she obeyed. I hit the straps on the saddle and fell from Ares, diving right atop the massive wyvern.

I avoided the claws with a well-placed Blink and plunged my sword deep into the wyvern's chest, my sword cutting through its hide like a hot knife through butter. Activating Speed Burst for another lurch of speed, I dodged a bite and kicked off the wyvern's chest, falling free from it. Ares was there only a second later, and I caught hold of her, pulling myself back into the saddle.

The beast wasn't done, but it was pissed. Streams of fire followed us, trees igniting from the wyvern's rage. All the while, we twirled and swooped, avoiding each strike. The wyvern was right on us, falling toward the ground more than flying, but it was clear we were going to land just shy of the village. This was good, as I didn't want the guardsmen to be consumed by the flames and Fred, along with the Runeforged, would be quick enough to join me in battle after only a minute or two.

That's if the thing was still alive, I could sense its life force diminishing as it flew, blood spilling off it from the massive rend I cut into its fleshy scales. We hit the ground, having put enough space between us and the falling wyvern that we were confident we'd be able to intercept. The massive wings spread out before it, and the black Chaos monster leveled trees as it came down hard.

Ares hopped back just as Fran and Kora appeared behind us, Fran immediately recalling her mount and Kora's massive bird like wings folding into themselves until she was flightless once more.

Before us was the black wyvern, maw open and ready to spit flames.

"I'll block the flames and immediately afterward we hit it with all we have," I shouted over the din of battle. I didn't look to see if they'd heard me, just trusting they knew what to do and when to do it.

Fran appeared to my left and Kora to my right.

I hopped off Ares, instructing her to stay clear unless she got an opening from above. She took off just as the fire roared out toward us. I raised my hand and activated Mana Shell, infusing it with a fair bit of essence. Black flames blocked out all light and for a moment, we stood in near darkness, only the slight blue glow with crackling green lightning from the essence giving any light. Several cracks formed as the flames continued, but I pumped more Mana into the Shell barrier and they closed, keeping us perfectly safe against the brutal attack of the wyvern. A few moments later, the flames ended, and I allowed the barrier to fall as well.

If it were possible, I'd say the wyvern had a surprised look on its face when it saw its prey still alive. It even took a hesitant step backward and I felt the beginnings of another power growing on its claws. Before it could form, Ares slammed into its head and tore at its face. Before the wyvern could react, all three of us rushed it, weapons ready.

Kora had turned her hands into long lance-like instruments, throwing copies of the weapon in a glowing yellow light, and Fran had her sword out, already throwing a slash through the air at the wyvern. I decided to join her slash with one of my own. Using Speed Burst to more easily chain my skills, I activated Power Strike, Swift Strike, Force Wave, and Light Blade at once, while infusing a few hundred essence. The cracking slash that appeared to shoot from my blade tore at the very fabric of reality as the air trembled around it.

It moved with such deadly intent and absolute assurance of death, that it passed up the other two strikes. The wyvern, free of Ares for the moment, saw the attack coming and could only move so much to avoid it. Its left wing caught the attack at the shoulder and to my utter surprise, slashed right through it. A massive wing came falling to the ground and then came a cry of pain so fierce that it brought me to my knees, along with my companions.

It filled its cry with power, and it shook the air around the wounded wyvern. But the power waned, and the beast was already on death's door. We managed to get back to our feet and continued our assault, the wyvern moving sluggishly as its life blood poured freely from it. Just when things seemed sure, a rip in the air around it appeared, and two adult drakes stepped through. Behind them, stood the Chaos Knight I'd been searching for.

My heart skipped a beat, and I lunged forward, infusing my movements with essence and imbuing the blade. I moved faster than the wind, but I was still too slow. The tear closed, but not before I got a good look of where the Chaos Knight was, standing with her back to a great open ocean. She must be in the elven lands, and I would find her.

But now I had to focus on not being overwhelmed, as fire poured from the maw of the two adult drakes. The wyvern was left to my comrades, both stabbing and slashing it to bits. Meanwhile, the Drake to my left was suddenly swarmed by bodies as Ventus and his kin appeared. They'd be enough of a challenge for it, so I turned my attention to the final Drake. White fire slammed into it just as it tried to shoot more flames in my direction.

I turned and saw Fred had joined me, his white robes

billowing in the air around him as flames circled him, powerful and deadly. "I've calculated our odds of defeating this Drake as extremely high," Fred said, his voice most academic and calm.

"I concur," I said back, laughing.

The drake lurched with unreal speed and grabbed hold of me by the arm, throwing me through a tree. I felt the pain as the Chaotic creature somehow bypassed my armor's defenses and cut into my flesh beneath. I stood and Blinked back to Fred's side as he threw white fireball after white fireball at it. It lost ground with each attack.

Just as the drake went to unleash more fire, I pointed my blade and lightning danced from its tip, the strands of electricity bouncing off the ground and forcing the maw shut. Meanwhile, white flames took chunks out of its massive black hide, scales and all. Running forward, I infused my body and my blade, ready to end this beast before the fight had a chance to progress much further.

Standing my ground, I waited for the Chaotic beast to charge. I felt a sense of peace begin to wash over me and when it finally did, I ran headlong toward the monster. Mighty jaws of powerful teeth attempted to consume me, but I was too fast. My blade cut deep into the soft under-belly as I slid under it, pouring out its guts and remaining life force.

A distinct 'caw caw' from one of the trees pierced through the sounds of the skirmish. It was so clear that I recoiled when I saw the black bird watching nearby and its feet moved in a dance-like rhythm. What in the hells was going on here?

Now wasn't the time to waste thinking about some bird that may or may not be stalking me. Rising to my feet, I gripped my sword, preparing to take on the next Chaos monster, ensuring their demise. But as I surveyed the scene, it was evident that we had prevailed, and I was now one step closer to finding the Chaos Knight.

# CHAPTER 15
## A WEDDING

Alayna wasn't happy to hear that we had encountered three powerful Chaos beasts instead of just one. However, the reminder that our wedding was just three days away cooled her rage. Galt further added to the tension, informing her that I had gone off on my own again, referring to me as a 'foolish child at times'. He wouldn't meet my eyes on the way back and kept to himself after he saw the wound I'd taken on my arm.

It had healed easily enough, but I had assured him before that I was in no danger. He seemed to think that it was his duty to keep me safe, but I was just glad only he seemed to be taking my small injury so seriously. Cam, on the other hand, asked for details of the fight and commented that he sure was glad we'd done the fighting away from them. He had faith in his abilities, especially with his new arm, but he wasn't in a hurry to get into a one-sided fight. And that is exactly what it would have been if the guards had been involved.

How many of them would I have lost, I told Galt, if I was too busy trying to keep them alive and not focused on the Chaos monsters? He didn't like my train of thought and accused me of purposely putting myself in danger because I liked the thrill. Then he went on about how people who are always looking for the next thrill will never live to see their grandchildren. Something about his last statement really dug at me, but I ignored him and let him stew. Though, now I was having to deal with Alayna, and her wrath was much worse than Galt's.

"If you have a death wish, Caldor, I can kill you just fine," Alayna said, not willing to let it drop.

Taking a deep breath, I tried again. "I love you Alayna," I said. "I do not wish to die; however, I do have responsibilities that will take me into deadly situations. You know this, I know this, so why are we fighting about it?"

"Don't try to reason your way out of this, you *do* have a greater responsibility now. To the people of House Variyn," she said, her words like hot metal searing into me.

I frowned at her words and knew I shouldn't say what I was about to, but I had to. "I have no greater responsibility than keeping the balance between Order and Chaos. I am also responsible, I know, for all the souls that live within House Variyn, but I cannot shirk one duty for another. I can and I will accomplish both. And remember, I love you. Together we can do this."

This seemed to pacify her more than enrage her, which I took as a sign that I was winning, but a moment later she turned her steely gaze on me, and I flinched back. "When we marry, you will only have one responsibility and that is to me. All else comes second."

I thought about that before responding. I loved Alayna and though we didn't plan it so soon, we did want to eventually get married as a way to solidify our bond. It was what my parents had done, and I wanted to follow the example of the best relationship that I knew of. And she had a point, my father had treasured my mother above all else, but he still did his duty and eventually died in the pursuit of it.

"I agree," I said simply, not wanting to drag on the argument any further. She knew I loved her, and I had responsibilities, so there was no need for a 'but' in my final words. I pulled her into a hug and was surprised to hear her begin to sob in my arms. I said nothing, instead, just held her close and enjoyed the warmth of her being so close.

This moment lasted several minutes, but never did I

consider pushing her away or not letting her finish. When she finally decided to release me, she looked up with bloodshot eyes and cheeks wet with tears. At some point, a few tears had escaped my own eyes, but I couldn't tell when.

"I'm afraid," she said, her voice cracking.

"I know," I said, kissing her on the forehead.

We stared into each other's eyes for minutes untold, saying no words but volumes worth of communication passed between us.

In that moment, we promised each other that we'd do all in our power to stay alive for each other. That we'd not let the fire of our passion burn out. We'd stand by each other no matter the mistakes the other made or wrong decisions were made. In my mind it was that moment we became wed, fully and utterly committed to each other. Through pain, fear, love, hate, whatever emotion would come, we would stand through it all. Never would we falter in these commitments and if death should come knocking, we'd blow down the door together. Nothing would stand in our way; no force would be equal to our love.

\*\*\*

When the day of the wedding came, I was pleasantly surprised at how little there was for me to do. It seemed like being the Lord of House Variyn came with more waiting around when things such as balls and weddings were to be planned. Servants moved here and there, preparing the grand hall for the occasion and, to my surprise, I'd received word that the King would be in attendance, even going so far as to be the one to join us together. I hadn't really thought of who would marry us, it was tradition for leaders or elders of towns or cities to do such acts, sometimes even a priest of the religion of Vanir.

But that wouldn't do for either of us, so I was actually glad when I got word that the King would be in attendance. It still made me nervous to think that he would be the one to join us together, but I pushed that aside and accepted it for what it was, a blessing. With the King here, I got my wish to trim down the guest list. It wouldn't do to have just anyone in attendance when the King graced your halls. Of course, my family and friends would be there, I'd even received word that Michael had appeared with the twins, having defeated their first dungeon and well on their way to growing stronger together.

In all, it was a wonderful time that I hoped to share with all those that I cared for. Beth and Adathin arrived that very day and I was on my way to greet them when Non appeared before my path.

"I must speak with you urgently about a threat against your life," Non said, his tone as monotoned and even as always.

Cam stepped forward along with another of my guards, as if protecting me from the bald man in his dark robes. I raised a hand and beckoned them to step back, and they did so, though Cam didn't look convinced at my safety.

"Can we speak of it here or did you want to go to my office?" I asked, being polite. We'd spoken at length recently and come to an understanding. Non repledged his loyalty to the kingdom and told me many deeds that he'd done while in the service of Lord Variyn. Nasty vile things that I did not approve of and immediately told him he would do no longer. One such task that he admitted to was having the explosive device placed in the city of Blalor.

If not for the blood already spilled, I'd have called for his own blood, but I knew that no further violence was going to bring back any lives. Instead, I would use this sentinel of death and with his hands accomplish greater tasks. Though, how exactly I'd do that still eluded me, but I was pleased to know he was under my control. So, it was with this attitude toward the man, knowing him to be deadly serious, that I walked him to my office to speak.

He wasted no time getting right to the point. "I've heard word that many of the collection devices we'd lost during the transition period, as you took control, have been used in dungeons all over the land. I fear that someone means to ignite another device and can think of no other target than your wedding with the appearance of the King. We must warn him and cancel the wedding."

I considered his words, and I smiled that I knew something he didn't.

Many of the missing devices had indeed gone missing while I took control of House Variyn. It had been the first thing I'd done when I'd gotten ahold of those in charge of it. Swearing and binding them with oaths, I sent them out to collect essence not for a new device, but to empower my sword.

"I am the one who took control of the collection devices, but it wasn't to empower enough of those deadly devices. Thank you for your concern, and I appreciate you coming to me," I said, then while he stared at me in surprised silence, I departed.

It felt good to put one over on Non, but I didn't let it go to my head. I'd needed secrecy for that project, and I should probably have trusted Non, master of secrets, to handle it. However, I lacked the trust I'd once had for the man, especially now that I learned of his involvement in the House Blalor incident. I met back up with Cam and my other guard, moving to deal with more Lordly business that I'd prefer to put off to someone else. Such was the duty that I now had to deal with, despite my many advisors and assistants.

"I have a gift for you," a familiar voice said from behind me. I turned to see Kora flanked by Ventus and another Runeforged I didn't know the name of, standing in the hallway. It was kind of nice how they hung around her now, guarding her like she was their queen or something. I supposed that she was in a way.

"Oh?" I asked, stopping my walk, and sharing a bemused look with Cam. I could tell he wasn't worried by her presence, well aware that she'd never raise a violent gesture toward me without cause. And I didn't ever intend on giving her cause, she was my friend and an opponent that I wasn't sure I'd be a match for the way she kept growing into herself and getting stronger.

"I know it is customary to present after the wedding, but I could not wait," Kora said, a quirky expression on her face that stood in stark contrast to the stony expression Ventus held on his own.

"Should I get Alayna? I'm sure she'd want to be here to receive any gift you have to offer." I looked around trying to remember where I'd last seen her or where she might be. Likely running around and tending to one thing or another.

"This gift is for you; I have already presented her with a gift of her own. Though, she too thought to gather you, but I assured her that I would find you next and here I am," Kora said, beaming brightly.

Whatever this gift was, she was obviously excited about it, so I wasn't going to stand in her way. "Let's have it then," I said, holding out a hand.

Kora stepped forward and looked me in the eyes. They blazed brightly for a second and when she next spoke, her words were solemn. "One of my kind fell, but not by my own hand. They were young and I know not the ways of our rebirth well enough to say whether or not she will be reborn. However, I can say that she has perished and what remains is her pure and powerful essence. Use it wisely, Caldor Miles." And with that, she placed a round gem into my hands, one that I recognized as I'd held a similar one before.

"A dungeon core?" I asked, completely shocked by the gesture. They were powerful reagents and known to be the rarest of finds, as destroying a dungeon was a punishable crime. How ever she'd gotten this, it was likely it either cost her a fortune or she had to go to great lengths to obtain it. It was very likely lives had been lost in the pursuit of such a rare item.

"Are you sure?" I asked, dumbfounded that, dead or not, she'd offer up one of her kind like this. "I'm not sure it feels right." I added, shaking my head.

"It is," Kora assured me. "Those that previously had it would have wasted the powerful essence inside. You, however, can put it to good use." Her eyes flicked to the sword at my waist, and I knew what she meant. She wanted me to infuse the sword with the essence from the Core.

"Isn't essence just essence?" I asked, wondering how

much could be within the dungeon core for her to be so excited about it.

"Is water just water, is all food just food?" Kora asked back in retort.

"Alright, I get it," I said, very pleased at the gift and the thought that Kora had put behind it. She understood my mission as well as anyone, it seemed. She knew that I had to face down the Chaos and darkness, and that without a powered-up Sword of the Ordu, I'd be hard pressed to do so. "When I have a moment of peace, I will feed the essence to the blade and with the offering I will strike down Chaos and fix the wounds laid down deep in the Wyrd."

"Good," Kora said, very pleased with herself. "Slay well, little Chaos Slayer."

\*\*\*

Bells chimed and the great hall of Keep Variyn buzzed with gossip and benign chatter. Lining the walls, blocking some of the decorations, were Royal Guards. Dozens of them stood in formation, and at the head of the hall on the raised platform, stood a stoic figure clad in resplendent golden armor – the King. I stood beside him in my traditional Arcane Knight black and blue formal wear, the white gloves on my hands each with the symbol of Evoker and a sword on them, the symbol of the Arcane Knight and a whisper at its class origin.

My mind was abuzz, and the time passed as if in a dream. The details were washed from my mind as I tried to focus on the moment and not the lavish decorations, or the finely dressed friends and family out in the crowd. It wasn't easy, but the moment Alayna appeared, escorted by Galt in full armor, my mind snapped into place, firmly affixed to her.

She wore the most beautiful gown I'd ever seen. It flowed behind her and sat on her in such a way that no words that I possessed could possibly describe it properly. It was enough to say that she was perfect, the dress was perfect, and the next few minutes were perfect.

The King spoke many words, but I heard them only as an afterthought, my entire being focused on Alayna as she stood in front of me. The time came when I could speak and I tried as best I could to express my love for her, mere words would not be enough, but I took a deep breath and tried to voice them anyway.

"Alayna, from the moment I saw you, I knew you were going to be special to me. While it wasn't the fabled love at first sight, your laugh, your wit, and profound wisdom drew me closer to you. You have the biggest heart I've ever encountered, and for that alone, I'd love you for a lifetime. While words may falter to express the depth of my emotions, I trust in our bond. You know that I love you, and I know that you love me in return."

Alayna smiled, her eyes beginning to water, but she held her emotions firm and kept the tears at bay. "When I was told to entertain a new knight, I expected I'd have to be the same stiff and serious person I'm forced to be much of the time." She blushed at the words and lowered her voice even more, despite the fact that our voices weren't carrying very far to begin with. "But the moment I spoke with you, I felt at ease, like I could be myself. Because of that, I fell in love with you far faster than I should have, but I don't regret it one bit. Together we will rise. I love you, Caldor Miles."

The King spoke some more and joined our hands with a simple white and black cloth. I then drew closer, sealing our union with a tender kiss.

We were married, now and forever.

"I announce to you, the Head of House Variyn and his wife, Lord Caldor and Lady Alayna Variyn."

That bit caught me by surprise, but I didn't let it show on my face. Was I to take the name Variyn? Because I wasn't sure I was okay with that.

But it was a small thing when weighed against what I'd just been through. I was married and in love with a beautiful woman on the inside and out. She was my partner in all senses of the word.

The rest of the night was a blur of activity and gifts. I

wanted to say that I paid rapt attention to all of it, but I was a man in love and lost in the moment. A part of me wished there was a way to capture the emotions and ambiance of the night forever, but I knew of no such device. So instead, I lived in the moment, talked long into the night with my wife, and received gifts from friends that I would cherish for a lifetime.

# CHAPTER 16
## PREPARATIONS

The core that Kora gave me lacked a certain feeling and brilliance that hers had when I'd held it, but nonetheless, I trusted her word that it was going to be useful. I held it out in front of me wondering if I should just get the transfer going so that I could get a sense for how much essence there was. I decided to probe it first with my ability and get a sense of the scope of essence before transferring it to the blade directly. What I found surprised me, several million, at least three, waited inside. This was enough to make a real difference.

I fed the essence of the dungeon core into the Sword of the Ordu and something marvelous happened. The sword flickered to full strength while the energy flowed into it. Runes blazed and the feeling of absolute power returned. Sitting where I was, alone in my room, I felt the need to move, to act, but I squashed it with great effort. Something about the dungeon core essence was kicking the sword into overdrive and it became clear what I needed if I wanted to be a match for this Chaos Knight.

This essence did indeed feel different as well. It was an immense amount, but it was more than that. Where the essence I'd given to it before had been taken by the sword, none had reacted so strongly with it. Almost as if they were similar creations and the transfer was the most natural thing ever. Could the sword and dungeon cores have something in common? They were both said to be created by the Ordu, but that couldn't be the end of the similarities.

The core cracked and shattered, turning to dust when the final transfer was complete some hours later. I collected the dust, knowing it too was a powerful reagent that I could either sell or keep for experiments of my own. My thoughts drifted back to dungeons and how I could possibly get more of this power.

Dungeons had reached out to me before, but I wondered if I'd be able to get more to do so or if just taking in the essence of the dungeon while inside it would be enough to get the same effect. I hadn't been inside of a dungeon since getting the sword, but I felt confident in my new plan. I would go and do as many dungeons as it took to empower the sword and make ready to face my enemy.

I found Emory just outside my main room playing cards with the guards.

"Time for a bit of fun," I told him, and he gave me his signature grin in return.

Before asking what I meant, he said, "I'm in."

I gathered together, Kora, Emory, Alayna, and Ismene, promising them drinks and a fun night so that I could discuss what I needed.

"The plan is simple," I said, looking at each of them in turn. "I need to run a few dungeons and get a feel for how much dungeon essence I can pull into the sword. Kora, do you think the dungeons will mind if I strip them bare without destroying their cores?"

She considered for a moment before speaking. "I know I would, but I think if you take me with you, we have a better chance at not aggravating them."

"Good," I said, I'd had a similar thought and it felt good to have it confirmed.

"Alayna, I know I promised you a trip, just the two of us, but—"

She cut me off with a raised hand. "It can wait. I will gladly accompany you and keep you all healed up."

"I can't go," Ismene said, looking a bit stressed. "Zander isn't in a good place right now, and I need to be here for him."

"I understand," I said, my mind already going to who else could fill in for her.

Fred and Fran had left with their parents after the wedding ceremony, as they hadn't seen them for a long while. Then there was Beth. She had been in attendance at the wedding, but I didn't know if she'd left yet. I'd have to send word soon and make sure she was able to come in Ismene's place.

"I understand," I said again when Ismene looked at me with worried eyes. "Please tend to Zander and give him my best wishes. I know he is hurting, but it was never my intention."

With that, Ismene nodded her head and left, likely to go find Zander and keep him from doing something he'd regret later. Honestly I'd love for Zander to come as well, but I knew he wouldn't right now. He needed time and I didn't have it to give yet. But I could give him space while I sought after my own needs.

I sent Cam off to find Beth, if she was still around, while the rest of us decided on the best dungeon to try.

"I think we should do one we've already done. It takes a measure of risk out of it," Alayna said, ever prudent.

I shook my head, I really wanted to have a new experience, but I might be convinced to go back to the dungeon where City Blalor had once been. "I want something new and exciting," I said, smiling. "It is our honeymoon after all, we ought to make it fun."

"This is not our honeymoon," Alayna insisted, giving me a mock death stare.

"So, does this mean I'm the tank? Come on man, I told you I want to be a damage dealer," Emory said, taking a few mock swings with a pretend sword.

He was a damn good tank, and he knew it, but I let him have his fun. "Yeah, and I will be the healer," I joked.

"You wish," Alayna said.

"Perhaps I can be the healer as well," Kora said, getting into the fun. She had an overly wide smile on her face, and we all laughed at the look of it.

"We can all heal, except for Emory, he has to tank," I declared.

Beth appeared around half an hour later, looking as wide-eyed and spunky as ever.

"We should try the Carnival dungeon," she said, very enthusiastic about her pick.

"I heard it can be a bit weird," I said, thinking back to what I'd heard about the dungeon. "What if we did the dungeon in House Thouca, I think it's supposed to be a dragon hunt or something?"

"Oh yeah, that one is neat," Beth said, nodding excitedly.

"If we are going to travel a bit, then I vote on House Qoswil's capital dungeon. It will be safer, as it is in the capital city itself, and the adventure is said to change monthly, so there is no telling what we'd face," Alayna said, and she knew she'd gotten me with the mystery aspect of it. An ever-changing dungeon meant it could literally be anything.

"Deal," I said. "We travel to City Qoswil tomorrow morning!"

"It's called Riverside, one of the few capitals not named after its House," Alayna said, smiling kindly at me.

I raised an eyebrow, I really should know stuff like this, but still, there was so much I didn't know it seemed. "Why?" I finally asked when she didn't offer up a reason.

"Capital city moved to the largest city when the territory was won over from the elves. It also has the largest non-human population, with the wife of Lord Qoswil even being an elf herself."

"Fascinating," I said, wondering what other interesting national facts were out there that I didn't know.

The preparations to travel to Riverside were more than I expected. First, we sent scouts to get permission to bring a small envoy of troops along with the Lord and Lady to visit House Qoswil. This took two days and delayed my immediate plan to leave. When that permission was granted, we then had to find enough flying mounts for a dozen troops, along with five extra servants that 'had to go' as well. In total, there were twenty-two of us, but I insisted we fly to make decent time.

So, after a bit of bartering, we had enough flying mounts together and we'd lost another two days. My advisors told me it was most unusual for me to go off 'gallivanting' into another's House territory, especially with my reputation, but I ignored them. I had a quest to restore the balance and it would be done. Along the way, we'd be stopping at two other broken Prime Mana Shrines. I had enough essence that I was sure I'd be able to fix one, if not two of them.

"And you're sure I can't go as well?" Galt asked for the tenth time just that morning.

"I need you here, keeping the keep safe and people in line," I said, meaning every word. I didn't trust so many under me, but I had no doubts in Galt. "Besides, I've got Kora with me, she's been given orders to keep Alayna safe at all costs. Between her and this sword, I'm sure we could remake the very fabric of reality to keep her safe if we had to."

This had the desired effect of pacifying Galt, the wrinkles on his forehead growing slightly less tense. He nodded and went to say goodbye to his daughter. To my surprise, Lady Variyn, Ceon's widow, stepped forward to speak with me.

"I wish to thank you for stepping forward and dealing with our mess. I pledge my support to you and the support of those that still have faith in my ability to lead," she said, her voice low and motherly.

I hadn't said so much as a single word to her since she came back to the city, so this was all a bit much all at once. Raising an eyebrow, I considered her words and decided it would be best just to be polite. "Thank you. I'm honored to receive any support you have to offer. And I promise that I will keep your daughter safe."

This seemed to be what she wanted to hear, because she lowered her head and nodded, before retreating.

What a strange day this was, Galt and now Lady Variyn, each wanting something from me and offering pledges of loyalty. A strange day indeed.

"You feeling alright girl," I said, patting Ares' head. She turned away, still mad at me. I guess I understood a little, but I didn't want her to be mad at me. I could feel the hurt and why it still stung, which made me just as irritated as she was, though it was my own damn fault.

She felt like she was a close friend and partner, so she ought to not only have been invited, but have been a part of the wedding. However, it was inside, and I didn't think she'd care for a human celebration. Of course, I'd been wrong and now I was paying for it. She was not going to make this a fun or comfortable ride. I almost, just barely, but didn't, thought about getting a pegasus to ride just to spite her. I didn't hold onto the thought long, it felt wrong, and I didn't want to walk down that path.

Ares sent thoughts to me of mistrust and annoyance, and I bore them the best I could.

"I am sorry, you were there in our minds, it was a humanoid gathering was all," I said though I barely believed my own excuses.

Before too long, we were off and flying in the air. Ares made sure to make many quick dips and turns that were wholly needed, but I stomached her punishment until she grew bored of it. Then the flying wasn't bad, though she didn't want to share her eyes with me, so I only saw it through my limited sight. It was two days of travel, as we could only push the Pegasus mounts so hard, as none of them had the extra power they would gain from being bound to an Awakened.

This was fine and it gave everyone a chance to truly appreciate the view. My mind wandered as we went, from what we could expect inside the dungeon to how I'd find the Chaos Knight. I'd already sent word to the Elven Queen that I believed she was in her lands, so perhaps she would do me the task of finding her location. I just hoped she wasn't sending anyone foolhardy enough to engage the powerful fighter, as with her sword she was likely a match for any that would be sent.

The air was chilly, the seasons pushing onward, and all was still and peaceful in the air. It was a comforting, even soothing, feeling flying up above it all. One could almost pretend like all the pain and anguish were someone else's worry. But no, not only were my own demons something I would need to deal with eventually, the future and safety of all below me fell more firmly into my responsibility now.

Responsibility.

It was a heavy weighted word that more and more took me into its clawed grasp. Like a never-ending surge of water from the great oceans, it seemed all consuming in its need to take away any freedom I might once have had. That I'd been able to get away to do these dungeons without taking half the court with me was a miracle. Several Lords and advisors expressed a desire to come, but I'd turned them down.

It wasn't like I wanted any of this responsibility in the first place. The only singular thing I'd taken that I didn't somewhat regret, was the role as an Arcane Knight. Despite the heavy weight of that, I'd gladly take up the mantle again. I was, as my father was, and I would continue to try and live up to that great legacy. But I was also my own man now, much changed and different than my father. I recognized both facts and accepted my reality for what it was.

We made camp that night and the dungeon group gathered around the fire for some drinks. It was pleasant and helped me forget my woes. By this time tomorrow, we'd be at the dungeon, and I was looking forward to seeing what lay in wait for us. I was a bit nervous about meeting the Head of House Qoswil, but it wasn't anything I could avoid. As a visiting House Head, I would need to take my time, meeting and greeting those whose House I was visiting.

The next day came, and I repaired two Prime Mana

Shrines, draining the sword of its remaining essence. By day's end, we found ourselves at the border of the city Riverside, appropriately named as it laid beside a mighty river. Tall walls surrounded the city and miles of farmland spread out before it. It was equal to City Variyn in size, but there was something about it, maybe the taller buildings and the numerous farms, that set it apart in my mind.

The introductions were quick and dirty. The old man who ruled House Qoswil said all of three words to me, before having an advisor take us around to give us a tour. It ended at a massive complex of buildings surrounding the dungeon proper. We got to skip the line and soon we were standing within the Dungeon starting room, a fountain of pure essence water in the basin before us.

Taking a final look at my group, we stepped into the dungeon.

# CHAPTER 17
# BIBLIOMANCER'S LAIR PART 1

"Welcome Librarians," A deep voice spoke out in the darkness and suddenly a light appeared, revealing a cloaked figure in purple robes. "You have come here to delve into my Lair, the Bibliomancer's Lair. You have been tasked with recovering two powerful artifacts and clearing the pesky beasts that have slunk into my territory. Are you up to the task?"

Before any of us could answer, he chuckled, low and hearty. He waved his hands and a purple magical fire appeared, flashing here and there. I got no sense of danger from him, but still, my hand went to my sword belt.

"Oh, it would seem you are more than prepared, allow me to increase the difficulty to something you will find challenging." With a grunt of effort and more waving of his hands, the Bibliomancer did something, what it was, I couldn't say. "There we are! Oh dear, it seems there will be four artifacts to recover now, but you should find what lies ahead to be well within your range of talents. I aim to please, of course, no boring deaths here."

Before he'd even finished his sentence, he began to fade away and his voice trailed off as well, ending with two words. "Good luck."

Suddenly, light blossomed from all around and we found ourselves on a cliff, water splashing in waves against the cliffside. A massive, mountain-sized keep laid before us. Its massive doors were bound in iron, and flanking its entrance were two colossal golems, constructed of boulders and etched with magical runes.

"Time to get to work," I said, looking at what lay ahead. "I bet those artifacts lay within and we have to defeat those guardians to gain entrance."

Several nods followed and Emory stepped forward, raising his shield before him, ready for anything. That is when one of the golems reached down and pulled a section of rock off itself, throwing it at Emory. To my surprise, Emory took the hit and was bowled over, end over end, grunting in pain as he went.

"Shit," I said, pulling free my sword and charging forward.

This dungeon had increased its difficulty, and it might have ramped it up too hard if Emory couldn't even take a single hit without being knocked off his feet. My sword came down, infused with mana and the golem raised its arms in defense the same moment that I struck down. The strike was devastating, crumbling the left golem to nothing within moments. My sword licked up the remains, gaining much more pure essence as it went.

The right one wasn't idle, a fist slamming into me and taking several hundred health points as I went flying. I used Blink to position myself for a strike and took it down before my team had time to do much more than blink at the exchange.

"Damn, boy," Beth called out. "You've really upped your game since I last did a dungeon with you."

The doors creaked and opened before us, revealing a massive library and hundreds of enemies waiting within. These weren't the massive stone golems we'd encountered outside, but rather, paper golems. They looked less ominous than their stone brethren, but the sheer number presented a problem, and I looked over the room to get an idea of a plan.

At first it looked like a massive hallway, two story tall shelves stuffed to the brim with books, running several hundred paces long and ending at a massive door. None of the paper golems attacked yet, and as they moved, I noticed a few spirits in their midst as well. Along with a few ink-black blobs that I could only guess at how to kill; magic would likely be necessary.

The room had no lights, yet the light was bright

enough to read yet not so bright as to tire the eyes. The 'hallway' opened up every hundred paces or so into a maze of more bookshelves, or at least I assumed as much, as I saw directly to our left and right more bookshelves and a narrow opening between the variable sea of books. In all, it was like being deposited into a dream, with so many books. I wondered absently, if they all contained real knowledge or if merely dungeon fabrications.

Something whispered at the edge of my hearing that they were real books, and the sheer amount almost brought a tear to my eye. I could spend the next two hundred years in here and not get through the books that I could see just in this first hallway.

"Incoming," Emory said as my eyes ran over a ladder that swung down the length of the bookshelves with a spirit on it. I looked down to see that a pack of five paper golems had broken off and were headed in our direction. The harder I looked, the more I could see their composition. They were built from real book pages, with words noticeably all over them like scripts or lettered tattoos on a flesh of yellow parchment.

As much as I hated to do so, and I did hate burning anything related to books, I began casting Firebolt to deal with this incoming group. I spared a glance at Alayna, and she was just as lost in the vastness of the dungeon library as I was, her eyes glazed over and her mouth open. As I turned my attention back to my casting, my spell went off.

Crackling fire sparked from my fingertips and smashed into the first golem. Even without empowering it with essence, the golem went up in flames, screeching out in pain. The sound disturbed me, even more so as the flames spread to the next golem then the next. By the time they reached us, all five were alight, but still coming on hard. Emory shot me a look and I shrugged apologetically.

Flaming parchment met wood and steel as they crashed against Emory, burning at him through his armor. I rushed forward, rearing back, and bringing down my sword in a devastating slash. Doing as I'd done before, I sucked up the essence of the monsters as easily as taking a sip of cool water, then the additional damage of my slash left them as a smoldering pile of ash. Repeating the process as fast as I could, I sucked in several hundred essence and the sword's runes flashed as it was fed.

Beth and Kora hadn't been idle though, each of them cutting or in Beth's case, shooting, apart a golem each. Kora looked annoyed at how easily the golems fell to pieces, but I was just happy to be able to feed the sword.

"What are the chances we can talk to the dungeon and ask if I can just start sucking up as much essence as they can give?" I asked Kora, not actually expecting an answer but getting one anyway.

"I believe we must venture deeper before our words will be heard. This dungeon is much more ancient than I, but I feel her, and she feels me. If we prove ourselves worthy of her time, she will come to us eventually," Kora said, then giving me a stern look she added, "But don't expect that she will give anything freely."

"Well, we ought to clear out the monsters and look for any clues," I said, my gaze running over the sea of monsters still left to be defeated. We needed to find four powerful artifacts, though he'd given no hints on where or how to find them. Like most dungeons, I imagined it would be as straightforward as plowing our way through and finding them after defeating a boss of some kind.

But I kept those ideas to myself and instead, focused on defeating the monsters that lay out before us. Cut by cut, firebolt by firebolt, my enemies fell before me. It was almost too easy once we got the hang of it. Where was the challenge that had been promised to us?

As I defeated each one, I made sure to suck up the pure essence they provided, feeding my sword. A few times I wondered if I should focus on leveling myself up a bit, instead of feeding everything into the sword, but I stopped myself. This weapon was all the power I needed right now, I just had to feed it the necessary fuel to guarantee that none could stand against me. Not that I planned on stopping my growth completely, that would be foolish. No, I took a tenth of all essence earned for myself but kept the lion's share for the sword.

Once we'd cleared the open area, we spread out into the maze-like space, defeating all the paper golems in the side halls as well. A few of the ones we found here were magical in nature and shot out arcane blasts that really stung. From what I could tell, the further from the center we got, the harder the monsters were. With that in mind, we cleared out as much as we dared before the fights became too difficult. When it became apparent that there was no end to the maze of books, we returned to the center.

"Should we check out some books now?" I asked, already walking over, and grabbing a random tome off the nearby bookshelf. It was titled, "Musings of the Bibliomancer Volume 241". I nearly put it back without even reading a passage, but something urged me onward.

It took me all of five minutes to determine the value of the book and it was priceless. Each paragraph shifted to a new topic, seemingly without rhyme or reason, but every segment was detailed and brimming with insights. For example, I found a passage on essence and learned that there were in fact different types of essence, but we processed it almost entirely the same. That hadn't been the case before the Ordu, or so it read. Before the Ordu, you'd have to focus and pull in the essence that most suited the affinity of the person.

It was an odd, yet interesting fact, and inside the tome were so many more. One paragraph detailed knowledge of toxic dust from Jewelcrafting and how most Awakened were poisoned several times over. Though, their increased constitution took it all in stride, never putting the crafter in true danger. I'd learned a bit about the toxins that could be released from Jewelcrafting, and I took as much protection as the next. This particular section interested me enough to skim several more pages until it continued seemingly the same train of thought.

This section went over a variety of ways to avoid poisoning and then randomly went on to talk about how even Un-Awakened were now stronger than people had been before the Ordu. It was odd to see so many references to 'Before the Ordu', but I skimmed over them, far too excited in general about the usefulness of the book.

"This one is all about History and a world whose name I can't even begin to pronounce. It talks about a race of people who called their Awakened, Champions, and then mentions something called the Titan System. This is all so fascinating," Alayna said, from where she'd sat down with a particularly large tome.

"Shouldn't we focus on, you know, finishing the dungeon?" Emory asked, a nervous chuckle escaping his mouth.

"He has a point," Kora said. She shut a book that she'd been looking through and added, "I know most of this anyway."

"You do?" I asked, Alayna saying the same thing only a moment later.

"I've lived a long time, but I can't imagine why this

dungeon has laid out all its knowledge in book form. Seems like a tedious process, even for a dungeon," Kora said, sliding the book back onto its shelf.

"They're right," I said, shutting my own book and replacing it on the shelf, very careful to put it back where it had been before. "Let's see if we can find a clue to where the first artifact is, if we have four to collect then we've got a bit of work ahead of us."

We went the one direction we'd been avoiding, forward. It led to a mighty door, large and imposing, which opened before we even made it all the way there. It looked, at first glance, to be a child's room of some kind. A vast chamber filled with children's toys of every make and model. It was brightly decorated and had paintings of silly dragons, bears, and even a few donkeys on the wall. Walking around the room were small toys, what looked like a cookie shaped like a person—all brown with gumdrop buttons—and a hulking figure toward the back with a red scarf over its head.

In the very back of the room, behind the hulking figure, was a pedestal bathed in light and sitting atop it was a Quill and Ink, all gold and silver. I didn't know much about random artifacts that might be found, but that screamed, 'take me I'm a treasure'.

"Seems easy enough," Emory said, strolling into the room first and walking past one of the small foot-sized cookie men.

They took displeasure at this, pulling out candy swords and spears, some even ripped gumdrops off themselves to throw, and then they attacked. At first, I thought we'd be able to just sweep them aside, but they were aided by the toys all around the room, jumping to life. Emory was being swarmed and taking several small knicks and cuts.

"Take them down?" I half asked, half commanded, unsure how to even begin this fight.

What followed was half an hour of clearing the room by kicking, smashing, and dismembering toys and cookie men. All the while, the hulking figure stood with its back to us, some two hundred paces away, waiting.

"That was the most ridiculous and annoying fight I've ever had," Emory complained. He'd taken the brunt of the damage if you could even call it that. Alayna had been wary of even healing him, but he insisted, saying that the many hundred tiny cuts stung to no end. When everyone had been fully healed and the room a wasteland of cookies and broken toys, we advanced on the hulking figure, easily a head or two taller than Emory while hunched over.

"Hah, hah, hah," came a voice from behind the figure. A creepy little girl walked into our path. Creepy was definitely the right word, because how else could you describe a child wearing a wolf's skin as a mask, while holding two tiny axes. She repeated the same laugh as before, as she regarded us with pure white eyes.

"You want my treasure, dontcha?" She asked, her voice high pitched and childlike.

"Yes, we do," I said, raising my sword toward the diminutive child. "Any chance you'll hand it over without a fight?"

Her laughter came back in earnest. Child or not, she was a monster, I reminded myself, but it was hard to think about attacking such a figure. That was the moment that the hulking figure she'd been hiding behind turned and I nearly lost my lunch.

It was a massive wolf man, but most of its face had been cut off in order to make the mask the little girl wore, and it hadn't been a clean job. Red flesh hung about the face with one eye hanging out of the socket completely. A row of sharp teeth could be seen as all ability to hide such teeth had been stolen from the poor creature. Other than the face, the rest of the body was intact, save for lines of red where the small axes the girl wielded must have cut into it.

Surely this monster would want the girl dead as much as we needed her to be, maybe if it had intelligence enough to be persuaded? "Look what she did to you," I said, trying to get it to raise its eyes to meet my own. When it finally did, I realized my mistake. It had eyes of red, but they showed no gleam of intelligence, just animal hunger directed at our party.

"Oh, yous think you can sway my baby wolfy, do ya? Go get your lunch, Mr. Wolfy," the axe-wielding girl said.

The hulking wolfman moved with a sudden, frightening speed, but this wasn't our first dungeon. The team reacted perfectly. Emory stepped forward, catching the wolfman's charge and I sidestepped an axe-throw from the small girl, as Beth released a volley of arrows at her. Kora cut in beside Emory, slashing with her sword arms into the wolfman.

She'd adjusted her fighting style a good bit from what I was used to seeing, preferring to attack up front with her sword arms and barely, if at all, relying on her summons. My guess was that she felt like there was no need, so I followed suit, attacking with just my sword and the moves I'd learned from Michael.

First, I sliced a line down the crazy wolfman, slashing and slamming into Emory like he was the only target, then slipping past him I engaged the smaller axe-wielding girl. One, two, three swings and she dodged them all expertly.

"Little Red won't be taken out so easily," Little Red said, slashing hard across my chest. Despite her small form, I felt it, but my armor did its job preventing any real damage.

This back and forth continued with me not hitting her and her strikes unable to penetrate my armor, then I stopped messing around. Putting just a touch of mana into the sword, my body surged with speed and strength, my mind reeling from a sudden desire to claim it all for myself. Before I could stop myself, I began to pull at Little Red, her essence resisted me, and I struck out recklessly before gaining control once more.

I needed to focus on controlled and skillful movements. First, I Blinked behind her, tired of not using my full abilities and uncaring anymore with the power of the sword running through me. Next, I activated Speed Burst, time seeming to slow around me.

Then, I struck with a thrust into Little Red's back, using Phantom Thrust at the same moment. She screamed, a distorted thing with Speed Burst active, but she blurred and with blood flinging around her, caught the edge of my sword on her two axes. I pushed against her, but she matched me in strength despite her small form. Stepping back, I activated Power Strike and slammed into her axes, causing them to fall to the side. I scored a devastating slash into her shoulder, and she screamed again, blurring away from me to attack Kora.

Blood ran down her in spurts, but she fought all the harder for it. Kora was pushed backward, her speed not a match for whatever skill this monster was using. Though, as with all skills, the time ran out and she slowed. But the moment of relief was just that, a moment.

A red glow covered her and the wolf. I watched in horror as they both jumped back and suddenly, despite arrow after arrow hitting her chest, Little Red opened her mouth much, much, too wide. So wide, in fact, that it could almost be comical, until she jumped and ate the massive wolf in a single bite.

"Hah hah hah," Little Red laughed as her body morphed and changed. Little Red was no longer little, her form equal to the size of the wolfman, but thinner and more grotesque in its appearance. She took on the features of the wolf man, but her skin ripped and split as her form outgrew it. What we were left to fight looked like a hairless wolfwoman with red lines running up and down the naked form, any clothing she'd worn had fallen to pieces during her transformation.

Then, her form blurred, and pain shot through me as teeth sunk into my neck. How she'd so easily bypassed my armor's defenses, I didn't know, but everyone except for Kora was staggering from a similar blow. Yet, Little Red had returned to her starting position, seemingly unbothered by the speed she'd just moved.

I flicked Speed Burst back on just as a heal washed over me and I Blinked forward, blade at the ready. My attack met open air as the whisper of 'hah hah hah' filled my ears from behind me somewhere. Pain ran down my back as Little Red's slashing fingernails, as long as claws now, ignored my armor and cut into my skin.

But the attack only made it halfway down my back before I turned and activated Swift Strike, followed immediately with a Lighting Strike. My blade met flesh and my spell slammed into my target. The moment my sword was within her flesh, I pulled and felt a wash of essence run over me.

The 'hah hah hah' cut off and became a snarl of rage. "That's mine, stop it!" Little Red screamed in a distorted version of her original childlike speech.

The flow cut off and a kick sent me flying backward. I saw my team react as my Speed Burst ended and time became slow once more. Beth loosed exploding arrows into Little Red, while Emory threw his shield and called curses down on her, getting her attention. Meanwhile, Alayna hit me with a heal and Kora began chanting the words to a summoning spell. What she'd decided would be a match for this one's speed, I couldn't say, but I was glad she was taking this seriously at least.

A few moments later, her spell finished, and nothing appeared. Or at least nothing that I could see at first, several seconds later her Disruptor Cat appeared, all black and ready to eat. It was a sneaky thing, and it caught Little Red by surprise, biting into her neck and giving us all the chance we needed to strike.

I slashed out using a combo of Power Strike, Swift Strike, Light Blade, and Force Wave, sending a sparking arc of attack energy through the air at the exposed chest of the once diminutive girl. Though she was no longer that same small girl, she took the attack in stride, even as it ripped another line of red down her chest. Then the arrows came, followed by a spear of light, and a powerful shield smash by Emory, and lastly twin sword arms through her chest.

The monster flickered red, then I struck, stabbing her through the heart before she could enrage and put us through another volley of attacks. I began to pull in essence, and it was like a dam had been unleashed, filling the sword by the thousands.

"Hah hah hah," she whispered as she fell to her knees, dead.

# CHAPTER 18
# BIBLIOMANCER'S LAIR
# PART 2

The artifact was easy enough to collect after that, but I looked around confused at why we hadn't gotten any loot yet. I tried to loot the fallen golems before, but they'd given nothing, and now even the boss had no loot to speak of.

"What's with the loot?" I asked, and Emory nodded along as he tried to loot the boss and got nothing as well.

"All loot is being withheld until I've decided you've earned it," A familiar voice said, a purple robed figure, face obscured, appeared before us. "Thank you for returning my Quill and Ink to me, now hurry onward and see about really showing me what you can do. So far, you've weaved an exciting tale of victory by strength of arm. How well do you do when it is your minds that must be tested and not those brawny arms of yours?" His voice seemed to quaver with excitement as he spoke, and I didn't like the sound of it at all.

The back wall, where only a child's painting of a door had been moments before, now held a massive wooden thing with metal bands running across it. The purple robed figure gestured at the door and then disappeared, taking the Quill and Ink with him.

"Onward and forward," I said, shrugging. "Beth, stay on alert. If my guess is right, we are going to be dealing with either traps or puzzles, but I don't want to get caught in a trap if we can help it."

"I'm on it," Beth said, pushing her way past Emory and holding out her arm as if she could feel the traps with her open hand. She pressed onward and we entered a nondescript hallway that, given how harmless it looked, practically screamed, 'I am filled with traps'. Sure enough, Beth held up a hand to stop us.

"Oh boy, this is going to take some time. Did I tell you I improved my ability to sense traps? If I hadn't, this one would have totally fried us. It's a pit trap filled with fire runes meant to cook us alive," Beth said, nonchalantly.

What followed, was nearly two hours of Beth clearing traps and slowly progressing forward. At one point, we triggered a wall moving trap, but she disarmed it, sheepishly throwing me an apologetic grin for not catching it. With the first hallway taken care of, we went through a medium-sized door that led into a larger circular room with a domed ceiling and six tables set up with some kind of game. Each table's game was in a different stage of completion.

"Chess games," Kora said, her face a mask of amazement.

"What's that?" I asked, not recognizing the game at all.

"It's an old game, played by very few people in the Wyrd," Alayna said smartly. "It isn't as popular as some other more prominent games, and it is fairly similar to others, so it just never got very popular."

How she knew this bit of information or why Kora was excitedly sitting at a table and moving pieces around, was beyond me. Walking to stand beside her, I watched as she moved a thick tower-like piece into place and she spoke the word, "Checkmate."

The side opposite her had black colored pieces and one of them fell over at her words. The room thrummed and a voice rang out.

"One out of six challenges complete, you've added thirty seconds to your time. Four minutes remaining." It wasn't a voice I recognized, and it sounded very flat.

With a new sense of urgency, I followed Kora to the next table, where she was three moves into what looked like a game halfway complete, she exclaimed victory once more with a, "Checkmate!"

This followed several minutes of tense gameplay

culminating in the final match, which she didn't appear to be winning. She was down to only three pieces and the black side had a solid eight, but she moved her pieces skillfully, trying to maneuver her opposing side into a losing position. I didn't really follow how, but she moved several times and lost another piece before finally claiming checkmate. She'd had to sacrifice a piece to make the victory possible and I wondered if or what the dungeon was trying to tell us.

With those puzzles complete, we were led into another room, this one filled with the same small tables but with square puzzles on them that could be moved either left, right, up, or down. Each of the six sides had different matching symbols on them and again, Kora went to work without a word. She was our official puzzle master, and I was glad to have her. These tests took her a good bit longer and several times the voice of warning spoke saying there would be consequences if the puzzles weren't completed in time, but each time we avoided any punishment by mere seconds.

So it was, we got to the second artifact, a locket that looked much like a puzzle itself, with so many rods that interconnected and seemed to swirl as you looked at it. The Bibliomancer appeared, said a few meaningless words and we were off once more.

The next door took us into a grand open area, set up like a tournament stand or something similar. A voice, ever-present and vibrating with power, spoke once we'd stepped through the door.

"You have entered the Hall of History, now tremble in fear as you face some of the greatest challenges of your past. First up, is the mighty Iron Fist, but this time he won't accept anything but victory!"

And just like that, an armored figure that I recognized intimately appeared before us, old Iron Fist. He wore grizzled armor, worn and weathered; his helmet covered his face, but I could feel the same intense power coming off him as before. However, this time I had a team behind me, and I was much stronger than before.

As if reading my thoughts, he spoke, the same surprisingly fatherly voice echoed from within his helmet. "I'm much stronger than I once was, prepare yourself and let's engage in honorable combat. Your forces, versus my own."

Several soldiers appeared, eight in total, wielding spears and going into formation behind their general. This was not going to be a quick and easy victory, that much I knew just by the sheer weight of power coming from these figures.

"I'll keep Iron Fist busy, you guys deal with the soldiers," I said, not waiting to see if they'd agreed with my plan or not. Instead, I launched myself forward, letting the sword whisper to me of my overwhelming strength and power to change reality itself.

As stalwart and deadly as ever, Iron Fist brought up

his sword and stopped mine just as I activated Power Strike. The open arena rung with the sound of battle as my team engaged the soldiers, and I traded blows with Iron Fist. He moved with speed akin to my own, but he was trickier than I remembered, grabbing at my feet with his earth abilities and tripping me up to get a strike in here and there. It was enough that the battle didn't seem to be going my way at all, but I had tricks up my sleeves as well.

First, I started things off by closing the distance once more, using Blink the moment he swallowed up my feet with the dirt ground. Immediately after, I activated Speed Burst, infused it with essence, while also infusing essence directly into my muscles. The results sent me practically flying across the battlefield, sword posed and ready to strike. I did my usual combo of Light Blade, Swift Strike, Power Strike, and Force Wave to send an arc of damaging attack energy at him as I approached. He blocked it away, but that was fine, because I had my opening.

My sword came down hard on the opening between his neck and helmet. Blood sprayed and I thought for sure that I'd taken his head, but when I looked up to see him fall to the side, he punched me right in the face, sending me sprawling backward. It didn't really hurt, my helmet took most of the blow, but it caught me so much off guard that I stayed on the ground for a second too long as I tried to figure out how that hadn't worked.

Earth pulled me into the ground, and I realized I'd

made a huge mistake. Blink was still on cooldown, but I was free enough to still cast other spells. So, laying there I unleashed all I had to keep the titanic man at bay. I started with a Lightning Strike, which he brushed off casually, strolling forward. Next, I hit him with Channel Lightning, pumping essence into it to push him back. It worked! He staggered and I could tell it was doing significant damage to him.

Letting the spell drop, I prepared a Fireball, easily my strongest attack when infused. Letting essence build into it as I poured more and more mana, it sparked and sizzled. This attack would likely blow me out of the ground and injure me just as much as Iron Fist, but I had few options until Blink came off cooldown.

I was able to charge it for a solid three seconds before unleashing it. Iron Fist put his hands up to block, earth surrounding him like a shield. The Fireball hit and detonated, throwing debris and rock everywhere. As I thought, I was blown free of the ground, but I was battered by immense force and as I got to my feet, I found myself spitting blood.

There was no waiting around now. I rushed forward and activated Phantom Thrust. My attack hit where Iron Fist had been, and I heard a grunt of pain as it hit home.

"Got you," I panted the words. My battle sense screamed at me, and I jumped back just in time for a sword to slam down where I'd been just moments before.

"Not yet," came a response. Old Iron Fist wasn't out of the fight just yet.

Spears of rock followed, one after another shooting like speeding arrows toward me. I erected a Mana Shell around me and caught them easily against my barrier. After half a minute, the barrage ended, and I let my barrier flicker away.

Iron Fist emerged, badly battered and blood running down the front of his armor. "Will you defeat me as you did before or will I retain some honor in this fight, defeating you as I should have the first time?" He asked, his voice strong once more.

"I won fairly, and bloodshed was avoided," I said, not sure what this fake Iron Fist was getting at.

"Using a technique that allows you to fight far above your station is not honorable. Stop these antics and face me as an equal," Iron Fist commanded.

I started, looking at him with new eyes. Is this really how he felt or was this just dungeon madness? I couldn't help but consider his words and nod my head to accept his terms. "I accept your terms, let us fight, man to man. I will prove that I have what it takes without essence infusion," I said, despite knowing that any skill or ability I had should be considered fair game.

But I had faith in my ability to deal with this threat. Iron Fist would fall this day and any doubt of my strength and abilities would be put to rest. For, I was Caldor Miles,

Slayer of Chaos and Defender of the Balance. Nothing would stand in my way when it came to accomplishing my goals.

I started things off with a Chain Lightning, not infused with essence it didn't hit quite as hard, but it did the trick of staggering him while I waited out the last seconds of my Blink cooldown. The moment I felt the pressure ease and it was able to be used again safely, I struck.

First, I threw a Lightning Strike right in front of my target, obscuring his view, then a Blink to the side. Using my favorite combo, I infused them with the power of my Light Blade ability. But this time, I struck so close as to be impossible to dodge.

Iron Fist cried out and blood spurt from his helmet's visor as my strike hit his side. It wasn't enough to completely rend his armor, but the force of it would do work against his internal organs. Rearing back, I struck, unwilling to give him a moment's respite. A sword was not an ideal weapon against someone in plate armor, but when wielding an instrument of the Ordu, it proves to be more than enough.

Slash after slash staggered the fake Iron Fist back further and further. Until finally, he caught my blade in his outstretched palm, causing significant damage to his hand to do so. He roared an inhumanly loud bellow into my face, and I nearly took a step backward. Keeping my composure, I let the blade blink away and appear back in my hands a moment later, freeing it from his grip. Next, I slashed down with Power Strike, slamming past his slow guard and bringing him to his knees.

This fight had never been about honor or saving lives. I knew now that I would do whatever I needed to win, but I had nothing to prove. I thrust my blade into the rip in his armor and began to consume his essence. It took surprisingly little time until he fell apart into motes of light. The battle around me had ended seconds before my own, none of my teammates looking worse for wear.

"That was intense," Emory said, gesturing at the damage I'd taken. My armor was intact, but pain riddled through my body in waves as my regeneration tried to fix all the injuries I'd taken internally.

"I wonder what other threats we will face from our history?" I asked, a bit unnerved that this was the first fight the dungeon had chosen for this section of the dungeon.

"We are about to find out," Kora said, as mist swirled, and the arena was cleared.

"Hello Beth, my dear sweet lady," said a slimy voice as a tall dark figure stepped out of the mists. He held two daggers and wore the attire of a rogue. Looking over to Beth, I saw her eyes had gone as wide as saucer plates.

"No," Beth said, and the battle was on as she loosed several arrows at once.

The battle wasn't nearly as long as the first, and we won with only minor injuries. But Beth was clearly shaken by the appearance of the man, and I couldn't help but wonder why.

"You okay Beth?" I asked, she was still looking at where the man had fallen.

"I will be," she said, her voice tense.

Unwilling to push it any further I waited for the next challenger to arrive. One by one we faced off against specters of the past, Emory against an entire dungeon party, the one he blamed for his slow progress at the start of his journey. Kora faced off against an Owlbear, though I didn't get the feeling it bothered her much. And lastly, Alayna's specter from the past was her father, a battle I wasn't keen on repeating. I ended it fairly quickly, using the sword's unfair advantage to suck the fake Variyn dry before he could make any headway on us.

In all, it was a disturbing challenge that ended with us getting the third artifact and returning it to the Bibliomancer, a Tome of Time. It was a large gold embossed book with an hourglass atop its cover.

# CHAPTER 19
# BIBLIOMANCER'S LAIR
# PART 3

The final room we entered was a spherical shaped prison. Three platforms rose up on the sides, connected by staircases. The room was lit dimly by torches on the walls, but the dozens of cells remained dark behind thick iron bars. But each cell contained something, I could feel the immense power inside them.

"Welcome to my Room of Sealing," the Bibliomancer announced. "Here I will have you defeat three monsters of your choosing. Of course, nothing here likes to be known in the normal sense of the word, so it will be random as ever. Unless, of course, you can divine what lies behind a door before opening it. I warn you," his voice stiffened, "there are monsters here more powerful than even you, Chaos Slayer, so choose wisely and defeat only those that can be defeated."

With that, the purple clad figure rose up in the air, and instead of disappearing as he had so many times before, he just hovered there, cloaked in shadows. What a riddle filled mess, what was I to do with this?

"Any ideas?" I asked, looking from one cell to another. I had some skill reading auras, but monster auras were tricky. Each cell gave off the sense of immense power and I couldn't sense much difference as I focused on one after another, until I came to one on the very bottom, directly in front of us.

From that cell, I at first felt nothing. But I sensed something, though, it was so faint as to be easily dismissed. I scanned the rest of the cells to make sure, and as expected, I found three rooms that gave off very little aura at all. Thinking I'd cracked the code, I opened my mouth to declare our first challenger, when a feeling in my gut stopped me.

I knew of two figures that could cloak their auras well enough as to be considered nothing at all, the King of Newaliyn and the Queen of the Elves. What if this was a trick, and these three cells actually held the most powerful monsters, not the weakest. I decided to focus more on the ones I could sense and try to determine which, out of all these powerful auras, was the weakest.

"I can sense three masking auras, but I can't get a finger on how much power they are hiding," Kora said, surprising me with her ability to sense auras. Beth, Alayna, and Emory looked utterly bewildered just looking from cage to cage at random.

"I felt the same," I confirmed, then looking up at the Bibliomancer I added, "I think it would be best if we left those three alone. The unknown variable is potentially worse than one of these stronger auras. Give me some more time and I will find the weakest of the strong contenders."

I continued my scan, until I finally came up with what I was certain was the weakest of the options. It was faint and the difference was almost small enough to be worth ignoring, but I wanted every advantage we could garner.

"I pick that cell, the second to the left on the third floor," I said, cracking my neck to the side as I waited to see what came.

"Fair enough, enjoy your fight with the bloodsucker, but be warned, the more of you that he gets inside of himself, the stronger he will be," the Bibliomancer said, laughing as he faded from view and the cage, I'd specified opened.

Out walked a well-dressed figure that looked like he'd just stepped away from a ball. He even held a glass of red wine in one hand. Taking a long pull on his glass, his skin went from an ashy white to a pale pink and his eyes flared red.

"It has been a while since I've been invited to a party, allow me to introduce myself," the figure said, his accent was odd, not one I'd heard before. "My name is Count Valetine, and I will be feasting on each and every one of you before the night ends."

"That's a vampire," Beth shouted, loosing an arrow at it. "Don't look it in the eyes and don't let it get any of your blood!"

I'd heard of vampires before, they were folklore and myth, not a monster I'd ever encountered. In all the stories I'd heard, you needed silver or wood to take care of a vampire and, as far as I knew, we had neither.

"Are we going to be able to kill it?" I asked, just as Count Valetine grabbed the arrow from the air and snapped it casually in two. His form blurred and he appeared before a surprised Beth before she could answer.

I unleashed a Lightning Strike just as Beth made eye contact with the vampire, my attack had the desired effect and Beth rolled away smartly. The vampire slashed out with claws that appeared at the end of his fingers, just missing Beth as she rolled to safety. Emory was there a moment later, throwing his shield. It hit the surprised vampire, bouncing back to Emory just in time for him to shield bash the well-dressed monster in the face, sending him to the ground.

I used Blink to put myself behind him and plunged my sword down, but the vampire, like all the monsters we'd faced here, was fast as hell. It rolled out of the way of the blow and tripped Emory as it stood, sending him to the ground. The Count was atop Emory a second later, biting for his neck but finding only plate armor. With a frustrated sigh, the vampire stood just in time to get stabbed twice by Kora's bladed arms.

"Oh, and you don't have any blood to speak of, do you?" Count Valetine asked as he lazily grabbed hold of one of her arms and at the same time, kicked at Kora's body. To my utter surprise and astonishment, one of Kora's arms ripped free of her body with a sickening screech of ripping metal.

With this new weapon, the vampire swatted arrows from the air and kicked Emory again as he tried to get to his feet. Then, slashing out, he scored a direct hit on my armor as I prepared another swing. He was fast, so I made myself faster with Speed Burst. Back and forth we fought, he seemed almost bored with the exchange, using Kora's arm as if it were a weapon he'd trained with his entire life.

I finally scored a lucky hit with a well-placed Swift Strike, cutting him across the chest and disarming him. Kicking away his makeshift weapon, I saw Kora grab it and sparks followed as she attempted to reattach it. As my speed advantage went away, I kept the attacks coming to keep the vampire occupied. Out the corner of my eye, I could see Kora taking the fight seriously and summoning a monster. What she summoned I didn't know until I heard it roar above me.

A giant T-Rex appeared, suddenly looming over me. It

moved with a determined slowness, latching down on the vampire's entire body and swallowing it whole. There were some screams, but mostly they were drowned out as the Bibliomancer appeared in the air again.

"Choose your next challenger," he said, his voice a bit deadpan. Likely he didn't like the way we'd won that last fight and truth be told, neither did I. If I couldn't suck the essence dry of these monsters, then what was the point?

With that in mind, I sensed out another monster, going for one that would be a little stronger, but only marginally than the last one. I called out my choice and the Bibliomancer chuckled.

What came out of the cell as the doors swung upward wasn't something I could easily describe. It was a monster for sure, but what kind, I couldn't say. It had what looked like several parts all sewn together. The arms, hands, head, feet, legs, and torso all belonged to vastly different monsters. Red scaled arms, fish-like claws on one arm and a massive fist on the other. Its middle torso of white flesh pulsed a radiant golden color in an almost rhythmic pattern. The head was the most disturbing part, it was human, but lacked human eyes. Instead, someone had put two massive yellow eyes into eye sockets not big enough to fit them.

It left the monster with a bugged-out look in its eyes and when it opened its mouth and spoke, I couldn't believe how normal it sounded.

"I am the next to fall, it would appear," it said, almost wistful in recognition of its fate. "I will give it my all and be none too upset when I fall, for I am a freak of nature. However, it is that very nature that will not allow me to give you an easy victory. To that extent, I will have that large reptile and add a part of it to myself."

He held out a fishy hand and his middle torso glowed more fiercely. Suddenly, Kora's summoned T-Rex faded into motes of light that zipped right into his torso. Then his face morphed, and I was sure he wouldn't be talking much after this most recent change. His face elongated and he gained several scales. When he opened his mouth next, he roared, showing several rows of sharp teeth.

"Fights on," I said, checking that my team was ready over my shoulder. They were and we ran into battle, Emory leading.

The amalgamation of a monster met Emory's shield with his ham-sized fist and the resulting force sent Emory off his feet and flying toward the group. I had the genius idea of stopping the flying man, but I didn't take in his full weight or the force behind it. I was bowled over as well, but I managed to somewhat catch Emory and together we made it to our feet.

"Watch out for that punch," Emory said, his eyes blinking maybe a tad too fast from the sudden blow.

"You alright?" I asked, looking up to see that Kora was going head on with the monster, bobbing and weaving its strikes expertly. Meanwhile, both Beth and Alayna shot projectiles at it, some hitting and some not.

Spears of light came crashing down on it and that seemed to get its attention, focusing on Alayna. I flexed my muscles and leaned into a jumping motion, ready to flush my body with essence to put myself between the two, but Emory held up a hand.

"I got this," he said, rolling his neck and picking up his shield. He used a skill that propelled him with unnatural speed toward the monster, slamming it hard enough with his shield raised to knock it off its feet. But he wasn't done there, he raised his weapon and began to strike repeatedly as they went down. Then, as he began to fall forward as well, he activated a skill that made his foot glow a hazy red. Slamming down his foot, a shockwave shot out, knocking the stumbling monster fully prone.

"Hell yeah," I said, pointing my sword and casting Lightning Strike. Lightning arced down from above and struck the target, sending it back to the ground as it attempted to turn and get to its feet. Not wanting to give it a chance to breathe, I followed that up by sprinting into position beside Alayna and flanking the monster.

Lightning sprung from the tip of my sword as I focused my Channel Lightning spell, infusing it with essence. It went from its normal white lightning to a hue of blue green with additional sparks as the potent energy of life itself was infused into the attack, strengthening it beyond what I'd normally be able to accomplish.

The continued strikes from my lightning kept the monster slow, and Kora, her arms working as if they'd not been pulled off recently, sprung atop the beast.

"This is for stealing my summons," she said, cutting and stabbing with mad vigor. "Its! Not! Nice! To! Steal!" She enunciated each word as she stabbed the life out of the powerful monster. This fight was not going its way and we were in no mood to show any mercy.

Suddenly, flame and water materialized all around it and Kora was sent sprawling along with Emory. My lightning cut off and my was vision obscured by a thick mist that had begun to spread out all around the monster.

A scream echoed through the room as Beth took a hit or was startled by something. But no matter how hard I tried to see, I couldn't make out any movement. Closing my eyes for just a second to adjust myself I began to sense auras. Beth's was weak and getting weaker. A huge flame of an aura, more powerful than it had been only moments before hung over her. I ran in that direction, activating Speed Burst as I cut through the fog.

The monster was using its new distorted human and T-Rex hybrid face to tear into her neck and Beth wasn't moving anymore. I could still sense her aura, but it was faint. I stabbed with all my might, cutting deep into its neck and with my other hand I summoned a quick Fireball, smashing it on its back. The blow from even a small fireball blew away much of the fog and finally the beast, bloody and with a chuck of Beth's neck in its mouth, turned its attention back to me.

"You son of a bitch!" I shouted, cutting and slashing away, activating skills without thought or care for my stamina.

"I've got her," Alayna's voice came, and she began to chant. After four solid seconds she laid a massive heal on Beth as I battled the monster, slowly pushing it further and further away from the injured Beth.

Emory and Kora were there a moment later, and all three of us closed in on the monster. It was strong and had a red haze all around it, meaning it had enraged, but we were a match for it. Cutting, stabbing, and slashing we took it down piece by piece. Every once in a while, it got a hit in, and the two that weren't knocked off their feet redoubled their efforts until finally I stabbed in one final time with my sword and pulled.

Then I pulled some more, forcing the monster to submit to the tool of the Ordu. Its essence was mine by right and I would have it! Nothing would stop me from accomplishing my goals! Essence by the thousands filled the sword and I came one step closer to bringing it back to full power. If I could bring it up to full strength instead of just giving it a few million here and there, I had a feeling something inside the sword would solidify and I wouldn't have to brute force my way into fixing the Prime Mana Shrines or the ley lines anymore.

Until I could do such a thing though, I was stuck doing what I knew would work and I still had several more Prime Mana Shrines that needed to be reconstructed. Not to mention all my work would be for nothing if I couldn't also stop the Chaos Knight from poisoning more of the ley lines, by taking out more Prime Mana Shrines. There was a balance that needed to be kept and I was the one to do it. I needed to kill the Chaos Knight and end her reign of terror.

It was a bit upsetting to me, I thought as I finished slurping up the energy from the fallen monster, that the answer to everything seemed to be death and killing. In a perfect world, I'd be able to solve these problems without taking life or being forced into impossible situations. However, I knew that even if I disarmed this Chaos Knight and took from her the greatest of her power, then I'd still be faced with a decision. Kill her or allow her to live and possibly cause more damage later on in her life. There wasn't a single part of me that thought a prison would hold her forever, so raw and intense her power had been.

No, I knew what I had to do, but facing it and coming closer to my goal left me wishing there was another way.

Any way other than the path I knew I must walk.

The Bibliomancer spoke, breaking me from my thoughts.

"Oh, look at what you've accomplished and without a single death and only a little dismemberment!" He exclaimed as if he were truly excited for us. "I think I am changing the rules a bit. Forget the last artifact, I have it here anyway." He lifted up a golden scroll and tossed it up, catching it deftly. "Instead of a final sealed opponent, I think you will face me, the mighty Bibliomancer! Make ready and let's have a change of scenery."

Suddenly the world around us shifted, like sand being poured down a drain until everything snapped into place. We found ourselves in the first huge library, the main hallway lay just in front of us and behind was the exit.

"One last fight," I said, cracking my neck to the side and checking on each of my team members. Beth looked pale and sickly, but she was on her feet, looking alert with an arrow strung. "We got this. Give us your best shot!" I yelled to the Bibliomancer, and the fight began as he started to chant the beginnings of a spell.

# CHAPTER 20
## DUNGEON GIFTS

"For my first trick, allow me to introduce you to a few of my friends," the Bibliomancer said, his spell finally finished. Several books flew off the shelf of their own accord and smashed into the ground.

With each hit, a flurry of paper morphed into one of the weak paper golems that we'd defeated by the handful before. Was this really all the Bibliomancer could do? One after another a horde of paper golems began to form before us. But that wasn't all he had in store for us. Next, he pulled out a large staff in the shape of an oversized ink pen. He began burnishing it around and ink splattered on the ground.

Wherever the ink splash hit, black ink oozes sprung to life, ready to fight us. All the while, we stood ready to face him, but as we braced ourselves for the attack, something occurred to me.

"Why are we waiting? Beth, attack the Bibliomancer directly!" I yelled, readying a spell of my own. Mana poured into a Fireball spell, and I took aim at the purple robed Bibliomancer.

However, just as I loosed my attack, several of the paper golems threw themselves in the way, preventing my damage from doing much more than thinning the ranks.

The fight continued on as we shredded golem after golem, avoiding the blobs while they slowly advanced. The blobs finally got into a position to be a threat and I raised my sword, readying a deadly combo. A combined Swift Strike, Power Strike, and Force Wave took care of the first one and I followed up with a release of my Light Blade ability to finish another.

Beth and Emory were there to deal with the last ones, arrows and shields flying at the targets.

With that taken care of, we rushed the Bibliomancer before he could summon any more monsters. My sword cut into his flesh and a look of surprise fell over his face as the tip of my blade pierced his heart.

With that, the Bibliomancer fell, dead. But then the oddest thing happened, his body knit back together, and we readied ourselves for another round of difficult fighting. However, I didn't get the sense that he was here to fight us this time, as he stood, hood over his head, he held out his hands.

"Easy now," he said, his voice less playful than it had been this entire time. "I'm here to talk to you about rewards. I have a choice for you."

"Let's hear it," I said, wiping blood from my face from where I'd been struck. "And no tricks."

"No tricks," the Bibliomancer repeated. "You have two choices. I can empower your sword with enough essence to fuel your journey for weeks to come or I can give each of you crafted items of such quality that it will change your journey forward."

I could barely see beneath the hood, but I could swear the figure before us held a smile on its lips. As if to punctuate the point, he suddenly laughed.

"Not an easy choice is it," he said, and I turned to my teammates to see what they thought.

Obviously I knew what I wanted to do, there was nothing more important than finishing my mission and saving the world. But I wasn't the only one to be considered here and I cared what my teammates thought.

"What do you think?" I asked, turning to them.

"New items are nice, but the whole reason we came here was to get that sword working, so just get on with it," Emory said, surprising me as I would have thought he, more than any of them, would want a new powerful item.

"But what about the item you could get? I've already

harvested enough essence to maybe fix another Prime Mana Shrine, a few more runs and we ought to be alright," I said, trying to convince myself more than anything else.

Beth spoke next, stepping forward and rolling her shoulders as she recovered from whatever injury she'd taken during the last fight, Alayna's healing doing an amazing job of patching her up.

"We stand with you," she said simply. Everyone nodded and I turned to the Bibliomancer, the sword held tight in my grip.

"We defeated your challenges and collected your artifacts. We choose to have the sword empowered, keep your loot," I said, trying to project an air of confidence that I didn't feel at that very moment.

"So be it," the Bibliomancer said and with a wave of his hand, I felt a surge of essence begin to fill the sword. I fought back a grimace as I dealt with the intoxicating effects of the sword being empowered.

The world stilled as I battled the feelings, coming out on the top of it, if just barely. It was an odd sensation, overpowered by rushes of strength and feelings of invincibility. I knew without being told that I could reshape the world around me and for a moment, I almost tried, reaching out toward the Bibliomancer, but I caught myself. It wouldn't do well to piss off the dungeon that had just helped me.

Instead, I opened my eyes, unaware that I'd shut them. And faced the Bibliomancer. "Thank you," I said simply before turning and walking toward the exit.

We didn't stop for pleasantries with the locals, escaping out of the city in the cover of darkness and back on our way home. I needed to take care of several more Prime Mana Shrines, but that was a task for me and not the entire group.

# CHAPTER 21
## SWORD PLAY

I stood alone in a training yard outside the keep, having sent away all the guards and attendants. My sword cut through the air as I considered my next steps to end the Chaos Knight. I cut low, the air screaming from the speed in which I struck, and I imagined my blow ending the wicked woman that had caused me so much trouble. I could feel the sword wanting to obey my commands and erase her from existence, but that wasn't within its power, not yet.

After meditating over the sword and then beginning my combat exercise, I realized a shocking fact about the sword. It was an endless pit of hunger when it came to essence. I thought that perhaps I'd be able to fill it and then that would be that, but I could feel now that it had more essence than ever before, that it would never truly be satisfied. A piece of that hunger entered me as I trained and I felt a need to act, a need to consume.

It took more focus than I cared to admit, but I mastered myself and continued my sword training. Strike, swipe, and a phantom block as I wove myself through a battle, long commenced, yet recently rehashed by a dungeon. My thoughts wondered at what old Iron Fist could be up to now? We had several border disputes still going on, despite my best insistence that we deal with them another way. Ever since I'd taken the role of head of House Variyn, the bordering Houses wanted to test our defenses.

The only time it had stopped was when the King had visited, so at least there was some peace in the matter. No troops had fallen, but several dozen had been injured and eventually, if not dealt with, the situation would get worse. But I was getting off track, I'd been planning out my next move against the Chaos Knight, not worrying about the politics of a position I wished I never had been given.

I paused my training and focused on pulling up my map. A translucent overlay of the magical map I'd purchased showed up before me and I studied the marks Mah'kus had added. There were three more Prime Mana Shrines to fix, two of which were in the elven lands and the other on the way. I decided I would slip away from the Keep alone and deal with them in secret. I'd leave a note of course, but I was done putting others in danger when it wasn't necessary.

Of course, that was it right there. Soon it would be necessary, and I'd likely need to raise a small army to deal with the Chaos Knight and her growing power. I had no doubt that I'd be able to match her now, sword against sword, but she had many powerful Chaos Beasts and who knows how many followers that would need to be dealt with. But that wasn't for now, no for now, I'd escape into the night and deal with these issues.

But, I knew that leaving now would be too soon. I needed to keep training and master myself with this sword before going on such an endeavor. With that resolve, I continued my workout. It was hard work, but the longer I kept in contact with the weapon, the more I felt like, just maybe, I could control the flow of the power and keep it from overwhelming me. One second at a time, I mastered myself and the sword.

Just another hour of training and I'd be alright, just one more swing of the sword, just one more.

But despite my mastery of the sword, I felt those familiar feelings creeping back, the ones that always consumed me when alone. This wasn't the influence of the sword, but the shadows of my past coming back to haunt me. My left arm wavered, and my next strike was shaky. Before long, my entire rhythmic shadow fight disintegrated, and I found myself on my knees, panting. Even though I had sent everyone away, I felt the presence of someone approaching.

"You alright?" Cam asked as he held out a hand to help me stand.

Tears wet my eyes, but I didn't know when they'd appeared or why they'd made an appearance at all. I swiftly wiped them away and tried to master myself, before taking his hand up and looking him in the eye.

"Thank you, but I believe I said I needed some privacy," I said, leveling a measured look at the young guard captain.

"Galt told me I had to watch out for you, that you might run off if left alone, so I sent everyone else away and I watched you from a distance. No harm done," Cam said, his usual smiling face bringing a measure of light into my soul.

"Thanks, I guess," I said, putting a hand on his shoulder before I had an idea. "Want to spar?" I asked him.

Cam smiled, took a step back and pulled free his long sword. I'd been sure to teach them all how to use a blade and a spear during our lessons during the war, but he would be no match for me, strong arms or not. As I thought this, he moved his sword to his left artificial arm and gave it a few practice swings. The sword screamed as it cut through the air, as fast, if not faster than I was able to do myself.

"I'll go easy on you," Cam said, a wiry smile on his face.

"And I'll do the same," I said, stepping forward deftly and slashing for his armored chest. He caught the blow, turning it aside, which was good, as I was only going about a quarter of my possible speed.

We danced back and forth trading increasingly fast and powerful blows. His footwork and general speed were lacking, but his ability to strike with that sword arm was incredible. He even forced me to take a step back once, before I landed a flurry of blows on his armor, adding a few gouges into the metal but leaving him mostly unharmed.

Cam panted hard from exertion, but we continued. I even yelled out a few pointers as we went, until he finally made his move. His arm came down like the very jaws of death itself and I realized my mistake too late. Stepping to the side, I was prepared to catch the blow on my armored chest, but it stopped a mere inch from impact. He had a huge grin on his face, obviously proud of himself.

"That was damn fine swordplay," I said, putting my sword away and feeling a weight come off my chest. It was such a burden to wield a weapon that could literally pull apart the fabric of reality. At the last moment before Cam's strike, I'd felt the urge to undo his attack, perhaps even his entire self, but I'd squashed it like so many other impulses the sword sent me.

"You let me get that attack through," Cam countered, though he looked proud, nonetheless.

"Honestly, I didn't," I said, shrugging. "Just very distracted right now. Either way, you did well, and that arm is a real boon. With more practice, I bet you could surprise and kill a good many Awakened with a weapon like that."

My words fell hollow at the end, and I wondered why my mind had gone straight to killing. Hadn't I had enough of it already? The bloodshed, the names, everything weighing so heavily on my soul.

Cam seemed to be able to sense the direction of my thoughts and he frowned, putting a hand on my shoulder. "We lost a good many men, but without all you did, it would have been worse. Can I tell you a something?" Cam asked.

"Anything," I said, returning his reassuring look with one of my own, though I didn't feel reassuring.

"Sometimes I wonder why I made it back when so many others, like Dan, didn't. Was it something I did or earned or just the dark black luck of fate? It haunts me some nights, when I'm alone and even sometimes when my wife is in my arms. I think that perhaps I should have died out there with them, but then I look at all I have now. Children who love their papa, a wife that would go into battle for me if I asked, and a friend whose given me more than I could ever think to ask for," Cam said, his eyes watering over.

I didn't know what to say. I'd thought Cam was immune to the very feelings that haunted me and yet, here he was telling me that he struggled with the very same thing. I held his gaze for a long time before I answered him. "Cam, I understand, I really do. Together we will walk free of this darkness, the little lights in our lives guiding us back to safety. Stay strong my friend, the end is not yet upon us."

Cam nodded and wiped free his eyes. "Shall we go again then?" He asked, his composure returned, and his breathing back to normal.

"Let's do it," I said, smiling.

We spent the next thirty minutes pushing each other, with my sharp focus returned, he didn't get any strikes on me, but it was a rewarding bout, nonetheless. We talked for a bit longer after our match and he told me he'd learned a few new skills as he leveled his guard proxy levels under Galt. I had him show me, they were interesting and effective at closing the distance quickly. One particular skill allowed him to do a shout that slowed opponents for three solid seconds, and not even I could shrug off the full effects of it when he used it on me.

It was so interesting to me how proxy levels really could turn a normal person into something exceptional without even being Awakened. It also made me wonder at the nature of the advancements and why proxy levels could do all this. Surely, if they could use skills or even spells through proxy classes and levels, then they ought to be able to be Awakened and do the same? But no, that just wasn't the way it worked and holding the sword I could feel a bit of the connections of the system and the limitations.

While pondering that, it was almost like I could feel or understand the system better, though it was superficial at best. I doubted my mind was strong enough to hold the intricacies and complexity of the system that controlled the very universe around me. No. But I still tried, feeling out with my mind, and trying to understand why certain things worked the way that they did. While doing so, I had a bit of inspiration regarding proxy levels.

Awakened individuals were directly connected into a network of powerful ley lines, pulling power from it as needed. Proxy level holders did the same thing, but instead of always being connected as Awakened folks were, they had moments of connection. So small and quick that it did almost no harm to their souls, or risking unbalance. But I did sense that even proxy levels had an effect on an individual, leaching away a tiny portion of their life force in exchange for power.

That meant that those who used proxy skills or abilities too often risked the same thing that those who tried to Awaken before they were ready. This bit of inspiration hit me hard, and I didn't know what to do with the information. I'd make a note of it and perhaps pass it along to someone more well-studied into system theory. Looking down at the Sword of the Ordu, I sighed, then sheathed it.

\*\*\*

Edward Nums really put me through the paces when it came to my profession. I spent the rest of the morning working on a new set of gems for my armor, but each time I came up short and Edward was there to tell me to do better.

"Tell me what I'm doing wrong, not just 'Wrong again young master'," I practically spat the words at the old man.

He had white hair and wore simple, yet elegantly tailored fine silks. He had an ever-present scowl on his face, but when he smiled it appeared grandfatherly and kind. He gave me one such smile and nodded his head.

"You are close enough, young master, that if you just push yourself even a little, you will find success. Try again," Edward said.

I did so, and again, and again, each time I was met with his smile or a scowl and failure. Taking a break, I took out the book that I'd been reading to teach me this particular cut and enchantment combination. It wasn't easy and each time I'd had a flaw of some kind or another, left me short of the item I was trying to craft, and I needed twelve.

"Tell me again why I shouldn't just go buy these gems or perhaps even better ones?" I asked Edward, though I knew he wouldn't go for such an idea.

"Because you need to increase your professional level, and gems of the quality that you can produce are worth a small fortune. It is best if you learn to provide all you can for yourself. Plus, how do you expect to learn if you don't fail a bit first?"

I scowled at the old man and tried again. Cut by slow cut, using my enchanted tools when I had a bit of inspiration. After getting the rough shape, I put aside my enchanted file and began to use one of the many non-enchanted tools I kept laying around for finishing work. It took much longer, nearly two hours of work, just to get half the gem into the right shape, but the slower work meant more control. With less material coming off with each stroke, I was finally making progress.

Sparing a glance up at Edward I saw a smile on his face, he could have told me to use normal tools instead of allowing me to continue to mess up expensive gem after gem. But I couldn't feel too angry at him as I put the finishing touches on the gem and smiled wide.

"I did it," I exclaimed excitedly. "A Ruby that increases my Strength and Intellect by 30 each!"

I used Inspect to ensure I had done just that and was rewarded with exactly what I wanted to see.

"Well done, young master, now try it again but use the enchanted tools right up until the very last shaping step. You will find the same amount of control over the finished product that way," Edward instructed.

So, I did, and it was as he said. In the time it took me to make my first, I'd made three more. After several more hours of work, I had twelve and I pulled off my armor, piece by piece so that I could slot the new gems.

"So, Edward, tell me how you knew Regina and why she recommended you teach me?" I asked as I worked.

Edward frowned. "I've worked with her for years, providing gems and enchantments to aid her experiments. In fact, without her success rate in such endeavors I imagine I'd be much less well off than I am now. As to why she recommended I teach you, she didn't, not really. I approached her about getting an introduction and she all but promised that she'd be able to get me a job tutoring you."

That gave me pause and I considered the elderly man a bit more closely. He had kind blue eyes and skin so aged and cracked that he made Warrick and Merlin appear young. He was obviously an Awakened, but how old must he be to look like this? And why had he wanted to teach me anyway? he hadn't actually answered that question, so I posed it back to him.

"So why would you want to teach me?" I asked, popping out another gem and setting it aside on the nearby worktable.

"I've been around for a long time," Edward said carefully, as if gauging how to tell me something. "When I was young, I followed a specific creed. One that I think you now follow."

"I don't know what you mean," I said, stopping my work to give him my full attention.

"My master's class was called Twilight Guardian, but he told me before he died that he had named it himself. He was in fact a defender of the balance and I think you know what that means. I believe your father was much the same, which is rare to have so many active within a short period of time. But as I served him, I wish to serve you," Edward said, his eyes glistening as he spoke with power and strength beyond his fragile appearance.

"You knew my father?" I asked, stunned at this revelation.

"I did," Edward said, smiling. "I never got to aid him as much as I'd liked, but I provided him with the best enchantments and gems I could craft to aid his goals. Though, in the end, it wasn't enough. He fell when he should have risen. Just as my master fell and all the few that followed his footsteps. It seems being the scale that holds in place the balance is no safe path. But you are young and sharp-minded. I believe you could go the distance, bringing this world into an age of peace unlike any other we've experienced before."

I took a sharp breath and blinked, trying to get my mind to work again. This old man was saying he'd served several of the Chosen, the keepers of the balance. How old was he? He had a powerful aura, but it wasn't even as powerful as my own. I'd wager he wasn't even past level forty or fifty, that, or his aura had diminished with the weight of time. Determined to truly know this man now, I decided I ought to just ask.

"What level are you?" I asked.

The elderly man chuckled and wagged a finger at me. "That is considered a very private question. I have levels enough, but what I have in even more abundance is wisdom and skill. Allow me to impart this little bit of knowledge to you and let me earn your trust. Let's start by making better gems than those you've just slaved over."

I suddenly became aware of how long we'd been at the gem making and I shook my head. "These will do me fine for now, I've kept you long enough, go rest and we will try tomorrow."

"Tomorrow isn't guaranteed to any of us, besides what is the point of having an Awakened body if we don't push them to our limits," Edward countered.

I sighed and had to admit that I wasn't particularly tired, though I was hungry. "I'll send for some food, and you can tell me a tale about your first master, the Twilight Guardian."

And so, food was brought, and Edward told a marvelous tale of a young man, a childhood friend of his, who took up the mantle and began to fight back against the Chaos that consumed much of the world. He spoke of towns and nations I'd never heard of, but I let him speak, continuing to wonder at how old he must be. By the end, I wished only to know more about this brave and heroic warrior of the balance. He seemed to be more of a front-line tank fighter who excelled in using the phases of night and day to empower his spells and skills.

He sounded like he truly understood the balance and how to wield both light and darkness. It was a tale I hoped to hear more of someday, but soon enough, we were back at work, hours and hours going by while Edward reminisced about his life and gave small pointers here and there.

My mind wandered as I thought about the Twilight Guardian and his great deeds.

# CHAPTER 22
## INTERROGATIONS

I still couldn't get the stories and ideas about the Twilight Guardian from my mind as the meetings started. My advisors were telling me about one thing or another that required my attention, and I did my best to give it to them, but I had to admit that it wasn't easy. I would give them another day or two, then I was escaping to deal with the Prime Mana Shrines. Why couldn't they understand how important it was that I be able to fulfill my role for the Ordu?

Without meaning to, I'd missed what one of them had said, so I inclined my head and he repeated himself. "We've uncovered a plot against your rule inside the city and those responsible await your punishment. They've been close-lipped but Non assures me it was a plot by

House Attra. They've been biting at the bit ever since we ignored their requests for recompense."

"What recompense?" I asked, trying and failing to remember anything about House Attra wishing recompense for anything.

"It was discussed roughly a week ago and decided that they were owed nothing."

I looked at my head advisor, Arnold, and then at the younger advisor who'd been speaking, Harold. "Why didn't I hear about this?"

"You were off doing your duty as it were," Arnold said, his voice like aged parchment being crumpled into pieces. He emphasized the word duty to ensure I knew that he didn't approve of my Chaos Slayer activities. More than once he'd lectured me that my time as an adventurer should end, that I had responsibilities to attend to here now, but of course he didn't understand the true extent of my responsibilities.

"Thank you, Arnold," I said, doing all that I could not to roll my eyes at the man. As if my personal improvement and leveling up was secondary when my strength was what had won me this office in the first place. What would happen the next time someone did what I did, and I wasn't strong enough? But I was letting myself get distracted, I wanted to know more about this recompense that House Attra felt they were owed. "Tell me more about House Attra and their recompense."

So, they did, starting at the boring beginning and going through every detail just to spite me, but I bore it and kept rapt attention. As it turned out, House Attra felt that they'd been wronged by Lord Variyn when their spies were found out, as well as several other conflicts afterward that I hadn't known about. In the end, I agreed with my advisors, House Attra was just looking for a reason to push their borders and I wouldn't have that.

"I'll see those responsible and pass my judgment, are we done here?" I asked, standing and ready to end the boring meeting.

A round of head nods followed and I stood, meeting Cam and Galt at the door. "Take me to the cells, I've got some prisoners to speak with."

"We could bring them to you one at a time?" Galt suggested and I paused to think it over.

"Yeah, that will probably be best, how many were captured and do we know who their leader is?" I asked, a plan forming in my head.

"Seven men captured, six dead but we are sure we've caught their leader. He is a brutishly large man with scars up and down his arm. He holds the Monk class but is currently restrained and unable to use his skills or abilities. We believe one more in his group is an Awakened, but our mages were unsure. All the rest have disciple proxy classes, benefiting from the leaders Monk class," Galt said.

"Perfect," I said, smiling. "Go ahead and bring me

them one by one but find someplace new to put them after I've talked with them. I want the leader to go last so he can sweat it out. Bring more guards than you think necessary, because I was able to use skills when I was imprisoned, so he might be able to as well."

"Understood," Galt said, stepping forward and disappearing around a bend.

"Let's go to my office and await the first prisoner," I said, and Cam gave me a curt nod.

The keep bustled with activity, between servant girls and boys running about and nobles going from one activity or another. Cam was joined by four other guards as we walked, standard procedure nowadays. They liked to keep a tight leash on me, but I'd slip their knots eventually and get back to my duty. After my sparring with Cam, I almost wanted to invite him along, but going alone would be best.

If alone I could get in and out without issue. I just hoped the remaining Essence would be enough to close up the last ones and that the Chaos Knight hadn't reopened any new ones. Hopefully, if she did, Mah'kus could update my map as easily as he had before. That would be convenient. Turning the last corner, all the guards took up position at the door and I signaled Cam to come in with me.

"How's your family?" I asked. I sat down behind the desk and Cam took up position to my left. He leaned on the wall in a very unguard-like gesture, relaxing before he responded.

"They are getting used to the city life, though I can't convince Tyrza to stay in the keep. Thank you for offering by the way, but she's says she's happy in the little property we purchased. So strange having two houses, but with all the money you gave us I think we could afford a third and still not be hurting."

"Glad to hear she is settled in, what of the newest addition, have they shown up yet?" I asked, though I knew if they had Cam would have told me.

He shook his head and sighed. "We think it's close and we've lined up a healer and hired a live-in midwife, as our last birth was a bit difficult. I'm only slightly more worried about it than I am you being assassinated by one of the many attempts Galt claims to have stopped."

I raised a single eyebrow and fixed Cam with a look. "Still dealing with assassins, shame, I thought after that last public attempt they'd stop. I mean, I cut that poor man's hands right off before he could bring his blade down much more than an inch. Surely they'd try poisons or something different?"

It had been an interesting few months since I'd taken over and the assassinations were only part of the unexpected events that had befallen me. But I didn't want to think about that, I needed to work out what questions I'd ask these men and women who felt so strongly that House Attra was owed that they'd risk stealing directly from the city, as well as being caught planning their own assassination attempt.

I wondered what the assassins would think when they found out I was going to go off on my own? I'd only told Alayna so far, so I doubted any would know, but really, what could any of my guards do that I couldn't? I was as safe as I could be by myself or otherwise. If anything, my guards helped on the side of inconvenience, if anything.

The door swung open, and Galt escorted the first of the prisoners in, a young-faced boy of no more than twenty years. He had dirty blonde hair and a grimace on his face, blue eyes staring at me in fear. I took in his disheveled look and his fearful demeanor, ready to see what information I could get from him.

"Welcome, please sit down," I said, gesturing to a chair across from me. "I'm Caldor Miles, and you are?"

I did my best to remain polite, unsure of how to handle someone who had been a part of a plot to kill me and overturn the government. But I could tell by the injuries to his face and body that he'd likely been through enough physical persuasion already. It was time to try a different tactic.

"My name is Bernard, and you won't be getting anything from me, so you might as well let me go now," Bernard said, his face screwed up in a look of fierce determination.

"Well, I've just got something from you, your name. It's a good start, but we will need more than that if you wish to avoid the hangman's noose," I said, wondering why the man thought he'd be 'let go' after the crimes he'd committed.

His face paled suddenly, as if he hadn't even considered that death was an option. Was I ever so young and naive? It was a credit to my upbringing that I don't think I was ever so bad as this. Surely, he understood and was just putting on an act.

"I'm to die?" He asked, his voice hushed and low.

"Yes, surely someone has informed you by now that you are meant to face judgment and justice. Did you not think your crimes warranted death?" I asked, honestly curious at what was going through the boy's head.

"I was just following orders," he sputtered, his face slowly descending into grief. "What about my sister, surely you won't put our crimes on her, she was just helping with the food and cleaning."

I looked to Galt, but his expression remained hard. "Yes, even your sister," I said and his entire demeanor shifted from grief to one of steely resolve.

"I'll tell you whatever you need, but you must promise that she remains safe from death. I know stuff that Coolidge doesn't even know I know. Like, there is another group that is going to be setting some building on fire soon, if they haven't already, but it's just a distraction from another attempt to clear the throne."

There had been a fire a few days back and another failed assassination attempt did follow, so at least the boy knew something, as unhelpful as it was turning out to be.

"You will speak to your allegiance to House Attra and that they hired you to carry out these acts?" I asked, a plan forming in my head.

"Yes, I will say whatever you need," Benard said, his words coming out rushed.

"And so will your sister," I said. "If she and you both agree to share the same truth, then I will consider withholding death as a punishment."

He nodded vigorously and I motioned for him to be taken away. "Keep him separated and bring me his sister," I commanded Galt.

He nodded and did as I commanded, bringing a woman that must have been Bernard's older sister, for she was definitely older than he was. Where he'd been fresh faced and young, his sister looked weathered by years of labor. She had the same dusty blonde hair and blue eyes, but she had a fierceness behind them that immediately told me this wasn't going to be as easy as I'd hoped.

"You are Bernard's sister," I said, cursing myself silently for not asking her name from him. "What is your name?"

She glared at me from across the table and said nothing.

"I've made a bargain with Bernard for your life. Unless this bargain is kept, you and all your conspirators will be facing death," I said, but the threat of death didn't have the same effect on her as it did her brother.

"So be it," she said, raising an eyebrow.

Damnit. I'd gotten my hopes up after the first interrogation had gone so well, but she was definitely going to make this more difficult than it needed to be.

"You will let your brother die?" I asked, considering her false cool. "He was eager to save your life and yet, you are so quick to throw away his?"

Her mask faltered for only a second before the resolve settled back over her. "Coolidge says you can't execute us. House Attra will go to war for us, you just watch."

"House Attra has denied any knowledge of you or your operations but thank you for that confirmation of who you are working for," I said, a smirk on my face. She blanched and swallowed hard.

"I...I meant that," she tried to say something, but I held up a finger.

"Your brother has struck a deal, however, without your cooperation, it will be void. It is in your best interest to just go with it and tell me the truth," I said, striking while the iron was hot.

"I'll want a written guarantee," she said after several moments of silence.

I smiled and nodded.

The rest of the interviews went progressively worse until finally, I met with Coolidge, the leader of this particular group. He was a fierce man, who tried to attack me the moment he saw me and spoke only threats. I dismissed him to join the rest of the prisoners who hadn't been helpful, to await their execution. It was a task that weighed heavily on me, I wanted them to simply serve out time, but that wasn't the way of the land. We didn't have the resources to watch over so many prisoners, especially dangerous ones such as these. So, they would face execution the following morning.

# CHAPTER 23
## NECROMANCY

I stayed around to witness the event; it wasn't something I wanted to see or focus on, but it was a part of my new position. It was a sad affair that involved very few people, but I was happy in some small way that I'd been able to keep at least four individuals from death. Having had my fill of ruling, I was dead set on leaving tonight, but first I had to tell Alayna. A conversation I wasn't looking forward to having.

I found her in my office, toiling away as she did most days on translations of old runes and discoveries. Despite her work having been used for nefarious means, the academic inside of her was unwilling to give up on her pursuits. It was something I deeply admired about her.

"I'm leaving," I said, deciding to jump right to the

point. "I need to cleanse the last Prime Mana Shrines and locate some leads on finding the Chaos Knight."

Alanya looked up from where she was reading at the desk and smiled at me. "Okay," she said simply, then returned to her reading.

"I'm going alone, it won't be safe, but I'll do my best to keep myself in one piece," I said, confused by her sudden acceptance. I expected a small battle of words that I would eventually win by sheer force of will, not a silent surrender.

"I understand, come back to me safely please," she said, still barely looking up from where she worked at the desk.

"Are you mad at me?" I asked, getting a sense that perhaps I wasn't seeing something I ought to.

"No," Alayna said, raising her gaze to meet mine. "I understand you have duties that need to be tended to. I also have such duties, though yours are much more dangerous than mine. When we married, I accepted that this would be the case and neither of us wanted to give up adventuring. Do I wish you'd bring a team with you as back up? Yes, I do. Do I think you will do it if you feel you must go alone? No, I don't. So, I understand and please return to me safely."

I sat down across from her desk and just looked at her for several long seconds. "You are wonderful, you know that?" I asked.

"Yes, I know," she said, finally abandoning her work to stand and walk over to me. She sat in my lap, and I pulled her into a kiss.

It was a good way to go, and I felt relieved that she hadn't fought me over it, but now I wondered if I should be bringing some backup. Perhaps I could bring Fred and Fran, along with Emory, just in case.

I sent out a messenger to find them, they should still be around somewhere as I'd seen them just the day prior for drinks. It took all of two hours before I had them gathered and we ordered a round of ales.

We were in my office, all the guards outside, including Cam. Leaning in as if telling a secret, I revealed my plans.

"I've got some work to do, and I think I need a little backup, any chance you guys are free for a week or two?" I asked, sipping at my drink. I wanted to get a sense for their schedules before I gave away where exactly I'd be going.

Fred answered first. "I had planned on continuing my search of your library."

Fran snorted. "Bring the books with you, dork. We're in. Let's go smash some heads."

Emory looked at Fran and again I thought I saw something in his gaze, but I couldn't be sure. "Yeah, let's go do something. I'm growing moss on my ass sitting around here for so long."

Fran raised a questioning eyebrow at Emory, but he just shrugged and said, "It's an expression."

"Wonderful," I answered, and met their gazes with my own. "We are going to go hunt out some Chaos and fix damage done to the ley lines."

The sword had enough essence from the dungeon run that I could almost believe it would be enough to rebuild the remaining Prime Mana Shrines, but before I did battle with the Chaos Knight, I would need to dive into another dungeon to suck it dry of essence. It boggled my mind a bit, how much essence I'd just thrown away to the cause, enough that I might have reached level 60 and been all the stronger for it. I did take some essence for myself from the last batch, bringing me to a solid several hundred thousand.

I needed a staggering eight hundred thousand or so essence to get to the next level, but eventually I'd need to stop ignoring my own needs and grow even stronger. But I had my priorities in the right place at the moment. First, I'd save magic as a whole, then I'd worry about growing stronger. Until then, I had plenty of methods to temporarily grow stronger. Though, what the drawbacks were from those methods, I didn't really know.

Would the sword grow weaker if I constantly infused it with my own Mana or would my own pathways inside grow weaker as they were bombarded with extra essence to give me a temporary edge? I was alone in my use of such abilities, so their side effects, both short term and long, were a mystery.

We gathered supplies, I'd told them that we'd leave at nightfall from my room where I'd teleport us a ways away. It wasn't the nicest thing to do to Cam and the other guards, but it was the best way I knew. I'd leave a note explaining that I'd return shortly, and the guards were to pretend as if I was in seclusion, studying with Edward. To that end, I'd informed the elderly man who was all too ready to follow the plan, even saying he could go with if I wanted. Saying he still had a spark or two of fight left in him before the end, but I declined, seeing in his eyes that while he had the spirit to fight, his body was reaching its end.

Awakened or not, eventually the body failed and for some reason, I got the impression that he hadn't taken many life extending perks. Or if he had, he'd pushed them to their limit, with how old he was now. I'd tried to ask his age, but he scoffed at me saying it wasn't right to ask a gentleman such a question. Then he winked and told me he was a few hundred years old.

I guessed the truth was likely closer to a thousand years old, but I couldn't know for sure. Someone as frail as he was, would hamper our battle plans, powerful or not. It wasn't like with Warrick or Merlin, who despite being very old, had a vigor about them that couldn't be denied.

We teleported out of my room and went several miles west, ready to find the first Prime Mana Shrine and turn it back to the side of Order. What we found was a town in ruins. Burnt out buildings, and dead laid about discarded, as if forgotten. I checked my map for the name of the town, Winterfall. A town of thousands laid to waste. After walking the perimeter of the town for a solid hour, I gave the signal to venture in toward the Prime Mana Shrine.

Destroyed buildings by the dozens lay about us like black sentinels in the night. The smell of smoke was still strong in the air, however, there was no more heat coming from any of the structures, so this had happened some time ago. Bodies in various levels of decay were stepped around cautiously as we didn't wish to disturb the dead.

The closer we ventured to the center of the town, the more I swore I heard chanting of some kind. Signaling with my hand, my team gathered up.

"You guys hear that chanting?" I asked, my voice slightly muffled through my helmet.

"Whatever it is, it's making my skin crawl," Fran said, then looking at Fred she added. "You recognize any of the chant?"

"Necromancy," Fred said as he listened to the chant that seemed to be growing clearer and sharper as it went. "I've read a book or two on it and I recognize the formation of this spell. Some kind of reanimation chant."

"Not another freaking Lich," Emory groaned, and I understood his trepidation. The last one we'd faced had been a challenge and Liches were not easy opponents.

294

They had the ability to grow super strong in short periods of time, becoming even stronger the more corpses they had under their control. The last one had been weak enough to defeat only because it had taken such a small town as its victims. What we would face from a town this size was unknown, but I was suddenly happy I'd not come alone.

"We'll burn it to bits," Fred said, showing an unusual amount of gusto in his speech.

"Easy there, Firestarter," Fran said, laughing quietly. "Don't we have to smash its bobble or something?"

"Actually, it's called a Phylactery," Fred said, sounding his usual academic self again.

"We can deal with its Phylactery after we've dealt with the Necromancer. Let's scout out the area and see what we can find," I said, catching each of my teammates' eyes and giving them a reassuring nod.

"Come meet the masters," a voice from behind us croaked and we all jumped, despite being combat ready.

My sword appeared in my hands, and I readied a Lightning Strike, the air beginning to buzz around me as I looked for a target to unleash the spell on.

There was nothing but a few corpses nearby and suddenly I knew we weren't being as sneaky as I'd first thought. We all saw the corpse this time when it spoke. "Come meet the masters." It said, a decayed and nasty thing.

"Get ready, Emory you are in front, shield up. We hear it out and attack the moment I give the signal," I said, whispering the words so as not to be overheard by the undead around us.

As if we'd set something in motion, all the corpses began to stir and stand, but I ignored them. They were no threat to any of us and I was sure the necromancer knew that.

The chanting ceased as we made it to the town square, the moon high in the sky, its light shining through the clouds on a dozen figures, robed in black and purple finery. So, not a single Lich after all, but a dozen or so. Was that even possible? I wondered, as we grew nearer.

"Those are necromancers, but the centermost one is a Lich. He'll be their leader and the strongest," Fred said, his eyes glazed over in white, as if he were peering through the fabric of magic itself.

Necromancers were individuals given a class by the Ordu, but they tended to be outcast, much as Creed's class alienated him from his family as a Death Knight. I wished suddenly that I had him by my side, as maybe we could talk these Necromancers out of whatever it was, they were doing.

Purple fire began to burn on all the cloaked figures' hands, and I could feel the imminent battle approaching. But I had to try and talk to them before I let it come to blows, so I raised a hand and sheathed my sword very purposely.

"I want to talk," I said, stepping forward, my group staying in formation around me. "This isn't a path you have to walk. Help us kill the Lich and end this abomination."

A wicked laugh sprung up, but instead of from a single person, it echoed from all gathered as if a single voice called out. Then, just the same as before, it spoke, but this time each of the necromancers spoke the same words at the same time.

"We are one in purpose and one in power. They are my arms of destruction and I am the vessel of rebirth," the voices came out raspy as if many whispers were overlapping each other at once.

"What have you done!" I yelled, feeling the aura surrounding them and cringing away from it. There was something awful about it, as if it were built of Chaos and not the Order of an Ordu class. They'd done something to the power.

"We reached into the opening our master made for us and we've strengthened ourselves beyond measure. Not even you will be a match for our power. We are Chaos as it was meant to be, unyielding and unbent by the rules of the Ordu. Outcasts, finally given home in the arms of our master. Prepare yourself, Champion of Order, for you have come to meet your end."

A dozen balls of purple fire came hurling toward us, Emory raised his shield, but I knew it wouldn't be enough. I stepped forward and raised my Mana Shell, infusing it with essence to strengthen it. The balls hit, one after another, each sending cracks throughout the barrier as I flooded it with more mana. It shattered as the last one hit, and Emory caught it on his shield, deflecting it into the ground.

I panted at the quick release of mana; I'd been forced to feed nearly five hundred into it in seconds. The spell wasn't meant to take so much, so fast, nor was my body so easily unaffected by such a massive release. Staggering briefly, I righted myself, unleashing a Lightning Strike on the closest cloaked figure. It cracked the air but instead of striking home, it hit a corpse that lay nearby.

"They've set up a protective field, fueled by the corpses," Fred said, his eyes glazing over white again as he peered into their wicked magics. "I'll burn it down. Step back."

We all moved, giving Fred room to work his powerful white flames. He stepped forward, his cloak fluttering around him as he moved ever closer to the Necromancers. Flames of white, like spindles of fire, circled him and rose up to a fiery cone of death.

In an instant, several corpses popped up around the Necromancers, their arms outstretched and ready to grab hold of Fred. At my side, Fran stepped forward as if ready to defend her brother, but I laid a hand on her arm, giving her a reassuring smile.

"He's got this," I said. No sooner were the words out of my mouth, than the white flames began to smash into the corpses, burning them apart almost instantly.

But the Necromancers, or the Lich using them, was not done yet. Purple flames roared to life from the hands of each of the Necromancers, hitting Fred over and over again. His white flames pulled apart the power on contact, but I could tell it was straining him.

"Time to get our hands dirty," I said, signaling Emory and Fran to follow me around the side.

We'd flank the Necromancers and be sure that Fred could see us clearly. He'd gotten so much better controlling his flames that I was only a little worried that he'd fry us while we tried to help. There was a reason we gave him a large girth, those flames sucked in essence and matter like nothing else I'd ever seen.

Fred caught my eye and nodded ever so slightly as he lashed out with his flames, finally taking down one of the dozen Necromancers. They all cried out in alarm as one, their voices slightly losing sync as they did so.

"You will pay for that," the voice cried. "Feel the true power of a Lich!"

Instead of the purple of the Necromancers' fire, there rose up a green flame in the center, surrounding the one Fred had identified as the Lich. It burned at my skin, even from this distance, and I knew I had to do something before he unleashed that attack on Fred. But what could we do? We had just gotten into place on the left of the small force of cloaked Necromancers, when an idea struck me.

Could the sword absorb even the tainted essence from the ley lines? Surely, it wouldn't hurt the blade to do so, and I needed some way of draining the power of that attack, fueled as it was, from the very depths of the ley lines. I activated Blink followed by Speed Burst, putting myself amongst the Necromancers, sword already in hand and striking into the green flames. As I'd hoped, the attack was laced with extra essence, giving it unnatural strength. I tried to pull it in, but the sword resisted my command.

What was happening? I'd just put myself in the worst possible position, banking on this tactic to work, because why shouldn't it? Essence was essence after all. Unless...I decided to use another feature of the sword, forcing outward its power, and purifying the essence as I'd done when rebuilding the Prime Mana Shrines. The Lich screamed in anguish, his voice like a thousand needles in my head. But still, I purified and as I did so, the sword drank up the essence by the thousands.

This Lich had poured and continued to try to pour so much essence into this single attack that he might have wiped Fred completely off the face of the Wyrd. That my enemies were learning the secrets I kept to myself as an edge, was troublesome, but I had a way of winning this tug of war now, so I took it.

Point by point, I purified and sucked clean his attack.

His screams became a mental attack and finally, I had to stop my assault or be overtaken by it. Focusing on creating a structure in my mind that could not, would not, be intruded upon, I stood fast against his attacks, even able to sink my sword back into the green flames. The power of the flames waned and suddenly I could see the figure within them, his robe burnt away and a mostly rotten looking corpse remaining, hand lit by green flame.

"You will not defeat me!" All the voices screamed at once and I saw where the Lich's other hand was. On the ruins of the Prime Mana Shrine, drawing forth power. Before he could swell his attack once more, I swung, just as Emory and Fran cut into the Necromancers. All around, risen villagers and skeletons took up anything that could be used as a weapon and charged in our direction.

My attack came down and sliced cleanly through the Lich's hand. I knew it wouldn't be so easy to kill one such as him but disconnecting him from his power source had an effect I didn't anticipate. The entire rest of his body, gross and rotten flesh as it was, began to bubble and boil. He screamed, this time a raspy singular voice, and suddenly, he exploded.

I was hit by the gore and bone, being thrown off my feet and flown into a group of risen villagers. They began to beat on me, but it was nothing worrisome, as weak as they were. I stood and batted several away with my arm, a part of me not wanting to disturb the poor undead by cutting them to bits. Instead, I shoved my way through to where a ring of Necromancers still fought.

"Feel the wrath of Nelson!" One of them screamed, purple flames smashing into the ground in front of Fred and hands reaching out and grabbing hold of the startled white-haired fire wielder. He yelped as he fell and his flames extinguished around him, even more hands grabbing hold of his cloak as he squirmed on the ground. They didn't appear to be doing any damage, but they held him fast and took him out of the fight.

Nelson, I assumed that must be his name, let his hood fall back, a satisfied smile on his pimply face. He was in the process of summoning more purple flames when a blade sprung from his chest.

"Don't mess with my brother, dick," Fran hissed the words in his ear as he died from the strike. If not for my enhanced body I wouldn't have heard the exchange, but I did, hearing Nelson's final words as well.

"Shit," he muttered, his voice a very nasally. "I'm dead."

Yes, yes you are, you extremely stupid Necromancer, I thought with a smile, as I plunged my blade into another Necromancer. Without the Lich, they were proving to be rather weak opponents, each of them dying like nearly raised Awakened. Still, as we finished up the battle and killed the final Necromancers, I wondered at how so many could have been found by the Chaos Knight and put to work for her.

Sure, it was common enough in the past that Necromancers and the like would sometimes turn to aid the side of Chaos, as they felt alienated by their own kind, but for twelve fairly new Necromancers to be in a single place, it boggled the mind. Unless...I looked down at the sword I held and wondered suddenly, at the extent of control it had over the Ordu System that controlled Classes and Awakening. Could I possibly...

I sent out a thought to the sword and it responded as it did when something was within my ability, sending a gentle warm pulse back to me. So that was how the Chaos Knight had done it. She was able to wield the very system of the Ordu in her defense now!

I'd asked or prompted the blade to create a new class for someone and felt without any hesitation that it was definitely something I could do. I bet it required a fair bit of essence and would have to involve remaking the person to an extent so that they fit the criteria of an Awakened, but I could feel that it was something that, with how much essence I had, I could do.

Oh hell, the Chaos Knight had done it at least twelve times, so perhaps it didn't take much at all to make those changes. I looked over to Fred and another thought crossed my mind. Perhaps I'd be able to restore him as well, but even if I could, should I? He'd grown into his new powers, and he was obviously stronger than he was before, would he want to change back? I concluded that it wasn't for me to decide or even ask just yet. I needed strong allies and he'd learned to control his abilities well enough that he was no longer a great threat to those fighting around him.

"Well, that was messy," I said, seeing that Emory was covered in blood and gore as well. I unsummoned my armor and resummoned it, a little trick I'd learned. It took with it all the grime and blood I'd accumulated. Where it went, I wasn't sure, just being happy to have an easy way to clean my armor. A black bird made a sound from above, it sounded almost cheerful, but I ignored it for now.

"Fred, you alright?" Fran asked, holding out a hand to help her brother up.

"Yeah, that last attack was..." Fred started to say but was cut off by Fran.

"Pretty handsy attack, eh?" She asked, elbowing him in the side as he stood.

We all laughed at her lame joke and surveyed the scene around us. I had much work to do, but beyond that, we needed to care for these bodies. "Let's get a pit dug and put these bodies to rest, then I'll fix the Prime Mana Shrine."

"Great," Emory said, sighing. "I hate manual labor."

Fran laughed at this, more so than the rest of us. She walked over to Emory and pushed him lightly, saying something I didn't catch as Fred started speaking to me at the same time.

"We didn't find its Phylactery. We will need to before we can be sure the Lich is dead," Fred said, looking around the sea of dead bodies as if he expected one to rise up.

"He will be fairly low in power after blowing up, I think we have time. And if we can't find it, I'll send out word to the Adventurer's Guild to set up a quest to hunt it down. We've more important duties to attend to right now," I said, summoning the door to my dimensional space and walking through. I had tools inside if I could just find them in the mass of items I'd collected.

A voice caught me off guard from inside and I nearly jumped out of my armor.

"You are on the right track, but you need to send word to gather your forces. War will be upon you before you realize," Mah'kus said, from the plush leather chair beside the fireplace. A fire crackled in the hearth and Mah'kus sipped at a dark red drink, wine most likely, while eating a round pastry. "Care for a donut and some wine?" He asked when he saw me looking.

# CHAPTER 24
# WAR IS COMING

The door behind me shut, though I'd intentionally kept it open so I could see my friends. Annoyed by the visit from the god-like being, I kept myself on task, finding the shovels and rooting through a few other stacks of items before finally answering the relaxed figure in the chair. I walked over and sat across from him on the plush velvet red chair that was my favorite thinking chair, so soft and comfy.

"War is coming?" I asked, repeating what he'd said. "I assume you don't mean the war between the Easternlands or even my conflict with the Chaos Knight? You speak of the darkness that is coming our way?"

"Wrong," Mah'kus said, taking a bite of his donut. "While the black dragons that travel the space between worlds are coming, this time I meant now, as in your conflict with the Chaos Knight. It is as you feared and rightly guessed. She is building an army of Awakened fueled by her twisted Essence that you are depriving her of with each Prime Mana Shrine you fix. She will notice this next one and bring her forces to bear against you."

"An army of Awakened, are they all Necromancers? Because they went down pretty easily," I said, fixing him with a look. His dark brown eyes looked right on back, unblinking. Then he turned his attention away from me and took a large bite of his pastry.

"Oh, excuse me," he said as if realizing something. "Did you want a donut?"

"You asked me that already," I replied, but Mah'kus continued to look at me, waiting for an answer, so I added. "No thank you, I'm fine."

Hunger was the furthest thing from my mind at the moment.

"Shame. They are quite delicious." Mah'kus took another bite of the round pastry.

"So, how many are we talking about?" I asked, turning the conversation back to the problem at hand.

"Several hundred, but only a few possess strength that your allies should be wary of. The Lich you slew here, and it is dead by the way, was one of her lieutenants, left to slow your approach as you took back the Prime Mana Shrines."

"Can't she just destroy more and infect the ley lines

over again?" I asked, his 'donut' as he called it looked pretty good, now that I gave it a second glance. It was glazed over with some type of sugary surface that flaked off a bit as he bit into it.

"As much essence as it is taking you to fix them, she has to use nearly as much force to break them. It takes time for her to gather her strength, but she is close to having enough to break through another one. You must stop her before she does, or the damage might be too great to reverse. Even now, the bandages you've put on the ley lines are slow to spread, but they are working. It takes time to heal, and she might be able to deal a lethal blow if she isn't stopped soon."

"I understand," I said, feeling the pressure of the situation tighten around my chest.

"Do you?" Mah'kus asked, his usual jovial tone slipping for just a moment to a more serious one.

This caught me off guard and I looked at him, but he sighed and took a drink of his wine. Before I could speak, he continued, his jovial tone returning. "You've been warned more than any other, yet you really do enjoy taking your time about it. I know you have many responsibilities that seem important to you but believe me when I tell you, that dealing with the Chaos Knight right now is the very most important thing you can do before the arrival of the true darkness. Of course, it would be helpful if you could also unite all the nations of this world into one, but I don't want to ask too much of you."

"Yeah, can't ask too much of me," I said, shaking my head and standing. "Your message has been delivered and I understand my responsibility. I will tend to the matter now."

With that, I turned and walked toward the door. Mah'kus appeared a step ahead of me holding out another donut. I took it and smiled.

"Take care, Chaos Slayer."

\*\*\*

"Emory, I need you to do this for me," I said, trying to get the bullheaded man to understand.

"Why would they listen to me? Why not just teleport all of us back and gather the troops?" Emory said, he did not like the idea of going back to Keep Variyn alone to request a military force be gathered.

I'd given him a sealed letter and my signet ring along with it as proof of the orders, but still he resisted. I guessed he was more worried that I planned on going to the next Prime Mana Shrine without him that was really bothering him, but he wouldn't say as much.

"I have told you already, I have to fix the last two Prime Mana Shrines. I've given instructions on where to meet with the forces. Get Warrick to teleport the troops to the location in five days. I will be there, and we will face the final Prime Mana Shrine together," I said, working out the details had been hard, but I was certain that the final Prime Mana Shrine would be defended by the Chaos Knight herself, because of its location.

It was in the middle of nowhere, an ancient Ordu ruins that my map had very little information about, only saying that it was searched and deemed worthless due to the level of decay. My thoughts ran a bit differently those claims. I was convinced this was where she'd found the sword and perhaps even where she first took down a Prime Mana Shrine. If not for Mah'kus marking the locations on my map, I'd have never known to check the location, as it wasn't marked on the map as having a Prime Mana Shrine.

"I'll go, but I'm not going to like it," Emory finally said, giving up his fruitless arguments. We all had a duty to attend, and he knew his. Fred and Fran stood not far off, waiting for me to finish with Emory. Both were ready to fight with me to the end, oaths, or no oaths, and I was glad to have them at my side.

However, if Emory did his duty, then I'd have all my friends and allies, at the ready. Ismene, Kora, Creed, Beth, Alayna, Adathin, and even Zander. It was important to me that we gather the strongest Awakened we could, so I'd requested that even the likes of Non and my Barons lend their support if they were battle ready. My letter made clear that a force of powerful Awakened was likely waiting for us, and I would not be able to do this alone.

I stopped short in asking aid from the King, already I'd asked him to help with the situation in the Eastern-lands, and I couldn't expect him to solve all my problems for me. No. House Variyn, under Alayna and my watch, would deal with this issue, along with our allies. This included the elves, as the ruins were in their territory, but I'd instructed Warrick in my letter to send word to the elves as well.

Summoning forth Ares from a hunt, she was still sore at me, but when she felt the state of my emotions, she soft-ened and approached, nuzzling into my side. "It's alright girl," I said, assuring her that I was okay.

Ares looked at all those present and gave them sharp glares. I chuckled at the feelings I felt from her and communicated her message to them.

"Ares wants to know why you've allowed me to become distressed," I said flatly.

Fred and Fran looked taken aback but Emory laughed.

"Hey Ares, come here, I gotta tell you something," Emory said, leaning down to get face to face with the majestic animal.

Ares inclined her head and awaited Emory's words.

"He's safe for now, but you are on duty from here until I return," Emory said, his humor gone from his voice. "You keep this knucklehead in one piece until I can get back to help. He likes to think he is the strongest thing around, but even the strongest fall. You keep him out of trouble, okay?"

Ares nodded, understanding his words perfectly and then she did something that surprised even me. She stepped forward and nuzzled her head into Emory as if to reassure him as well. Stepping back, she made a call into the air, and I understood the meaning through our bond. She was calling out anything that dared to attack me, that first they'd have to go through her.

Tears began to well up in my eyes and I quickly blinked them away. I had to keep a strong face for those around me, but damnit Ares, I love you. I sent the feelings through the bond, and she returned my affection with more of her own.

"Get ready," I told Emory and put my hand on his shoulder. After a time, I gathered enough power, doing as I'd been taught by Warrick. The air in front of my left hand began to shimmer and change into a swirling mass of color and shapes. After a minute, perhaps two, as it was hard to keep track of time when in a state of such concentration, the portal firmed and solidified.

I was getting better at making them with each new one I formed, but I was still nowhere near as good as Warrick or anyone else that studied portal magic as a main focus. But if I was familiar enough with the location and it wasn't too far, then I could do it. Distance, Warrick told me, was irrelevant, but it was hard for me to think of it that way. Which was too bad, as it added a layer of difficulty in producing portals as a portion of it played off of your own understanding of dimensional transportation.

Warrick had explained it more like a single plane of existence that could be bent in places so that two points existed next to each other, so close you could step through. But my own understanding and what clicked for me, making portals possible, was seeing it as more of a tunnel between two points where the door was visible on each side, but the hallway was not.

Warrick had been surprised when my conceptual understanding, being wrong as he put it, still resulted in the formation of a portal. I argued that I must not be wrong if it worked, but he just huffed air at me like he did so many times growing up when I asked him a question he didn't or couldn't answer. I missed my old friend suddenly, and I focused up, Emory having already passed through to the other side. I let the portal drop and turned to Fred and Fran.

"You ready to face what awaits us at the next Prime Mana Shrine?" I asked, we were heading into House Athesh lands unannounced. If we were stopped by anyone official, our cover would be that we were headed for the dungeon. However, my true intention was to visit a fairly large city that had lost their Prime Mana Shrine. It wasn't the capital city, House Athesh having at least three Prime Mana Shrines in their territory, but it was a bigger city.

"We're ready," they said in unison.

We set off and I wondered what we'd find in the city. Surely, the entire city of over a hundred thousand couldn't have been burnt out and killed, not even the Chaos Knight had that kind of power to do something like that unchecked. No, I suspected the Prime Mana Shrine would be watched over a bit more discreetly this time, but what foes we might face, I couldn't say.

We reached the city quickly, our mounts carrying us with incredible speed. There was a distinct lack of burnt-out buildings visible from the sky, so that was good. However, the massive walls were manned heavily, so we decided to land a ways off and enter by foot. Ares still refused to be unsummoned, so I left her to hunt and told her to be careful if she flew into the city, as they might have weapons meant to take down flying mounts. She understood and assured me that she'd be safe, of which I had no doubt. I still remembered how she'd flown into the city during the war, so fast and impossible to see against the night sky.

"Let's do this," I said, waving Ares away and heading for the city.

# CHAPTER 25
## DIREFIELD

The city of Direfield bustled with activity in the early morning and, despite the heavy troops on the wall, we made it into the main fairway easily enough. As adventurers, getting most places was easy, and a quick flash of our Adventurer's Guild coins confirmed us being adventurers without any need for personal identification. Had they asked, I would have refused, but they had nothing to fear from three random adventurers.

I began to worry that we wouldn't get to see the area where the Prime Mana Shrine was when we got near to the location. It was behind a large fenced off area, my map clearly marking it as inside of a huge keep area, or right behind it, it was hard to tell.

"We'll have to wait for nightfall and see if we can sneak

in," I said, keeping my voice low so the hustle and bustle around us didn't hear. Fran and Fred nodded, and we left to find a nearby inn.

For some time, we sat in silence until the tavern emptied, then we all retired to the larger room I'd rented. It wasn't your basic one room rental, but a suite that had two rooms and an entry room, likely set apart for nobles and such to rent. I'd gladly paid the steep prices for privacy, and we sat, sipping at our ales when Fran spoke up.

"We've come so far and changed so much," she said, for once not making a joke out of the situation.

"Never thought I'd be adventuring until my hair turned white," Fred said, pushing a stray strand out of his face.

Fran and I both laughed, Fred joking about anything was always a treat, as he lacked the sense of humor his sister had, preferring to be straight and logical about most things.

"I'm serious," he added, shaking his head a bit but it just made us laugh all the harder for it. Some of the tension we'd felt released during that laughter, fueling it.

"What if you didn't have to have white hair?" I asked, feeling around the subject very carefully, a part of me not wanting to offer a change, though I might be able to do it. I had enough essence to cap off one more Prime Mana Shrine, so it might not even be practical to offer what little we had to fix him now, but maybe I could tell him it was a possibility.

"I don't mind it," Fred said, oblivious to the truth I was skirting around.

"What about the other changes?" I asked, probing further and drawing a critical look from Fran. She'd not been happy about the harm that had come upon her brother and for a few weeks I'd thought for sure that she'd blamed me for it. Maybe she had, but now she seemed alright with me, and it helped to release a weight that rested on me from the entire situation. "Are you happy as you are?" I asked, being more pointed in my questions.

Fred took his time to seriously consider my words, scratching at his chin and even going so far as to summon a tiny bit of white flame above his open palm. Then, with a wink, it went out and he closed his hand. "I don't like the emptiness I feel, like I'm even more disconnected from my emotions than I was before, but honestly, if I had to change anything, I don't know that I would. Cause and effect, what could have gone differently if I hadn't had such an odd boost in my power? I prefer not to think about it if I'm being honest."

Fran came to his defense then, changing the subject with a rapid-fire suggestion. "Why don't we play some dice, or cards, you have cards, right Caldor? Fred likes cards, but I think he cheats."

Fred looked taken aback and answered with a sly voice.

"It isn't cheating per se. I just remember the cards really well."

"Let's play dice," I suggested, we had plenty of time to kill before nightfall.

What followed was a pleasant evening of dice, then a few games of cards—Fred won each card game with ease —ending with each of us speaking of home and how our parents were getting along with the changes we'd all experienced. Fred and Fran's parents moved to the city, saying they wanted to be closer to their kids and because they were independently wealthy from their time as adventurers, they kept both their old home and the new one they found in the city.

I told Fred and Fran about my mother's own struggles to maintain two residences, as she wanted to be around for me when she could, but she still had a business of her own to run, keeping the orchards producing fruit and attending meetings with merchants. The farm was doing better than ever before, but with my thoughts focused on my family, I inevitably ended with a comment about my siblings.

I worried for them, but from our brief interaction at the wedding—which they attended and left promptly after—it appeared, even according to Michael, that they were thriving in their roles as adventurers. Defeating dungeons and roaming monsters with ease. Neither mentioned anything about the dungeon groups they'd gotten together with, but I was sure they were finding stand-up folks to explore the world with. What surprised me most was how my sister had seemed to take to the life, she spoke animatedly about different monsters she'd defeated, while my brother just smiled and nodded along.

Before too long, the time came for us to go try and sneak into the complex around the Prime Mana Shrine. I nudged Fred, waking him from where he'd fallen asleep on the armchair. He startled awake and I raised my eyebrows at him. "Ready to go?" I asked, he nodded, and Fran laughed at him as he struggled to stand, his robes having gotten tangled around him while he slept.

The inn below was quiet and no one stopped us or saw us as we left out the back door. The streets were lit with mage light, similar to City Variyn, but the streets were far busier than I would have expected. Several dozen people just outside the back alley were walking from one place or another. Luckily, by the time we reached the section of gate I'd decided to try and jump, no one was around.

I started by lifting up Fred, then Fran over the fence, when my turn came around, I easily jumped right over the ten-foot-tall wall. Having an enhanced body such as mine had its benefits. Neither Fred nor Fran had a strength attribute quite as high as my own, which meant they needed an extra hand. Now safely over the wall, we peered through the shadows, looking for any sign of movement. We saw none. In fact, it was so quiet as to be suspicious.

Surely, if this place was being watched or guarded, there would at least be a patrol of some kind that we could see or sense. I turned to Fred; his keen senses of magic beings more finely tuned than even my own since his accident.

"Can you sense any Awakened or anything for that matter?" I asked.

Though I couldn't see it in the dim light, I imagined Fred's eyes must have glazed over white as he peered around the complex, searching for any signs of magical interference. He gasped suddenly and rubbed his face. After recovering himself he spoke. "Something inside is so bright that I can't see anything else."

I turned my own senses toward the building and felt it immediately. It was a huge concentration of essence, so huge that if it were coming from a person, it would rival even the King's aura. We would need to be careful; something was not right here.

"We move in slow and careful. Fred, if things get bad, you go for help," I said, though what help we'd find in this city, I did not know. Fred must have had the same thought, because in the dim light he gave me a confused look but said nothing.

We approached the massive, abandoned manor one

step at a time, the darkness and silence covering us like a suffocating blanket. What foe could possibly hold that much power inside and why did I feel like we were heading right into a trap? A part of me wanted to call the mission off until we could watch the place some more, but I knew we didn't have the time. Instead, we marched right up to the front door and slowly swung it open.

There were no locks or squeaky hinges to bar our path or give away our approach, yet still, I felt as if I was being watched. A bird suddenly made a cawing noise from behind me that had the distinct sound of warning in it, though how I knew what one bird sound over another should mean, I cannot say. I turned, spotting the bird in the moonlight sitting on a dead tree some dozen paces away. That damn bird followed me everywhere and if I had my guess, I was beginning to understand why.

"Thank you, but I already know it's likely a trap," I whispered the words, yet the bird inclined its head as if to say, 'I understand'. Emotions threatened to overtake me as I imagined who was behind the messenger bird, but I squashed them and focused on the task at hand.

"You think so?" Fran asked, clearly hearing my words despite my attempts to hide them.

"Yes, so be ready to overcome whatever they've laid in wait for us," I said, my mind going over scenario after scenario trying to prepare for any eventuality.

The inside of the manor was even darker than outside,

if it were possible. So, despite not wanting to, I cast Light and illuminated our way forward. The entryway opened into a grand area with dust covered floors and a massive staircase leading up to the second floor. There was furniture laid about the room, but it was covered by dusty white sheets of cloth, giving the room a very deserted feel. I could make out a large light fixture above us on the domed vaulted ceiling, but it gave off no light, whatever spells or enchantments set into it were now dormant.

With each step we took, the feeling in my gut tightened. We were walking into a trap willingly, and I knew I had no other choice but to grin and bear it. This wasn't smart or healthy, but we had to fix the Prime Mana Shrine if we were going to come out of this on top. I had just enough essence that I was sure I'd be able to fix it, but it would be close.

"Looks like whatever we are looking for is somewhere in the back of the manor," I said, taking a second to gaze through at the powerful essence mass somewhere in front of us.

"There's a door there," Fran said, pointing at a door to the left of the massive staircase. "Perhaps that leads deeper?"

I nodded and we headed in that direction. Upon reaching the door, I heard conversation on the other side. Slowly opening it, the words became clear.

"I know you are here," it said. "Come on back and let's get this over with."

The voice was relatively normal, a male by the sound of it, but nothing distinct that would set him apart in my mind from just another random person on the street. I shared a look with Fran and Fred, then shrugging I called out to the voice.

"We are armed and ready for a fight, so don't try anything stupid," I said, hoping my words might give the person pause.

"I am unarmed and just here to talk," the voice came back, echoing from further down a long hallway. "Take this hallway down to the end and come through the door on the left. I'm where the Prime Mana Shrine used to be. Funny that this family had exclusive rights over the shrine before my master slaughtered them. Do you think many cities have a shrine and don't know about it?"

The voice was almost friendly in the way he spoke, and it caught me off guard. Not knowing what else to do, I stepped forward and made my way down the hall to the last door. Walking through it, I was met with a gruesome sight.

Around the ruins of the Prime Mana Shrine and in a room that was open to the sky, was a mound of dead bodies, mangled and bloody. Yet, they seemed to have been here longer than the first town and were already decaying by the smell of it. Sitting to the left on a simple crate, was a man in purple robes, his hood down.

He had dusty brown hair, a kind smile, and my light illuminating sparkling purple eyes that reminded me of Ismene or Alayna. Nothing about the man spoke of him being dangerous, other than the massive amount of essence that seeped all around him. Had the Chaos Knight learned how to infuse a person so full of essence that they'd be a match for even me? His relaxed posture and tone of voice scared me most of all. This man was dangerous, and he didn't care at all about three, armed Awakened finding him, though he had no visible weapons. A caster perhaps?

"You're here to talk?" I asked, my hands ready to strike if needed, my ability to summon my sword itching to be used to cut down this threat. But I would hear him out and see what he had to say.

"My mistress asks that you step aside from the side of Order and join her," he said, smiling all the while, as if we discussed a simple matter like what we'd be wearing today. He held up his hands as I began to respond, cutting me off. "Now I know what you want to say but just hear me out. She can give you anything you want. You want to rule the Human lands under her? Done. You want to save the lives of thousands by stopping suffering and blood shed? Done. There is nothing she cannot give you if you join her side. You want power? She can do as she's done for me, enhancing you and making you even more unique than you already are. Please listen to her words and submit. You will stop so many deaths if you just stand at her side."

"You have to know that I'd never even consider siding with her," I said, dumbfounded at the earnestness I heard in his plea. "It would literally go against everything I stand for, everything I've worked for."

A bead of sweat fell down the man's forehead and he began to look distressed. "Surely, you can be intelligent enough to examine why you want the things you want, then perhaps I could help you understand that they are still goals you can accomplish under her guidance. Please hear the reason in my words and submit yourself."

I let my sword appear in my hand and readied a spell but didn't cast it. "And if I don't?" I asked.

His face fell open as if he could not believe that I wasn't taking up his offer. Then suddenly he calmed again, wiping sweat from his forehead. "So be it. She told me you'd not listen, but I was sure that I could get you to at least examine reason, but you are brainwashed against the truth and her way is the only path forward. She bids me to tell you to meet her at the final Prime Mana Shrine, that she will face you with her gathered forces and crush you. Not that you'll live another minute. Goodbye, Chaos Slayer."

The man lifted his hands up to his head and I attacked, not waiting to see what awesome powers he might have. But my Lightning Strike smashed into an invisible barrier surrounding him and his hand hit his forehead. A sudden flash and his body began to glow fiercely, followed by an impossibly loud scream of anguish.

"He's going to explode!" Fred shouted, white flames appearing all around us like a dozen vipers, striking out at the invisible field.

I activated Speed Burst infused with essence to give myself a moment to think, time slowed to a crawl, and I gripped my sword tightly. I could see, inch by inch, cracks appearing all over the man. His mouth opened in a scream that had been silenced, yet his mouth remained open in his final act. Scanning him with my senses I felt the powerful essence inside of him roiling around and getting ready to be let loose in what must be a final desperate attempt to kill me by the Chaos Knight.

It was no wonder that this man had been so eager to end this conflict with my submitting, I doubted very much he had a desire to die, yet I could see no other outcome as his body was literally being torn to pieces. The cracks continued to ripple through him, and I rushed my mind to come up with a solution.

I could set up a barrier and flood it with essence and mana, it might be enough to keep us alive, but how big was this explosion going to be? Was the entire city at risk?

Should I do the opposite and try to put a barrier around him and myself, saving the city but leaving the world without a Defender of the Balance? I could save countless lives or perhaps none if the barrier failed during my death.

Whatever I was going to do I needed to figure it out, time was not on my side and only moments had passed, yet he already looked ready to explode, pieces of his flesh flying off him. Then a sudden idea hit me, and I looked down at the sword. I sensed an enormous amount of essence and the sword needed as much essence as it could get, so what if I? No, it was too risky, but what other choice did I have?

With my mind made up, I plunged my sword through the barrier, easily cutting through it, despite the power, and I slammed the tip into the man's face. The pulling started immediately as the sword rushed to suck up all the essence before it was ignited. I felt some of the essence leave the sword as I willed changes around me, expanding a barrier of pure will and force around the four of us. Fred and Fran worked feverishly, knocking bits of essence rich flesh out of the air, each one exploding and throwing them back to the edge of the barrier.

But it was working, mostly. If I could just get the rest of it before it hit critical limits and all ignited. I felt the spark within him, and I reached out with the power of the sword, empowering my left hand. I plunged my hand into his chest and held fast to the ignition, despite the damage it began to do to my arm. I could feel my flesh being torn away, but the sheer power of the sword kept what was left of my skeletal hand gripping over his power and stopping the final ignition.

Then, just as everything seemed impossible and unlikely to succeed, the sword finished siphoning away the essence. It seemed to groan under the speed at which it had to do the task and I almost sensed a presence inside the sword, as if it had a will of its own. But just as I brushed against it, the feeling faded.

I pulled my skeletal hand from the burnt-out husk that was this mysterious messenger and looked down at it. "That sucks," I said, as at once the pain of it all assaulted me and I took a step back in shock.

"Your hand is gone!" Fred said, utterly bewildered.

"Do you need a hand?" Fran asked, seeing my hand and grinning.

"Terrible timing," I said, hiding a grimace of pain.

While staring at my hand and wondering if my body would be able to heal such an injury, the sword tingled in my grip and suddenly I wanted to hit myself upside the head. I had the very weapon able to warp reality and change the structure of essence beings with ease. I placed the flat of the blade on my stump of a skeletal hand and willed it be restored to its previous condition.

Just like that, the world blinked, and my hand was restored, the sword losing only a tiny portion of its overall essence stores. The Chaos Knight had given me the means of her own destruction with the amount of essence she'd packed into this single person. I felt the temptations of the blade to change and warp reality, but it was more a distant thought than a persistent call. Instead, I reached out a hand and restored the Prime Mana Shrine. I then decided to take a look at my character sheets and look to see if I could afford any new spells or abilities that might give me an edge in combat against her.

*Name: Caldor Miles | Classification: Arcane Knight | Species: Human*

*Level: 52, 834,750 Essence to Lvl. 53 | Essence: 2,253 | Reputation: Rank 7, 13%*

*Health: 2,890/2,890 | Mana: 3,150/3,150 | Stamina: 2,300/2,300*

*Health Regen: 259 Per Minute | Mana Regen: 158 Per Minute | Stamina Regen: 210 Per Minute*

*Constitution: 259 (74 Base) | Intellect: 315 (80 Base) | Endurance: 210 (77 Base)*

*Core: 97 (74 Base) | Concentration: 144 (74 Base) | Strength: 386 (76 Base)*

There were countless spells and abilities that I could choose from, but nothing that would give me an edge over the Chaos Knight directly. So instead, I decided to spend the essence to upgrade my most powerful spells and abilities to the next Rank, increasing the cost and effectiveness. First, I increased Mana Shell, Blink, Channel Lightning, and Arcane Missile to Rank 3 to align better with Fireball and Lightning Strike. Then, I took Lightning Strike and Fireball to the next rank, bringing it to Rank 4, the max that I could at my level.

Next, focusing on my skills, I increased Speed Burst to Rank 3 as well as Hardy to Hardy IV which increased my health by 300 instead of 200. Then, taking my three most used skills, Power Strike, Swift Strike, and Force Wave, I increased them to Rank 4, draining nearly all of my stored essence and several rare reagents stored in my bags.

Having taken care of that, I turned to Fred and Fran, both still staring at me like I'd just done the impossible.

"You fixed your hand?" Fred asked. "You can fix me, can't you?"

"I can," I said, then thinking better of it. "I think I can, I honestly don't know for sure. What happened to you is rather unique in the scheme of things."

"Do it," Fran said, suddenly serious, but Fred held up a hand, never taking his eyes off me.

"I don't want it," he said, shaking his head. "Maybe someday, but I feel good how I am, I've learned to deal with it. Leave me as I am."

"Deal," I said, then added, "Any time you change your mind, just ask, and I will see what I can do."

Fran frowned and we left the manor, the room barely

showing any signs of what could have been a city-wide disaster. We'd gotten lucky today, but I wasn't sure if our luck would hold against the Chaos Knight. What new tricks might she have under her sleeve to challenge us, what strength does she wield herself now?

# CHAPTER 26
## GATHERED FORCES

We left the city and joined up with Ares, ready to go to our final destination in the elven lands. Fran was unusually quiet during our preparations, and she flew ahead enough that I wondered if she was worried about her brother. She tended to distance herself when she was worried. But atop Ares and with the wind beating around us, it wasn't conducive to easy communication.

That thought triggered an idea for communication stones that could be used by riders in the air to better communicate. I'd have to discuss the idea with Regina or Edward. Surely the transmission of sound over a short distance couldn't be too hard an issue to overcome. Suddenly, I envisioned a battle with such stones, and wondered if no one else had such a thought before. Maybe it could be Alayna and my next discovery if we worked together on it.

My thoughts tended to stray like this while I flew in the night sky with Ares. Her own thoughts were still and calm as she scanned the horizon and peered much further than my eyes could ever hope to. She was truly a blessing, and I couldn't imagine my life without such a friend at my side. This conflict with the Chaos Knight would be deadly, I was sure, but with Ares by my side, we'd meet whatever came.

A large encampment ahead came into view, and I directed Ares down to the ground. They'd done as I'd asked and raised a small force in record time as well. From the looks of it, we had at least a few thousand strong, not to mention whatever Awakened would be present.

The first sign of anyone I saw was Warrick walking out to meet us, Emory, Alayna, Beth, Zander, Adathin, Ismene, and even Creed walking behind him, all of them in full armor ready for battle. Creed had grown another foot, it seemed, and if I hadn't known, his armor's design I'd have thought we'd been infiltrated by one of the Chaos Knight's own.

"The forces you've requested have been gathered, as well as ten teams of Awakened from Blackridge Keep. Ready to fight whatever foul beasty you've found for them," Warrick said, a wide grin on his face when he finally stopped before me.

"You work fast. I expected you would take another day, at least, but this is good. Thank you, Warrick," I said, seeing Emory stepping forward, I inclined my head to him.

"You ought to thank me, I've been working my ass off to get all this together and your buddy Warrick was suspicious of me, like I'd be making this shit up," Emory said, Warrick looked at the tall man with a raised eyebrow.

"I said no such thing, I only urged you to be sure of your words, not stumbling over them like a drunkard," Warrick said, and I smiled, happy to be surrounded by friends.

I caught Zander glaring at me and met his eyes, but he averted his gaze and Ismene put a hand on his shoulder, giving me a reassuring nod. Alayna caught my eye next, and she just smiled, her visor up and her beautiful face giving me the comfort I needed in a stressful time.

Adathin and Beth stood together, they both waved, and I inclined my head to them in thanks. Creed sauntered forward and his voice was in its normal tone, meaning it had been a while since he used an ability, or he'd mastered that odd side effect of his powers.

"I heard you needed your allies close by," Creed said, speaking in a confident manner that I'd previously not have attributed to him. "We stand with you."

"Thank you," I said, putting a hand on his armored shoulder. His armor was cold to the touch, and I remembered fondly our first meeting when he'd helped me help Ismene become an Awakened. "Thank you for everything." I added, smiling at him.

"Together we will stand against the darkness, but we have work to do. Where have we set up the command tent?" I asked and we were off to plan and prepare for the battle. It would be a deadly next few days, but we needed to start by sending out scouts and getting a lay of the land. Once we'd done that, then we could see about where we'd place our men and how best to use our forces.

In the end, I knew it would come down to my skill against that of the Chaos Knights. Only one of us would be making it out of this alive, that much I knew deep down in my bones, I just hoped that I could overcome the obstacles she had planned for me.

*Caw. Caw.*

I looked up and the familiar black bird had found its way into the command tent and was looking right at me. But there was something different this time, there was something tied to its leg and as I went to grab whatever it was, I discovered it was a small roll of parchment. Inside were seven words.

*Her forces are on their way. Prepare.*

# CHAPTER 27
## UNEXPECTED ATTACK

"Send out more scouts then, I don't want excuses, I want action!" I yelled orders to my commanders, unwilling to hear excuses when the enemy might be on our doorstep. I'd expected her to wait in the ruins, I hadn't even considered that she might bring her forces out to meet us. Sure, we had scouts, and we'd have known soon enough, but this note and who it might be from, filled me with hope that we'd been warned in time.

Sure enough, less than an hour later, our second group of scouts returned, reporting a large force headed in our direction. They would arrive within the next six hours. We were lucky, and we had enough time to set a trap of our own. I sent the scouts back out to watch for any flanking maneuvers and had my men get into a ready condition.

Alayna found me while I was rushing about and giving orders, a question on her face, so when I had a moment, I gave her my attention. "What is it?" I asked.

"Reports are coming back that they have Chaos Beasts in their ranks. Our soldiers will be ripped to shreds. We need to reconsider the placement of the Awakened. We might even need to retreat and recruit more, I just don't know if we are up to it," she said, her face filled with lines of worry.

I knew this wouldn't be easy for her to accept but I knew what I was going to do. "I have a plan and it will work. Warrick left an hour ago to get us some reinforcements. He should arrive around the time the battle starts and if it pays off, it will take care of our Chaos problem. Just trust me and we will get through this together."

"I trust you," she said, though I could tell she wanted to know more. So, I smiled and leaned down to whisper to her directly what I had planned.

"But keep it to a 'need to know' basis, I don't want to cause a panic. You know how some people are," I said, and for a moment I wondered if Alayna was going to be one of those that panicked. But she pulled herself together and smiled back at me.

"That is an insane plan. Do you think Warrick can get them to come in force and will it—" I held up a hand and stopped her before she spoke too much about it.

"Let's keep a wrap on it, I trust Warrick, and I know

this will work," I said, then seeing the work on the temporary walls being erected, I gave her a nod and ran over to tell them I wanted them higher.

We'd begun using the Awakened to dig ditches and cut down trees, creating fortifications to prepare for the battle. When they got here, they'd find us in slinging spells from ditches and popping up behind them in hastily built tunnels. It was truly amazing what Awakened could do physically, and we were pushing them to their very limits.

"I've readied my people, but are you sure you don't want us on the front line?" Kora asked. She'd been busy when I first arrived, training some of her Runeforged, but I'd spoken with her in detail about our plan since then.

"I'm sure," I said, confident in my decision in how to use her powerful Runeforged. "You will act as our cavalry, crushing the enemies' flanks, while our mounted division rains hell down upon them."

"Very well," she said, then looking deeper into my eyes she nodded again. What she saw or what she was looking for I am unsure, but I took it as a good sign, as she went about her business to ready her forces. Chaos Beasts or not, Awakened army or not, we'd come out at the top after this. According to scouting reports, the enemy only numbered at barely a thousand, so we had an advantage in that aspect. I just hoped that not all of those thousand were Awakened soldiers.

I knew it was possible, but I didn't want to imagine.

There was a small village between us and the approaching army, but they'd stubbornly refused to leave or accept our protection. Instead, they'd informed us that they had places prepared for such events, and as I wasn't in Newaliyn I didn't offer any additional arguments. Adathin assured me that they would be safe, but I worried.

The time left before the battle ticked away much faster than I would have expected and there was still no sign of Warrick. Surely, he would arrive in time or shortly after the battle started, otherwise, it would be a mistake to have sent him away. His power alone was going to be something I wanted to lean on when fighting so many powerful opponents at once.

"Our forces are in place and ready for battle," Cam said, approaching with another commander at his side. I'd given him the position of commander of over a quarter of the assembled troops, each force meant to focus on something different. He'd gladly accepted it and, though I knew he wasn't eager for war so soon after our last experience, he stood strong by my side.

"And the scouts still report not a single flying unit among the forces or anyone that resembles the Chaos Knight?" I asked, needing final confirmation before I enacted the first part of our plan.

"That is correct," Cam said, all business. "You should

be clear to rain death down upon them with very little resistance if you keep your distance."

That was the plan after all. I'd take all those with ranged abilities or spells, even a few Runeforged, and fly over the approaching army and rain spells down on them. It wasn't the most honorable way to strike out at an enemy, but we couldn't afford to hold back any advantage we might have over them. Still, the fact that they didn't have any flying units really surprised me, and I hoped that I wouldn't be surprised when we arrived to deal our damage.

"Is Fred ready with the mounted forces?" I asked. I could feel Ares with him and was pretty sure they were ready. She'd put on her armor; she liked it and I was glad to have been given the gift all those months ago. We would go into battle together and be a scourge to the enemy forces.

I left Cam behind and moved through the open field toward Fred and the two dozen others that waited around him. Seven of them were Runeforged with specialty wings given to them by Kora, but the rest rode hippogryphs or pegasus. No other members of my forces were griffin riders and the Queen had been unable to have them assist us with their ranks so diminished. She'd sent me a message saying that additional troops were en route, but the closest teleport after Warrick's initial jump was a day's ride away.

So, we had reinforcements coming from two forces,

yet, would they arrive in time to turn the tide or would we even need them, having them so outnumbered as we do?

"I'm not one for speeches," I said, as I arrived by their side. "So, stick to the plan, stay in formation, and do as much damage as possible without putting yourself at risk. Be smart, not brave. Let's do this."

I got a round of head nods from the assembled humans, Runeforged, Orcs, Trolls, and even a Goblin shaman. We were a motley crew of mismatched races, but each of them were powerful casters that would be able to rain down hell on the enemy.

I took to the sky first, sending mental commands to Ares and merging my sight with hers while she flew. In the distance, I could almost see the approaching army, still an hour or two away. The plan was to hit them before they'd expected it, which was a small window before they arrived and not so far off that they'd be able to stop and recover. If they chose to stop and not continue the march, we'd bring the forces to them, seeing it as a sign of weakness on their part.

The air grew cold as we traveled, and I mentally prepared myself for what was coming. It was necessary, I told myself, holding tightly to my bond with Ares, to prevent any shakes or hesitation. She sent me a loving warmth and once more I was grateful for such a caring companion.

"Together we will figure this out," I said, though my

words were lost to the howling of the air around us. It didn't matter, we communicated beyond words, and she sent back the same idea but in her own way. She had a fierceness to her thoughts, and I knew she was ready for the hunt, wishing to dive down among the fray and do damage that way. But that wasn't the safest way, so we'd be sticking to my plan.

I gave the sign as we approached, lifting my left arm straight up. As a single unit we rose higher in the air and prepared our spells. Each of the ones I picked had a mana channeling spell that allowed for effects similar to my Fireball, so I was sure the distance wouldn't be a problem and I wanted to be out of range of any arrows.

High enough, I gave another signal and attacks began to be charged. I pumped essence and mana into my Fireball spell, not willing to hold anything back when it meant saving lives. In total, I put equal parts of five hundred points of mana, enough to guarantee that someone would expire from the force. Then, I unleashed my attack, looking down at the massive army below. My stomach lurched a bit in my stomach when I saw that there were easily three times as many as the scouts had reported. That had to be, at the very least, three thousand strong.

My Fireball sizzled through the air and along with white flames, lightning, beams of light, and sharp cutting wind, we laid waste to the enemy. My Fireball exploded and temporarily flashed bright enough that I had to avert my eyes, while the other attacks did damage, none, not even Fred's attack, left the impact crater that mine did. Bodies laid out as if they were sleeping all around.

Stop it! I screamed at myself as I imagined what their names might have been or why they'd decided to follow the Chaos Knight. I needed to focus and continue my attack, so I launched another Fireball, this one without essence and only half as much mana. It hit and threw people aside but left no crater. Over and over, we smashed our attacks against the enemy until only I was left with any mana, but even I was on my last twenty percent.

I made the signal to leave when I saw several black dots in the distant sky and once more, my stomach clenched. Merging my sight with Ares, I saw what was approaching, half a dozen black wyverns. Making the sign to retreat, I waited until all of them had turned before doing a bit of distance calculations. It was no good, they'd reach us before we could get back to our army and even if we did make it back, what would we do against six of those massive beasts?

"We can buy them time, buy Warrick time," I said, directing my words and thoughts to Ares. She preened, ready for battle and not at all afraid of the overgrown worms as she imagined them. She was the master of the skies, not them.

I pressed myself tight against her as she bolted with incredible speed toward the wyverns and what was likely to be a disastrous encounter. Something prickled on the back of my neck, and I turned to see the entire flight that I'd sent away to safety had turned. I made the sign for them to retreat, and I had to merge my vision with Ares, having her look back, and saw the determined expression on Fred's face. He had no intention of turning back and leaving me alone with these wyverns.

My heart swelled at the gesture, but I'd have to thump him after this. With just Ares to watch out for, we had a chance, but with all the others, I'd need to protect them and that would just slow us down. I asked Ares what we should do, but she sent back only steely resolve, unwilling to change her course of action either.

"You are all stubborn donkeys," I said, thinking back to Brea the Donkey and wishing I'd spent more time with her on my last visit home. Surely, someone was taking care of her though.

Focus! The black spots in the distance were becoming clear to even my eyes and I prepared myself, pulling out a Mana potion and downing it. I just hoped the others had the presence of mind to do the same. They'd need to keep their distance and try and strike out. Close up fighting would only work for us, and I'd be damned before I let any of these men go down today.

"Onward to victory!" I shouted into the air raising my sword into the air, willing us to be faster and stronger. I felt an aura settle around us and I actually felt a bit stronger, though I didn't know what exactly I'd just done. Raising the sword, a bit higher, I willed the same for my companions, and that time, I felt a noticeable draining on the sword. How or what I'd protected them with, I couldn't say, but something had happened.

The air screamed, and the wyverns came into view. The lead wyvern was huge, but the others were barely as big as Ares and I. This wasn't going to be as one sided as I'd first thought. Looking over my shoulder, I saw the Runeforged begin to ascend higher into the air. They were surely capable of fighting in close combat, so I was surprised to see them add distance until the first one changed course and dive-bombed toward one of the smaller ones.

I had no time to see how that worked out for them because I was faced with my own opponent. Ares threw her wings out at the last moment, claws open, and we tore a line into the massive wyvern's wings. In return it screamed at us with such force that I felt it on my skin, however, the call that would normally drop us from the air screaming and clutching our ears, did nothing. I spared a glance over to the others and they seemed unaffected as well. That was the kind of protection I could get behind!

Activating Speed Burst, I swung my sword down and used Phantom Thrust to cut into the large wyvern's chest. The attack barely pierced its scaley flesh, but it did cut through, so at least I'd be able to do some damage. Ares kicked off and I used Force Wave at the wyvern's face to buy us time to get clear and gain more speed. The sword was fine and all, but suddenly, I wished I had a long lance so that I could better attack other flying creatures in the air.

I felt the sword tremble, but nothing happened, so I ignored it. Instead, we circled back just as all hell broke loose above us. The largest wyvern spewed forth black fire at two of the closer Runeforged and they dropped from the air like smoking arrows heading for the ground.

"Get them!" I screamed, but Ares was already moving. As we turned, I let loose a Lightning Strike infused with essence at the massive wyvern, causing it to break off its attack and look at who had just put a sizable wound right into its neck. It screamed again, a roar so loud it should have destroyed our ears, yet we remained protected.

We reached the first Runeforged before it hit the ground, scooping it up in Ares' talons. However, the other one hit the ground, breaking through several trees and leaving a smoking crater in the ground. Ares swooped down low, dropping the other Runeforged lightly beside the fallen one and we sped off back toward the fight, unable to offer any more assistance until the conflict in the sky was resolved.

Fred took down the first wyvern, a smaller one that screamed as it fell. One of its wings had been completely burnt to a crisp by Fred's white flames, and suddenly I had an idea. If I helped take out the smaller wyverns, we could team up on the larger one and we might stand a chance. With that in mind, I sent a command to Ares and at first, she almost refused, wanting only to fight the strongest in the air to prove her own superiority. But she relented when I told her we'd still be fighting the larger one, just not yet.

My sword cut cleanly and easily through the long neck of the nearest wyvern, and I laughed a little at how easily it went down. The house-sized wyvern wasn't having any of it though, striking another Runeforged from the air and delivering a slash across the mount of one of the trolls, sending him flying from his saddle. Once more, we dove to save a falling member of our team. We caught him, but his mount was dead, so we set him next to the two Runeforged, each still moving but not taking flight due to damage they'd taken.

Getting back to the fight, I took out another smaller wyvern, then another, until, with the help of the others, only the larger wyvern remained. We'd lost a goblin and an orc, I was unable to catch either of them as they'd been burnt to a crisp or, in the goblin shaman's case, cut right into two. But the battle was coming to an end and the wyvern seemed to know this, fighting like a cornered animal.

I sent another barrage of Arcane Missiles, following them up immediately with my final attack before my mana was spent. I infused my Channel Lightning with essence and let loose as much as I could afford to, draining my mana to near nothing and giving myself a headache.

Lightning danced from the tip of my blade, striking the damaged wings and tearing new rents all down it, until the beast began to fall. Just as it let loose its final attack, my own cut off. Black flame came straight for us, and I saw my mistake. I should have kept some for a shield.

At the last possible moment, I heard a voice cry out behind me and I turned in time to see white flame pour all around us, slamming into the black flame. For a moment I thought it wouldn't be enough, but the white flames surged, and the black flames cut off. The wyvern fell then, unmoving and all fight gone.

I watched it go, turning to see Fred wobbling on his hippogryph, but the saddle held him in place and his mount was doing fine keeping him aloft. We'd won the first battle, but this was far from over. Checking that the wyvern had indeed died on impact, we landed and let our mounts rest while we recovered our injured and dead. Gonlak the Shaman, Neldon the Runeforged, and Gor'shaw the orc, were added to my list of names, but there would be time to mourn them later.

After carefully wrapping the bodies, I stored them away in my inventory and we took flight, eager to get back before the main forces of our armies clashed.

# CHAPTER 28
## OVERWHELMING FORCE

W e flew over the horde of enemies and once more, I was struck by how vast their numbers appeared to be. Using Ares' keen sight, I found out why. All around the armored and cloaked figures were corpses walking among them. They'd found dead to animate to fight for their cause and, while alone they wouldn't be much trouble to fight, with so many of them my forces would be in trouble indeed.

I needed to get back and warn them, we needed to focus on ranged attacks to further thin the horde. With that in mind, I threw a volley of fireballs, just normal ones with enough power to explode on impact, at the monstrous horde beneath us. None of the other riders followed my example, likely they were too far gone on mana and didn't have a regen as fast as my own. Even so, that little barrage brought back my headache and once more I had to focus on regenerating, so I didn't lose focus.

We made it past the forces coming against us and soon we were landing among our troops. The first thing I did was find my commanders and inform them of the change of events, we'd want to keep to our plan but be wary of so many extra forces. With a few adjustments, we were back on schedule and ready to meet the mass of undead and Chaos followers.

When the army reached us, we were ready, and I watched from a distance as the clash began. As I'd suspected, they started by throwing the undead at us, line after line, hoping to overwhelm our defenses. At first, I thought even our first line of defense would be enough, as they didn't seem able to do much other than throw themselves at the moat we'd built, filling it with their bodies. But then they began to climb.

Next, they came upon the wooden palisades we'd erected hastily and once again, I thought that would be enough to stop them. Hoping that the spikes and the rough nature of the wood would make it difficult for such simple undead to get through or over. But then, the purple flames came. The undead were unaffected, but where it touched wood, smoke filled the air, and it was set afire.

"Begin bombardment," I said, and the proper signals were given.

As the first undead got through the burning palisades, many on fire after the wood caught, they faced our trench system. Lightning struck, fireballs went out, and all manner of ranged attacks were launched. Next came a hail of arrows so thick that they provided shade before striking down with deadly force. All this went into keeping the undead back, yet still they came, ragged, and ripped apart but still walking.

Some had weapons, but most didn't, so when they reached the trenches, the melee fighters made quick work of them. Though, the sheer number made me send the signal to pull back and out of the trenches. We were losing ground much faster than I would have liked, but my army of soldiers were about to get their chance to wet their blades.

With the Awakened all fleeing the trenches, Cam called his forces forward to provide a wall against the undead. He led them from the back, as I'd commanded him. Even though we both wanted to be in the front lines fighting, someone had to call the shots. But soon it looked like it wouldn't matter, as we clashed, it was unlike any battle I'd been part of before. The mindless undead charged through the ranks, most not even stopping to attack, just pushing deeper and deeper.

At first, soldiers cut them down, but after a while and with so many thousands of them, they had to focus on those that were fighting. It was a mass of Chaos and when the purple fire came, many living died due to not being able to avoid the fires.

"Counterattack with the Awakened and call for the Runeforged to flank, I can sense the Chaos Beasts getting closer and we aren't ready," I yelled out the order and flags went up, signaling my words.

Several teams of Awakened appeared, cutting through the undead like a scythe cutting through wheat. It was a glory to behold, and each group had a freshly rested caster providing shielding from the necro flames, which allowed them to kill the undead with unprecedented speed. Minutes passed and finally I saw Kora at the head of her Runeforged, rushing into their side to crush the remaining undead.

Like hammer and anvil, the Awakened and the Runeforged came together, crushing all undead that dared walk between them. Soon, we had the upper hand and Cam was pulling his forces back as the more powerful military force crushed the remaining undead. It was a small victory, but we'd killed at least a thousand or more undead in the span of half an hour. Cam's men were beat and tired, if not for his quick thinking they might have been overrun.

But the battle wasn't over yet, and as many undead as we'd killed, I knew that there were that many more waiting to be sent at us to wear us down. It was a shame that our attacks hadn't killed more of them, but with how many we must have finished off, we'd at least bought ourselves some time.

"More undead are coming," someone called out and I looked, seeing that indeed, another wave was headed our direction, but what was more, purple flames were being hurled over at the undead already fallen and new corpses were beginning to stir.

"Bring in the reserved forces, we need to deal with the undead, they are rising again!" I yelled, giving my orders to the man beside me. He nodded and the signs began to be flown to direct the troops where to go.

They were fast to act, but even so, they now faced some of their fallen soldiers and the undead that weren't as badly dismembered. Then I saw another thing rise from the dirt and I nearly took up arms myself to take the abomination down. From behind the enemy lines came more purple fire, but it concentrated in a single spot, pulling together random parts until a thing made of too many arms, legs, heads, and more rose up standing some ten feet tall.

"Get Kora to push further back into their numbers, we have to break the concentration of those Necromancers if we are going to make any progress here!" I yelled the order, and the flags went up.

I saw the Runeforged make a push to go deeper into the enemy lines, but they faltered as they met a force of Chaos Beasts, their numbers becoming scattered by several massive drakes. I saw Kora call out something and suddenly they were retreating, their withdrawal protected by a massive T-Rex. It tore into one of the drakes and overpowered it by sheer force and strength of jaw.

The undead continued to creep ever closer, our men giving up space as they attempted to let none pass. Corpses piled up as heads were separated from bodies to never rise again. Just when it looked like we'd be over-whelmed by the sheer force of the enemy, I heard horns in the distance calling out a tone I'd heard before.

The elves had arrived!

Sweeping through the flank of the enemy and turning aside undead and Necromancer alike, a force of elves in golden armor cut their way through the battle toward the front. Adathin appeared before me, an excited glean in his eye.

"It's the royal guard, they've come to help us!" He exclaimed. "They are few in numbers but each of them is worth a hundred men on the field of battle."

"The royal guard," I repeated, and I could believe it, watching them work. Even the few smaller Chaos Beasts that got in their way fell as if a mighty wind assaulted them and they were defenseless against it.

This battle was far from over, but we'd just gotten an edge that I hadn't planned on using. I gave the order for several parties of Awakened to join the elves on their assault, then to order them back. We had more undead to cut through before the real battle could even start.

\*\*\*

Raging back and forth, the battle continued, the horde of undead thinning and then being reborn by Necromancers if there were enough pieces for them to work with. The abominations went down first, large targets both the elves and my teams of Awakened could sink their teeth into. As I watched everything unfold, I felt a deep sense of needing to do something more, but my place was giving commands until we absolutely needed me.

So, when the first group of what looked like Death Knights, each flanked by Chaos Beasts, took the field and began cutting through my soldiers with ease, I looked to my second and gave him a nod. It was my turn to get my hands dirty!

"Alayna, Ismene, Creed, Emory, form up!" I called and they did so. They'd just rotated out from striking into the enemy forces, but they still looked fresh, and their auras blazed with determination.

"It's like smacking around children," Emory said, as he cut down an undead. "But you know what they say?"

"What's that?" I asked, releasing the hold on my aura and letting the pressure of my power push back the weaker undead. It radiated out from me like a force of will that even the mindless undead heeded.

"Get enough children together and even they can kill ya," Emory said, laughing.

"I can kill many of these weaklings," Creed said, a bit more serious than I expected, it didn't help that his Death Knight voice echoed in its ethereal way as he spoke the words.

"Focus up," I said, running forward, my team all around me. The Death Knights and their Chaos Beasts were reaching the elven soldiers and my own and I would not allow them to be cut down so easily. If Warrick were here, I wouldn't need to do this or take this risk, but he wasn't so I did.

Our own soldiers pushed themselves aside for us and soon we reached our target, four Death Knights and three drakes. I wasted no time in throwing out a Channel Lightning filled with enough essence to drop two of the Death Knights to their knees and the Chaos Beasts to falter, taking a step backward.

"For the balance!" I screamed, rushing forward, and slashing at the biggest of the Death Knights.

He caught my blade, ethereal echoing voice laughing as he did and pushed back. But I wasn't so easily pushed aside, and he learned the hard way that you don't mess with an Arcane Knight. Instead of me being pushed back from his attempt, he stumbled back a few steps and I hit him with several sword swipes, ending in a Power Strike to his hardened icy armor. It shattered and sprayed red just as he unleashed an attack of ice from his hand that hit me in the chest, finally throwing me back as he'd intended.

But Emory was there a moment later, smashing his shield into the Death Knight's face as the others engaged the remaining ones. From the ground, I let loose a Lightning Strike, jumped to my feet and Blinked in front of a Drake to catch its maw as it opened to bite onto Alayna's shoulder. Activating Speed Burst, I marveled at this thing's strength as I was forced to inject a small bit of mana into the sword to surge my own strength. But I had tricks for days and these were the least of my enemies.

I threw the drake to the side by its mouth and roared into the sky, defying even the gods to stand in my way. I heard a caw from the side, and it snapped me back to reality. I had to keep a hold on the effects of the sword, otherwise I'd lose myself in battle. Keeping my mind together and looking across the battlefield, I chose my next target. With the effects of Speed Burst still going, I zipped across the field like a specter of death, sweeping in and delivering final blows.

By the time it wore off, another Death Knight was done, and I'd injured a Chaos Drake, nearly taking its leg off. Sweeping my blade around, I leveled it at Ismene's target and released an Arcane Missile. The five sparks of energy zipped out from me and smashed repeatedly into the Death Knight, staggering it enough to give Ismene the chance she needed to get a killing blow.

All around me we were winning, and my team showed off their powerful abilities. But suddenly, I realized that while we'd stopped this small band of Death Knights and drakes, we'd failed to see the dozen other groups just like it, pushing my troops back all around us. We'd been cut off and just now the enemy were looking around as if they'd caught us.

"Form up and retreat," I called, Emory snapped into place blocking the enemy from attacking us as we retreated, and I went to cut us a line through. First, I surged my aura, a trick I'd learned after my imprisonment, then as soldiers and Death Knights alike stepped backward, we fled.

We got into our lines, too many of my men lay dead on the way and I cursed this battle for all the lives that were being lost. Yet, of any battle I'd been a part of, this was the most needed and their lives would live on in my memory, remembered and respected.

Finally making it back to the command, I looked over the battlefield and saw the problem. Wherever the Chaos Beasts appeared, we shrank back, our soldiers unable to fight against such an overwhelming force. Our teams of Awakened tried, but even they gave ground as drakes weren't an easy foe to deal with, even the smaller ones such as these. Then I saw our end appear, three huge drakes from the back of the enemy's army began to walk toward our front lines.

This would break us, only my team being remotely able to take on such a threat. But we had no way to get to them without being outnumbered and overwhelmed. It didn't matter, I knew as I wiped black blood from my blade.

"I'm going in alone, I have to kill those three and I can't protect you at the same time," I said, turning my attention to Alayna, but speaking loud enough my entire team and command could hear.

No one spoke at first, then all at once they told me how stupid of an idea that was, but I held up a hand, my mind made up. It was simple really, I had ways of getting stronger and faster, but if I had to watch out for anyone but myself, I'd likely fall to a stray strike. But if I infused myself with essence and added mana to the sword, I might become strong enough to take them all on at once, buying us the time we needed until Warrick arrived with backup.

Come on Warrick, where are you? I wondered, as I looked over the battlefield one last time. I heard every objection; Alayna hadn't stopped hers, despite me silencing everyone else.

"You promised we'd live long lives together," she finally said, tears in her eyes. "Let me come with you at least, I can keep up!" Emory and Ismene shook their heads at this holding up their weapons as if to say they could as well, but I shook my head.

"You can't," I said, a sorrow filling me as I said the difficult words. "I'm stronger than you know, you can't keep up and you know it. But I promise I won't be dying in this battle. This is just one more crazy fight that will end in my favor, I'm sure of it."

I wasn't as sure as I tried to sound, but I could delay this group if not outright kill them. I'd be throwing myself into the deep end of the endless waters and hope to hell I could float.

In response, Alayna hugged me and called me an idiot. I knew she meant it this time too. I just smiled and lowered my helmet back over my head, ready to fight.

"Give 'em hell," Emory said, clasping me on the arm and pumping his other in the air.

"Our journey doesn't end today, don't forget it," Ismene said, tears in her purple eyes as well, though she was quick to wipe any away that escaped.

Creed gave me a head nod and, in the distance, I saw Zander returning with his group. I nodded in his direction just as I sprinted into the backlines of our army. My aura flared and people made way.

Before I'd made it to the front, I began to infuse my body with essence, each step coming stronger and faster, and just as I reached the front lines, I infused my sword with mana. Suddenly, I was filled with an arrogant surge of emotion, and I knew these peasants were no match for me.

To demonstrate my power, I did the impossible, surging my aura so hard that it split the enemy forces apart, creating a twenty-pace dead man's zone. Then, to further show them who they were messing with, I activated Channel Lightning, but with a surge of the sword's power I did it a dozen times instead of just once. At twelve different locations I did something I had no idea I could do with the sword's power, and lightning devastated the enemy's front line, killing Death Knights, undead, and Necromancers alike.

By the time I was finished, my voice was hoarse, and I realized I had been screaming. Another dozen feet had been cleared as the dead and dying fled before me. But I wasn't done yet, activating Speed Burst with essence infused into it, I began to rush into the line, cutting down all before me, using skills without thought or care as my resources slowly emptied.

So intoxicating was the feeling and rush of my power that I'd forgotten why I'd attacked in the first place, until three massive drakes appeared, and I screamed at their direction, using the sword to warp the very air around me until I'd created a dome around just the four of us, stopping all others from interfering.

"You die today," I said, my words barely a whisper and a touch rough from all the screaming. My aura surged and they attacked, uncaring for my powerful aura.

The first opened its mouth and unleashed fire, I cut straight into it and walked forward, uncaring. The next one slammed a foot into the ground and the ground opened up beneath me, but before I'd fallen more than an inch, I used the sword to reform the ground.

"You stand no chance," I screamed, the power intoxicating as I drank it in. Somewhere in the back of my mind I could feel my resources drain more and more, but I was too far gone to give it much attention.

The first one died by a simple Phantom Thrust into the eye, the next, I exchanged blows with and played with it while the other tried to fry me with its intense fire. I ended the game by removing its head with my sword, cutting through it like a hot knife through butter.

As I faced down the last one, something inside of me faltered and I suddenly felt like I'd throw up. Thinking fast, I activated Stamina Surge and really looked at my resources. I'd brought them all down to nearly zero and more than that, I'd been taking more hits than I realized, my health was at a few hundred under half. What was I doing and how had this happened?

The state of my body brought me back into focus and out of the trance the sword had put me under. I needed to end this quick and stop fooling around. Surging essence into my body, I moved, but as I traded blows with the drake, I felt the hardened air around us fail. All at once, icy bolts and purple fire came hurdling for me. This was it; I'd overextended for the last time. I had no time to heal, no time to take a potion, no time.

I activated Speed Burst and drank a health potion, cursing my stupidity. It would slowly recover my health, but not enough. Dodging and slashing to keep my foe at bay, I fought, determined to fight until the end came.

From a distance, I could feel my team coming, but I wished that I could stop them. It was too late, and I wouldn't make it in time. Fire slammed into me along with a bite from the mighty drake and I Blinked, using the tiny bit of mana that had recovered, just barely avoiding being bitten in two pieces.

My left arm hung at my side, my Blink not having been fast enough after all. Bloody, broken, and running only on essence infusion inside my body, I faced the dozens and dozens around me.

A final volley smashed through the air toward me, and I kept my eyes open, ready to face it until the end.

"You fool!" Yelled a voice I recognized, and I felt a glimmer of hope fill me just as fast as it went out. He'd arrived just in time to see me die; Warrick was not going to be happy.

I managed to turn my head to see him...flying? He was flying over the battlefield and his arms were wrapped around a gnarled staff, power gathering around it. Just as the attacks reached me, I felt a pull, and with a 'pop' I felt myself get pulled through reality. Suddenly, I was in the air where Warrick had been, falling for the ground. Warrick yelled in the distance, and I realized what had happened.

Somehow, he'd traded places with me and taken the killing blow meant for me. That tricky bastard. What had he done? I focused my mind, ready to Blink, but it was on cooldown still, so I was falling. Then, a familiar mind touched mine and I knew I was saved.

Ares, unable to hold herself back any longer, had already been on her way to help me. She swooped under me, and I grabbed hold as we rushed to Warrick's aid. Somehow, impossibly so, he was still alive and slinging spells like the best of them. The last of the larger Chaos Beasts had been half disintegrated and dozens of others had been beaten back by the fierce power of the ancient wizard.

We slammed down, Ares catching a Death Knight's blade in her maw and ripping it free before slashing down its icy armor. Dust billowed up around us as we joined Warrick in the battle for our lives. Just as we began to fight, the tide changed, my own strength all but spent, but Ares was fresh and shared in my powerful advancement. My team arrived next. No, not just my team, but all my friends.

Kora landed with a squad of Runeforged from the sky above, each of them fighting with a fierceness that boggled the mind. Emory appeared with Alayna, Ismene, Creed, Zander, Beth, Adathin, and Galt right behind him. Each of them fought with power beyond their own, cutting and unleashing abilities at more powerful foes. Their combined force was just enough to give us some space, but the battle was far from in our favor.

It did, however, give me a chance to speak with a weathered and tired Warrick.

"Did you bring them?" I asked, and he smiled at me despite our circumstances.

"Indeed, I did," he said, turning his head toward our forces.

Then, I saw it: a massive force, even larger than the army I'd brought, composed of blackened armored figures and, surrounding them, Chaos Beasts. At first, I thought we were doomed, that we'd been cut off by enemy forces, but no. These were not the forces of Chaos that answered to that Chaos Knight, these were our allies, as odd as it seemed.

I heard another 'caw caw' and looked to see the black bird eying me. It gave me a single nod of the head and then flew off.

What that meant, I wasn't sure, but I had no time to worry about it now.

"Fight them to the end, our reprieve comes but we need to buy them time. Let's show them what the forces of Order can truly do!" I yelled the words above the din of battle and my friends, my allies, all cheered in response.

We fought and my mind blurred. Would it be an epic ending to a battle we'd remember for all our lives? Perhaps, but honestly, I had more trouble keeping my blade up and relied on Ares more than any time before. She was more of a battle-hardened fighter than I'd ever realized, doing as much, if not more, damage than the gathered Awakened. Where she went, death followed.

# CHAPTER 29
## REGROUP

The enemy force, when met against people all too similar to themselves, seemed stunned and the strangest thing happened. All of the Chaos Beasts turned sides and joined with the stronger Southland Chaos users we'd allied with. The battle was over the moment that happened and the enemy either ran or surrendered. It was such a quick ending to what had been one of the most terrible battles I'd ever been a part of.

But we'd done it, we'd pushed back the enemy and now, with their surrender, the Chaos Knights that we could trust, for now at least, would take the beasts under their care and teach them not to be murdering monsters. I had my doubts on the matter, but it had been part of what Warrick had promised them if they came to help, so my hands were tied.

"Our problems aren't over yet," I said, as Warrick approached with a tired look on his face.

"As well I know," his eyes looked to the west where the Chaos Knight awaited me. "I wish you'd reconsider and let us bring the full force of our might upon her. It is no less than she deserves."

"She wields a weapon that might very well be capable of destroying our army and I won't risk losing any more people I love. Ares and I will go into battle together and we will be victorious," I said, projecting more confidence than I felt.

Ares preened under my words as if I was giving her some great gift by taking her into battle with me. I absently pet her head; the armor had served her well today and I hoped it would continue to protect her.

"Then at least you don't go alone," Warrick said, leaning down ever so slightly to peer into Ares' eyes. "She's one of our best, I think. Much love for you in those eyes. Fly swift and true great steed, for you carry on your back my truest friend."

She nodded once to Warrick and I swore I felt something pass between them, be it energy or magic, I couldn't tell. Perhaps the bonds of an oath. Either way, I put a hand on my friend's arm and went to find the others. I needed to say goodbye just in case the worst were to occur. There were no words I knew that I could say to Warrick, nor did any such phrases needed to be traded. For I loved him, and he loved me. Despite all we'd been through he had been my finest mentor and friend.

Once more, I spoke with all my loved ones, and they urged me to let them come. But this was different, and them rushing in to try and save me wouldn't win this battle. No, this was a battle I could win by myself. My strength, once I've fully recovered, against the Chaos Knight wielding a Sword made by the Ordu as well. This battle wouldn't be fantastic or anything, that I knew. We'd clash and one of us would fold to the other's power. It would be over quick, but I had confidence that I could do it.

I found a tent that offered some privacy and put myself into a meditative state, allowing my resources to fill all the more quickly. It was mostly in my mind, but I felt like relaxing myself really helped to repair the damage battle could do to me. It was during these moments of silence when my demons reared their head the strongest. After feeling my resources recover to full, I sought out Cam for a final report on how the battle went for his troops as well as the other commanders.

I found him helping with the body recovery efforts, messy work because of the Necromancers.

"Do you have a moment?" I asked him as he finished moving the mostly destroyed corpse of one of our soldiers.

He turned and I saw grief immediately clear on his face, but it was covered in moments, back to his normal cheerful self. "Of course, how can I assist you?" He asked with a bit more air of rigidity than I expected from him. I couldn't blame him though; it had been a terrible battle and losses were likely to have been high.

"I need to know how many we lost," I said, grabbing a shovel and jumping into a partially dug mass grave. Cam joined me and for a while we just shoveled away before finally, he answered me.

"A quarter," he said, his voice somber. "We lost nearly a quarter of the two thousand troops we sent to fight. I think the exact number was somewhere in the high four hundreds."

I didn't look at him for several long seconds as I kept digging. It was easier to focus on a menial task such as this than accept the reality that I'd just been apart of what might have been the worse battle I'd ever personally led. Was it some failing of my own that caused such heavy casualties or was it just the overwhelming numbers we faced? Would it have been so bad if I could have mustered a larger force perhaps? So many questions now weighed heavily on my mind but finally, I spoke up.

"I'm sorry," I said, not having any other words to come close to addressing the horror and reality of such losses.

Cam just sighed and put a friendly hand on my shoulder. "We knew going into this that it wasn't going to be an easy fight. You did all you could to save as many lives as possible and from what I'm hearing, you aren't even done for the day. When you face the person responsible for this chaos, give them a message via the tip of your blade for me."

"I will," I said, picturing the Chaos Knight and my blade piercing her chest.

I left Cam to his work after that and prepared to depart. Despite using essence and reshaping reality a time or two, the sword still bristled with essence, and I was confident it would be enough to take on this last challenge.

My mind wondered over our losses, the new list of names I'd need to memorize and what lay before me. It wouldn't be an easy task, nor one that I thought I'd truly make it out of without something to show for it, but I did feel as if I could beat her. It was this certainty that kept me from approaching my goodbyes in such a lax manner. I'd been more worried about going against three full grown drakes and the surrounding forces than I was fighting this Chaos Knight.

Perhaps I was being foolish but as far as I could see, we were on even footing. She had a weapon of the Ordu, a tool that could reshape reality, but so did I. My confidence in my mastery over the sword and what it was capable of, kept me confident, but I did worry about the tendency to feel overconfident while using the weapon. And it was truly a weapon, a device that could be used as a tool or anything really, but in my hands, I wielded it as a weapon of destruction.

Of course, the Chaos Knight did the same and she had been using it longer, even going so far as to use it on Warrick to temporarily drain him of much of his strength. I didn't know the process in which she had done that, but if memory served, Warrick had described her using other Ordu tools to accomplish it, not just the sword. That made me wonder that perhaps she'd have other tools at her disposal and maybe my confidence was not as well placed as I thought.

But no, even if she did, she'd been forced to subdue Warrick to use those tools on him and I wouldn't allow myself to be restrained while I wielded a weapon capable of distorting reality itself.

I sent out a mental command for Ares to meet me at the edge of our camp and headed in that direction. Despite having said our goodbyes, I was surprised to find Alayna there, waiting beside Ares.

"Don't go alone," the first words from her mouth being the last thing she told me when saying goodbye only an hour before.

"I'm not," I said, thinking back to my conversation with Warrick. "I've got Ares to watch my back."

At this, Ares preened, my thoughts open enough to her that she understood my words. Or perhaps she did understand common, I honestly didn't know now that I thought about it. I pulled Alayna into a hug for the dozenth time and kissed her on the cheek.

"You know what I mean," she spoke the words into my chest, and I hugged her all the tighter. Her armor pressed against my own and suddenly I had the urge to take her someplace private so that we could do a proper send-off. I kept my thoughts to myself, as I knew without a doubt Alayna would do anything to delay me at this point.

"I do, but I stand by it. I am not going in alone; it will be enough work to protect Ares and ensure that we both come out in a single piece. If I brought more, it would only split my focus. Warrick understands, why can't you?" I asked, a teasing tone slipping into my voice.

She wasn't having it though and pushed off my chest to look right up into my eyes, pure determination gleaming in hers. "Take Warrick with you, he is powerful enough to defend himself. He proved that when he saved your butt today."

She had a point there, but I wasn't going to concede it. "Warrick is tired and worn thin. Teleporting and doing what he did for me has already brought him to the point of exhaustion. I can't wait long enough for him to recover. This might be my only chance to face off against the Chaos Knight before she amasses more followers or does more damage to the ley lines. It has to be now," I said, my words firm at the end, all playfulness gone.

"Come back to me. Promise me that you will come back to me," Alayna said, deflating as she spoke.

"I promise," I answered back, a coy smile on my lips as I pulled her close and we shared an intimate kiss.

With that, she turned to Ares and whispered something to her that I didn't catch. Ares nodded and Alayna gave her a kiss on her armored head. I got the sense of protection and sacrifice from her, which only made me wonder what Alayna had told her to begin with. But I let it go, instead remaining content with knowing that both of these two loved me enough to want to keep me safe from all harm. Ares would fight like the griffin she was, with fierce determination and more ferocity than any other mount could hope to match, dragon and wyvern included.

I mounted her then, strapping in my legs and doing a final check on my armor to ensure everything was secure. I did the same for Ares, but I didn't need to, she was as set and ready as I was. So, with a singular mind ready for combat, we rose into the air and left the camp behind us, heading straight into the maw of the Chaos Knight herself.

# CHAPTER 30
## CHAOS KNIGHT

The closer we traveled toward the ruins, the darker the sky got. It wasn't even that there were clouds in the sky blocking out the light. No, there was just a darkness that seeped into everything and lowered the amount of light that could reach the area. Soon, it was like we were flying at the darkest part of the night, when in truth it was early morning already. My mind was focused, and I was ready to get this task finished.

The trees broke way to old ruins and in the distance, I could make out a single form sitting astride a massive wyvern, a dark red glow emanating from them just enough to make them visible from a distance.

"That's our target," I told Ares, and we adjusted our direction to land in front of them. No sooner had we set down, did I notice the raw power that surrounded the

Chaos Knight and her mount. This was not going to be an easy fight.

"Welcome to the birthplace of a new age," the Chaos Knight said, her voice carrying over the space between us loud and clear.

Between us, I saw the remains of the Prime Mana Shrine. This entire area had been cleared of stone, so it was easy to see the ragged remains jutting out of the ground. We stood amidst the remnants of stone and metal, warped by time and decay.

"Let's get this over with," I yelled back, not wanting to trade words with her. She knew her role and I knew mine, the time for talking had ended. Apparently, she didn't feel the same because she prattled on.

"You defeated my army?" She asked, then before I could answer she continued. "It matters not, they were merely tools and pawns to be thrown away as needed. Now that I have you before me, I will twist you into my perfect soldier. A Knight of Chaos born wielding a tool of those foolish Ordu. Together we will bring Chaos and ruin to this world and many more when my master arrives."

This piqued my interest, and I remembered back to what Mah'kus had said about her getting some assistance as well. Perhaps this master whom she spoke of was the help she'd been receiving? Again, it was hard to care. I had a duty to carry out, and I might as well get to it.

"I will never bow to your will," I said, drawing forth the Sword of the Ordu. It gleamed as if reflecting light in all directions, despite the darkness we were shrouded in. "Surrender now or die."

"You foolish boy," The Chaos Knight said, drawing forth her own sword. It was a match for mine, yet it had a darkness about it as if she'd somehow managed to bend it toward the will of Chaos and away from Order. What might that do to its abilities I wonder? "I will remake you from the inside out. Get ready to face your doom!"

With that, she pointed her sword at me, tip first, and a beam of black energy shot forth, right at me. Ares was quicker than it though, diving us out of the way as I unleashed a Lightning Strike. Each and every attack I planned on using would be expending what few thousands of essence I'd collected during the battle. It only took a hundred or so per attack to bring it up to the next level, damage-wise, so when my attack hit, it wasn't an easy strike to brush off.

Lightning ripped from the air above the Chaos Knight and struck her hard on the shoulder. Her blackened armor showed no signs that it did any damage, but her body jerked back from the force of the blow. She cut off her own attack and sneered in my direction before slicing through the air with her sword and taking flight.

Again, Ares easily dodged the slash of black energy

and followed the mighty wyvern upward, ready to show them that it wasn't dragons that ruled the sky, but griffins.

The wyvern must have had a similar idea in mind because it roared, and if not for some quick thinking on my part, it would have ripped our ears to shreds. The sword gleamed in my hand as the protection of the blade washed over myself and Ares, shielding us from the roar of the wyvern. I swore at that moment I saw an expression cross over the Chaos Knight's face. Surprise, maybe? It seemed odd. She'd chosen not to wear a helmet of any kind, but just as I thought that, she sneered in my direction again and a helmet appeared over her head like magic.

She must not have known how much control I had over my own sword. Had she been banking on the fact that I might be a novice in its use perhaps? This could turn the fight to our advantage if she continued to underestimate us. Ares flew us in close and she slashed out with her claws, meanwhile, I filled the wyvern with essence enhanced Channel Lighting, followed up by a powerful slashing combo of Power Strike, Swift Strike, Light Blade, and Force Wave. Both attacks hit home, and the wyvern roared in protest, bringing its long neck around to bite at us.

Ares, ever the quick combatant, dove out of the way and made room. That enabled me to strike out again, this time with Firebolt, multiplying the cast with the aid of the sword. Five Firebolts smashed through the air toward her, but she dispersed each of them with a wave of her sword.

Incredible! She had a fine control over her artifact as well. Seemed this fight was just getting started.

Back and forth we went, me draining my mana then backing off and using Stamina instead, never pushing either resource harder than I could recover from a dozen seconds or so of resting. Cycling back and forth, we kept this exchange going for nearly ten minutes before things finally shifted.

As we dove in close, I reached out and cut with my sword, extending the length using Phantom Thrust. The cut slashed opens the wyvern's stomach and put a line in its wings, but what was more, I drained out a measure of the creature's essence while attacking. It faltered in the air and began to glide down for a rough landing. I could tell the Chaos Knight was furious at this change, but in the air, Ares had proved herself the better fighter.

Darkness shrouded the two for several long moments and while I couldn't see them, I decided to act anyway, charging an essence infused Fireball. The same attack that had driven back the Chaos Knight at our last confrontation. I could feel the essence and mana pulling away from me, but more distracting than that was whatever the Chaos Knight was doing. She seemed to be pulling in essence from all around her.

I unleashed my attack and turned my mind toward the

essence all around. The place was thick with it, almost as much as the site of City Blalor. These ruins were rich in essence and the longer I focused, the more I sensed below. There was a dungeon beneath us, and it was calling out in fear. It came as a whisper at first, but then all at once I could hear it clearly, screaming in pain and suffering.

What I could do for it, I didn't know, but with another second of focus I blocked it out until I could figure out how to help it. My Fireball hit as I looked up, the exchange with the dungeon having only taken a fraction of a moment.

The darkness around the two broke as my fireball exploded, but to my horror I saw what she'd been doing. Where the large wyvern had once been, injured but strong, now stood a hideous twisted version of its former self. Green liquid dripped from its mouth and an extra row of teeth could be seen in its massive maw. Somehow, she'd turned the creature into something sick and awful.

The Chaos Knight waved a hand, and the creature took to the sky on a pair of massive wings. I dismounted and sent Ares a message. "Fight it but don't let it bite you or spray that green stuff on you. Be swift and cut it out of the sky."

She nodded and took off to fight while I stayed down below to face off against the Chaos Knight. I couldn't help but being distracted by the battle above, but I did my best to keep only a measure of my mind connected to Ares' mind. I had my own fight to tend to and it was going to take all I could to bring her down.

The screaming tried to overtake me again and I actually faltered in my steps for a moment. Blocking it out, I regained focus just in time to see an arch of blackness headed my way, far deeper and more menacing than the attacks she'd used during our first meeting. I jumped to the side, barely dodging the attack.

I was back on my feet a moment later and struck out with my instant cast Lightning Strike, following it up with my favorite arcing combo as I ran to engage her, sword against sword. She smashed apart each of my attacks, even catching the lightning on her blade this time. It appeared she had more to offer than I first thought, not a single attack getting through.

Taking my best swordsman stance, I slashed down at her with a practiced blow after practiced blow, but she was quick, far too quick. Her skill as a swordsman was the only thing that prevented me from losing an arm, so I activated Speed Burst and evened the playing field. All that did was put me just behind her for several seconds, but I forced her back first, one step then another and then the skill faded, and I was then taking the steps back.

Forcing mana into the blade and essence into my muscles, I felt my speed increase twofold and then some. Once again, I was on an even field speed-wise with her and we traded blow after blow, neither having the time or focus to unleash a skill or spell while we moved at breakneck speeds. Then the battle shifted as Speed Burst came off cooldown and I activated it without even thinking.

I struck her at the neck, and I was sure it would be a killing blow, but suddenly she poofed into a cloud of black smoke and she was behind me, slashing down. My back erupted in pain, and I felt blood flow as the blow cut right through my armor. I turned in time for her to poof again and appear where she'd been. Another slash came but I caught it on my sword and kicked her square in the chest, sending her flying some twenty paces back all at once.

Using Blink, I appeared over her and stabbed down, my sword sinking past her armor with surprising ease. She screamed in pain and stabbed at my face. Pulling out my sword, I stepped backward just enough to avoid the stab, but with that second I gave her, she was back on her feet once more.

She raised the sword above her head and screamed at me. "You can't comprehend the power I wield!" Her words echoed with power and all around me the darkness seemed to thicken as her sword gave off a half glow mixed with the deepest of blacks. In that moment, the screams from the dungeon became too much to push out and I heard the calls.

There was something coherent about it and the longer I focused the firmer the connection became. But I had to cut it off before too long as whatever attack the Chaos Knight had been preparing was ready to strike out.

Black tendrils of energy struck out from the ground and took hold of me. It was only with great effort of will and the power of the sword that I was able to shatter the spell before it did more than passing damage to me. But just as I broke one wave of the attack, another and another came at me, forcing me to drain essence to keep it from overtaking me. I needed a plan, but it was hard to match her in pure force, but I had proved that I could match or exceed her speed. There had to be something there I could use.

Increasing my speed once more, I dodged and weaved her strikes until I got close enough to deliver a few blows of my own. Then, just as before, we began a dance of steel, striking here and there and pushing each other back with each strike. I struck low, sweeping my blade in a practiced strike toward her knees, but she got her sword in place in time to block the strike. Then I went high, going for an over the head strike, but turned it at the last moment into a feign, before sweeping for her chest.

This strike had more success slamming into her armor at full speed and throwing her backward. I couldn't tell if it had done any damage, but she didn't look happy about being forced backward. In that moment, I heard a screech and looked up to see Ares fighting with her opponent, the huge wyvern.

She dove in, weaving around the larger and stronger opponent with grace and deadly accuracy. I felt, more than I saw, her claws tearing into the nightmare beast, but shadows gathered around the injuries, and they closed up as fast as she could deliver them. I could feel her strength and speed lessening with each passing minute.

I watched, keeping half my attention on the Chaos Knight, as Ares cut a nasty gash across the nightmare being's face, and it roared in anger toward her. Just when I was sure she had a good control over her battle, the tides changed. She was weaving about the massive beast when a clawed hand caught her wing, and a terrible snap filled the air. Ares screamed and began to fall from the sky.

Just then, the Chaos Knight was back on the attack, and I couldn't spare any attention for Ares. But using the sword and my healing spell I reached out with my mind, healing her broken wing. It cost me a strike to my own chest, ripping through my armor and injuring me, but it was worth it. I felt Ares in my mind get back to flying and attacking.

The battle felt far from over, but suddenly I opened my ears to the cries around me and heard the words the dungeon spoke. It wished to grant me its strength instead of giving it to the Chaos Knight. Readily, I agreed with such an idea, and I felt a flow of power beneath me shift and turn before slamming into me. Pure and powerful essence ran through me, and I funneled it into the sword.

Raising the blade up to the sky, I unleashed the might that was gathering there. The power to distort the very fabric of reality burst from within, tendrils of blue-green lightning reached upwards and outwards, piercing the sky above. As the power shot into the sky, it struck the hideous nightmare creature, unmaking it, turning it to dust. I smiled and turned to the Chaos Knight, using the power on her, as well. But I could feel her resistance, my attempts at unmaking her being pushed back through a will of her own.

Back and forth we fought, her power a match for my own. However, with the will and power of the dungeon below on my side, I had the edge now. Overwhelming force smashed down on her and I felt something give and crack.

Looking up, I saw the sword she held had splintered, several pieces falling free as she stumbled back stunned. I lessened the powerful attack then, ready to step forward and end her life the old-fashioned way. But just as I did, she reached out with her sword and black and purple lightning struck out from it. However, it passed by me harmlessly, as she'd missed me entirely.

That was when I heard Ares cry out and I knew I hadn't been the target. I rushed forward then, slashing and cutting at her. But something was wrong, I felt weaker than I should, and with a start, I realized I'd drained most of my resources during our fight and only the power of the sword was keeping me going.

I cut high and tried to come up with the focus needed to restore myself, but she struck out and my sword went flying from my hands. Lightning slammed into me, and I felt my vision blacken. The tables had turned so quickly and utterly, that I was stunned and unable to act.

The Chaos Knight stood over me, looming in her terrible armor with her broken sword crackling with menacing sheer power. She'd strike soon and I'd be dead, Ares soon to join me. In the distant parts of my mind, I heard her crying out to me.

"It has been my displeasure to battle you, now finally you die!" The Chaos Knight spoke her words just as a swirling portal formed right beside her.

"Not today bitch!" A voice roared and a shield slammed into the Chaos Knight's face as Emory stepped out of a swirling portal alongside all my truest friends. Next came Ismene, my loyal friend with her bow strung and ready, releasing arrow after arrow at the Chaos Knight. Then Alayna, her helmet down but her entire frame glowing in golden light as she threw lance after lance of light. Then pausing, she must have seen Ares because she began to chant a long and complex healing spell. One after another, figures appeared, striking out and disobeying my instructions to let me take her on alone.

I was glad for such rebellious friends as I struggled to

stand. A hand stretched out to me, and I noticed Zander there. I took his gauntleted extended arm and rose to my feet.

"Don't die yet, and don't think this means I've forgiven you," he said, then turning his attention to the fight, he began to chant. Last to step through was Warrick, and he looked pissed. His chants rose up above any others and the sky began to shine with a powerful light, as if the sun had cut through the darkened clouds above. Massive lightning bolts struck down on the Chaos Knight as Warrick unleashed the full might of his powers on her.

Strike after strike hammered down on the Chaos Knight, but she took each one in stride, using the power of her sword to deflect and control them. Even Warrick's mighty strikes only seemed to fuel her onward. I knew she'd be striking back soon and suddenly I was filled with new motivation to save my friends.

I looked where Ares lay, broken and barely breathing, her connection so weak that even my heals seemed to do nothing and I'd exhausted so much power from the sword that I couldn't just put her back together. I let the sight of it grow a red-hot fury inside of me, and I screamed as I charged for the Chaos Knight, my sword appearing back in my grasp.

"Hit me with all you've got," I screamed at her, and she did just that, but I had a plan. If she could take attacks out of the air and unleash them as powerfully charged essence, then so could I.

As she took the massive essence load from the attacks and turned it on me, I held the sword before me and used my last bit of will, to give the command.

Feed. And it fed.

I felt overwhelming power fill me as the blade began to bristle with power. She realized her mistake too late and cut off her attack. But by that point, I was already upon her with my blade rising to strike.

With one final sweep of my blade, infused with so much power that not even a mountain would have stopped my blow, she held up her sword and it shattered as my sword cleaved through it. With a burst of power, I took her head from her shoulders.

Thus ended the reign of the Chaos Knight that sought to change the world and plunge it into darkness. She ignored the balance and sought only her own power. She died for her mistakes; may she be forgotten in the passage of time.

# CHAPTER 31
## KOBOLD DUNGEON

It was done. It was finally over. Or at least it would be once I finished repairing the final Prime Mana Shrine and restored the planet's equilibrium. Walking forward, I found the correct place and did just that, cleansing the final ley line damage and restoring the balance. My quest 'Restoring the Balance Part 2' was finally finished and my new Perk Third Eye Open sank into my pool of Ordu given knowledge.

*Third Eye Open: Gives you the ability to open your third eye. While third eye is open, your spells are ten times more effective and powerful. You also gain the ability to perceive the true nature of the Cosmos.*

· · ·

I wasn't sure I was ready to use it yet, but I knew that I ought to try it out just to see. It was easy enough to activate, just focusing on the ability saw it done. Suddenly the world was open to me in a way, not unlike when I used the sword. I could see tethers that connected us and the Chaos Knights around me. In that moment, I saw that despite our differences, we were much alike, using a 'system' of sorts, each operating on another end of the spectrum.

Chaos ruled the unpredictable chaotic nature of magic and skills, while the side of Order seeing the Titan system observed. It was truly fascinating, but after only a few seconds of having my third eye open the strain was enough that I had to close it. This was an ability not meant to be used for prolonged periods of time. That was alright though, at least I'd gotten a glimpse at the true nature of the Wyrd. Chaos and Order, Order and Chaos, they rely on each other as much as they oppose each other.

With my third eye firmly closed, I turned my mind toward Ares, checking on her. She was alright, which I was truly relieved to find out, but the injuries she'd taken would take time to heal properly, so extensive was the damage she'd suffered. But the good thing was that she wasn't dead. I'm not sure what I'd do if something had happened to one of my friends.

Warrick was in recovery as well, having pushed himself in that moment far past his ability to safely wield his own magics. However, all the rest of my friends managed to escape with not so much as a scratch. They were gathered around me now, but I'd tuned out their voices as I sunk deeper into myself. I needed both to ponder and consider my next steps.

With the immediate needs of world destruction taken care of, I almost didn't know what to do next. There was a dungeon below us, buried in the rubble, perhaps I'd run it with my team and seek to strengthen myself once more. The mind of the dungeon was still close, and I could sense it preparing itself again, knowing that it might have visitors once more. How difficult would a dungeon be that had stayed hidden since the time of the Ordu? I wasn't sure, but I really wanted to find out.

"Who's up for a dungeon run?" I asked, cutting off a few conversations.

About half of them answered at once and their responses were lost in the muddle of the words smashing together. I looked at Emory, my loyal friend and tank, and raised an eyebrow. He took the hint and answered again.

"Hell yeah, I'm down," he said, ever the enthusiastic dungeon diver.

"Then we need a healer, a ranged damage dealer, and a melee damage dealer," I said.

In the end, I went with Emory tanking, Zander healing—Alayna needed to stay behind to help with matters more political than I wanted to deal with—Fred playing ranged damager dealer, and Fran as my melee damager dealer. As we prepared for the dungeon, which involved getting a bunch of help clearing rocks and debris, my thoughts turned to the war in the Easternlands and what lay ahead for me.

I'd need to meet with the King again and begin preparing troops for mass deployment. However, I planned on assigning generals to handle the day to day on that, my time as a commander was at an end. I refused to take direct responsibility of troops any longer. Instead, I would go out and fight beside them, consequences be damned. I was a powerful asset that couldn't be ignored. I might even take up the Royal Guard on their invitation to do some training with them, if they still would let me.

The future looked a mix of bright and grim. Perhaps I could go and speak with the Beastkin before any of the fighting happened. I remembered making friends with Grugssir or Grug as he liked to be called. Surely, such an honorable people would be open to hearing reason from someone they respected. I just had to work out a way to be considered respected among them and I might have a chance.

"Beth," I said, finding the attractive Delvish girl helping move rocks twice her size aside.

"Hey there Caldor!" She said brightly. "I'm getting as many rocks off as I can, but this is difficult work. What can I do for you, hun?"

She was always so happy and cheerful; it brightened

my mood just speaking with her. "Have you heard or spoken to Grug since he left to visit his homelands?"

"I have actually!" She exclaimed, excited to be asked. "He visited the elven capital and would have come if he wasn't on a 'pressing mission for my kin'." She added the last part in an impression of his gruff voice. "He is seeking allies for the war, but he wasn't having much luck as an ambassador. He's a bit short tempered."

"Would you take me to meet him after we finish this dungeon? I want to speak with him about something very important," I said, and she nodded.

"Sure thing," Beth said. "No problem at all."

***

The dungeon as it turned out wasn't so amazing after all. We entered the first room only to find that it wasn't themed, as we expected, and was instead an old-style room-to-room dungeon filled with blue kobolds. The blue kobolds were odd, to be sure, and the room that held them looked much more spherical than cave like, but we battled onward, never encountering a challenge all the way to the final boss room of the floor. Where we faced just a larger version of what we'd been fighting thus far.

It was after taking down this boss, it threw blue arcane balls of energy at us that weren't much of a threat to a single one of us, that I finally had a chance to talk to

Zander in private. Everyone else went ahead to explore, unafraid of what they might face without us.

I looked at him for a solid few seconds before working up the right words to say, but even so, he beat me to it, speaking before I could.

"I never thanked you for killing my father's murderer," Zander said, holding out a hand in thanks. I took it and shook it firmly.

"It was my pleasure," I said, then played the words over in my mind wondering if it had been the right thing to say. 'It was my pleasure' man what was I thinking, did I want him to be even more angry at me?

Zander just smiled and shook his head. "I want to hate you so much, but Ismene is right. You did what you had to do, and I'd likely have not done anything differently if I were in your shoes."

"Thanks," I said awkwardly, not knowing how to respond to that. "If it helps anything, I didn't want to do it, not really. In the end, if he'd just been able to change, it might have been enough. Though, he was changing, just not for the better."

"I know," Zander said, hanging his head. "Uncle had a tendency to lose himself in his work, so when his work became revenge, he became lost to it."

Just then, the group came back, all smiles. "It's just more kobolds, these ones were red and threw fire. We wiped out all of them up to the boss, but figured you'd want to see the boss fight. Emory figures he can take it by himself," Fran said.

"Hell yes I can. Just watch," Emory said, grinning ear to ear.

The cavern was dark ahead, corpses laid about here and there as we passed deeper into the dungeon. By the time we reached the boss room, the light had filled out a bit more, making it possible to see forward into the room without entering it. Inside stood a six-foot-tall kobold giant, hands engulfed in magical orange flames.

"Go for it, Emory," I said, actually curious to see how he did against the boss in a one-on-one fight.

Emory grunted in response and lurched forward, shield leading. He slammed into the massive kobold, causing both fires to fling harmlessly to the side in the process. He was relentless in his attacks, bringing down his weapon once, twice, and a third time.

Just those short few blows were enough to stagger the boss backward and a red haze surrounded it. The low health enrage that was so common in dungeon bosses had started already. Suddenly, it was moving twice as fast and I almost worried for Emory as the creature lurched forward, striking low and throwing a fireball with its other hand.

Emory caught both attacks with an ease that surprised me and even struck out again with his weapon. The mighty kobold fell backward, dead from his fourth blow.

"Did you see that!" Emory yelled, practically

bouncing from foot to foot.

"We saw it," Fran said, eying Emory with a curious expression.

Not for the first time, I wondered if something was going on between the pair of them, but I kept my thoughts to myself on the matter.

"Let's keep going so we can clear the remaining floors," I said, looking for the appearance of a staircase that would lead down to lower floors. Yet, as I looked around, I realized something. There was no staircase, which meant...

"This was the final boss," Zander said, finishing my thought.

"Lame," Fran said, then turning her gaze on Emory she glowered. "You hogged the last boss and now it's over!"

Emory visibly reddened as if actually embarrassed. He stammered his next words, and I couldn't hold back a laugh. "You...w-want to see the loot I got?"

Pretty soon the entire group had grins on their faces, even Zander, while Emory showed off what loot he'd gotten off the boss. Since he'd been the only one to participate, it looked like he'd been the only one to get any loot.

This dungeon had so little power and I couldn't help but wonder what it had been like before it gave so much of itself to the Chaos Knight and then to me? What grand adventure had been stripped from the world so that we could battle it out above? I would never know, only able to imagine what great adventure had laid here in times past.

Reaching out with my mind, I tried to sense the dungeon, but after several attempts, I decided it wasn't going to happen. Whatever power it had to communicate before must have been lessened by the fact that it had given so much of itself to aid me in the fight against the Chaos Knight. I wanted to pinch myself when it finally truly began to sink in. We'd defeated the Chaos Knight, the bane of my existence as a defender of the balance.

Truly, I was free from a great burden now and with this new freedom I wanted only one thing more than anything else, the truth about my father. For so long, I'd set it aside because more important things abound around me. But it was time to search out my father and find him, if he were truly alive as I believed. Making up my mind over the matter, I decided to have Beth go on ahead and ask Grug for a meeting, instead of running straight into that next.

The black bird that followed me around was my best clue, and I was now convinced it must be a messenger from my father, his attempt at watching over me. With Warrick's help, I was sure we might be able to trace the origin of the spell and finally have a decent lead on finding my father. So, with that in mind, we exited the dungeon and I went out to find Warrick.

# CHAPTER 32
## TRACING HIS STEPS

"I can't just trace a spell," Warrick said from the bed where he lay. He'd set up a small room for himself inside a massive tent in the Chaos Knight section of the camp, even going so far as to have dressers and a bedframe put in it.

"Sure you can, there has to be a connection from a messenger spell to the messenger, otherwise they'd not be able to get information. Can't you isolate that and try to create a portal to the location or place its transmitting?" I asked, working out how I'd do it if I had even the slightest knowledge around spell tracing and formations.

"Hmm. Yes, you have a good point. I might be able to get an image or two from the arcane manifestation that just might be enough to form a portal, but tell me, why are you so keen on tracing this particular spell. It could come from a number of people who are looking to spy on you. Your simple warding should block most of your actions so it's not like they are getting much," Warrick said, looking to me with keen eyes, weary from his spell workings.

I wanted to slap myself in the forehead. "I'll let you rest and think about it, I forget myself," I said, realizing I was asking him to do what might be impossible in his current state.

Warrick pulled the covers aside and swung his legs over the bed. "I'm as fit as a fiddle," he proclaimed. "Now, where is that pesky bird that follows you everywhere."

As it happened, we found the bird perched on our very tent just outside, it cawed twice, once at me and once at Warrick.

"Curious little thing isn't it," Warrick said, examining the bird from a distance. Then, holding out a hand he chanted a few short words, and the bird flew to perch on his outstretched hand. "Let's begin."

Moonlight lit the expanse, and I waited patiently while Warrick fussed over the bird, cursing at it at times and soothing it with a quiet word the next. I could feel every little tug he made at the spell and each time it threatened to unravel it completely. So entranced by his spell workings, I was, that I decided to open my third eye for a time to see exactly what he was doing. It was a mistake of course, but one that I had to learn eventually.

The bird shone like a blazing sun and the workings threading off of Warrick blazed equally bright. Whomever had crafted this spell had incredible power, all the more reason it might be my father. But in the moment of the painfully bright spell workings, I noticed a distinct difference between the two spells weaves. One was orderly and neat, Warrick's attempts at penetrating the bird. Meanwhile, the bird was chaotic in its formation, like it almost looked ordered, but several parts just spoke of disorder.

Parts sparked and flared, hindering Warrick's attempts. It was almost as if...

"Warrick wait, I don't think this is my father's after all," I said, but I was too late, he'd finally made enough progress with his workings and a small portal had begun to form.

Warrick, so bent to the task of opening a portal and connecting the images he'd seen, must not have heard me, because he didn't stop, the portal growing ever larger. As it turned from a hazy and milky white to a clear crisp image, I stepped back instinctually, calling my sword to my hand.

A figure in black armor sat on a throne of twisted metal and bones. He wore a nightmarish helmet in the form of a black bird's face with horns jutting up and around. He stood as the portal formed and a sword appeared in his own hand. Behind me, I heard shouts of alarm, as some of the Chaos Knights saw who lay beyond.

"It's the Chaos Lord, they've summoned a portal to the Chaos Lord!"

Warrick flagged under the weight of creating the portal, but as it began to flicker and close, the figure within held out a hand and the portal stabilized. I sensed an immense power behind it, but why was this Chaos Lord, the mysterious leader of the Chaos Knights, sending birds to watch over me?

As I watched, Chaos Knights beginning to gather around me, the Chaos Lord reached up to remove his helmet. Then my world came crashing down around me and power swelled up, threatening to strike out.

Warrick spoke before I could, his voice hoarse with surprise and exertion. "Elkor!"

It was my father, clad in black armor, sitting on the throne of the Chaos Lord and very much alive. Though his skin seemed drained of color from my last memory, it was him in every other way. Even the little grin he always had on his face when he'd come home from one adventure or another, was there. He stepped forward, his own sword fading away to black mist along with his helmet. Then, as he stepped through, even his armor faded away as if it were never there.

When he stepped through, he wore a simple white tunic and black slacks, looking particularly ordinary. His eyes, deep gray pools of power, pierced deep into my soul as he approached. I didn't know what to do, how to feel, but I needed to know that this wasn't a trick. I turned my third eye on him and opened it.

All around him, power buzzed and sparked. It didn't have the feel of an illusion at all, but rather, a powerful aura that he struggled to contain. This was my father, but at the same time it wasn't. No longer was this man an agent of Order, no, he was Chaos personified. Each step drew him closer and each step I knew him to be my father, but also a being of Chaos.

"You've changed," I managed to say as he stopped in front of me, a look of pure astonishment on his face.

"So have you, my son," Elkor said, his voice as rich and deep as I remembered it. It was like music to my ears and in that moment, I could no longer hold back. My sword fell from my hands, and I unsummoned my armor, pulling my father into a hug.

All around us, Chaos Knights knelt, but I ignored them and allowed myself to be held by my father. The man I'd once believed dead, come back to life as an agent of Chaos, the very thing he'd sworn to fight against.

Pulling myself free, I looked across and into his eyes. "What of the balance?" I asked, unable to wrap my head around how he could have become what he had.

"I am maintaining it even now," he said, giving me a knowing smile. "Unfortunately, the power I wield now is..." he paused to look around and with a wave of his hand a bubble formed around the three of us and sound from outside of it ceased. "...unpredictable, and for that reason and several others, I couldn't return home. But now that you've found me, it changes so much. You've become all I could ever hope and feared."

His words washed over me, and I struggled to comprehend it all, so scattered were my thoughts. "Mother suffered for years," I said, a sudden quiet anger bubbling to the surface. "You left us with so little and..." My anger turned to shame. "...I made several poor decisions, and we couldn't afford her treatments."

"I know, and if I had a way to send help I would have. How is she doing now, your mother?" Elkor asked, a sudden eagerness in his voice.

"She's fine," I said simply. "The twins are doing good too."

"I know," he said, smiling. "I've kept an eye on them since they Awakened, its easier to do so when they've been connected to the source of power on Wyrd. I've so much to tell you but I can't linger here. I need to return to my seat of power or our defenses around our capital will lessen and the Beastkin will begin their final push and invasion. Memorize my throne room and come see me."

"I'll come now," I said, blurting out the words.

Warrick spoke up then, his voice as struck with amazement as my own. "Elkor, what happened to you? I saw you die."

"Old friend," Elkor said, reaching out and putting a

hand on Warrick's shoulder. "Come with my son and I will explain all to you. I can also aid in your recovery; I can see the scars left by my adversary. Well done, defeating her, by the way," Elkor said turning back to me. "You did what even I could not, with her weapon of the Ordu she was beyond even my power. Did you recover her sword?"

"I did," I said, not mentioning that it had been shattered in the fight.

"Good," Elkor said, then putting a hand on our shoulders, he nodded. "Let's talk."

Together we walked through the portal into the Easternlands to speak with Elkor Miles, the once famed Arcane Knight, turned Chaos Lord. Finally, I had been reunited with my father and all the answers I'd hoped to have answered faded to dross under the joy of just having him back.

**The end of Arcane Knight Book 5**

**Come back for the conclusion in Arcane Knight Book 6.**

# LEAVE A REVIEW

Thank you for reading. Please leave a review at, My Book.

Check out my website at AuthorTimothyMcGowen.com

If you really liked the book, please consider reaching out and telling me what you enjoyed about it at, Timothy. mcgowen1@gmail.com.

Join my Facebook group and discuss the books at: https:// www.facebook.com/groups/234653175151521/

Join my Patreon at: https://www.patreon.com/ TimothyMcGowen

# ABOUT THE AUTHOR

 Timothy McGowen was born in Modesto, California. His journey into stories started with reading the Goosebumps books. Later he read a novel by Terry Brooks and became hooked on fantasy/scifi almost instantly. Shortly after that he was given a school assignment to write a 5 page fiction story, and 25 pages later his story was half done. He hasn't stopped writing since.

His popular Arcane Knight series has sold thousands of copies in both ebook and audible so far. Consider signing up for my newsletter for news on book releases as they become available.

facebook.com/timothym.mcgowen
x.com/TimothyMMcGowe1
instagram.com/timothy.mcgowen1

# LITRPG GROUP

Check out this group if you want to gather together and hear about new great LitRPG books.

(https://www.facebook.com/groups/LitRPGGroup/)

# LEARN MORE ABOUT LITRPG/GAMELIT GENRE

To learn more about LitRPG & GameLit, talk to author and just have an awesome time by joining some LitRPG/Gamelit groups.

Here is another LitRPG group you can join if you are looking for the next great read!

Facebook.com/groups/LitRPG.books

**List of LitRPG/Gamelit Facebook Groups:**

- https://www.facebook.com/groups/LitRPGReleases/
- https://www.facebook.com/groups/litrpgforum/
- https://www.facebook.com/groups/litrpglegends/
- https://www.facebook.com/groups/LitRPGsociety/

- https://www.facebook.com/groups/ AleronKong/

17244671R00246